COVENANT OF THE IRON CROSS

VATICAN ARCHAEOLOGY THRILLERS
BOOK ONE

GARY MCAVOY

LITERATI
EDITIONS.

Hardcover ISBN: 978-1-954123-60-1
Paperback ISBN: 978-1-954123-62-5
eBook ISBN: 978-1-954123-60-1

Library of Congress Control Number: 2024927416

Published by:
Literati Editions
PO Box 5987
Bremerton WA 98312
Email: info@LiteratiEditions.com
Visit the author's website: GaryMcAvoy.com
R0225

This is a work of fiction. Names, characters, businesses, places, long-standing institutions, agencies, public offices, events, locales, and incidents are either the products of the author's imagination or have been used fictitiously. Apart from historical references, any resemblance to actual persons, living or dead, or actual events is purely coincidental.

BOOKS BY GARY MCAVOY

FICTION

The Apostle Conspiracy

The Celestial Guardian

The Confessions of Pope Joan

The Galileo Gambit

The Jerusalem Scrolls

The Avignon Affair

The Petrus Prophecy

The Opus Dictum

The Vivaldi Cipher

The Magdalene Veil

The Magdalene Reliquary

The Magdalene Deception

NONFICTION

And Every Word Is True

PREFACE

TO LONGTIME READERS:

Welcome to *Vatican Archaeology Thrillers*, a new series featuring Marcus Russo, the Vatican's chief archaeologist. While this story places Marcus at the center of the action, familiar faces from the *Vatican Secret Archive Thriller* series—Father Michael Dominic, Hana Sinclair, and Swiss Guards Karl and Lukas—are present as needed, lending their expertise and support. You'll find Hana's role a bit more involved, something I've wanted to do for a while. Michael and Hana's personal dynamic, as ultimately revealed in *The Apostle Conspiracy*, continues to evolve, and their relationship and journey will take back center stage in the next installment of the *Vatican Secret Archive Thrillers*. Here, they serve as trusted allies to Marcus as he unravels his own dangerous mysteries tied to history, faith, and secrets buried deep in time.

PREFACE

TO NEW READERS:

If this is your first step into my world of Vatican intrigue, welcome! The *Vatican Archaeology* series begins entirely new adventures led by the Vatican's chief archaeologist, Marcus Russo, a skilled prehistorian confronting the dark intersections of history and power. You don't need to have read any previous books to enjoy this one—this story stands firmly on its own, introducing new mysteries, curious characters, and a pulse-pounding narrative that unfolds independently.

TO ALL READERS:

Whether you're a newcomer or a returning reader, this journey will draw you into the hidden corners of the past where every artifact tells a story—and some secrets refuse to remain buried.

PROLOGUE

OWL MOUNTAINS, POLAND - 1945

The night was heavy with the weight of a collapsing empire. Across Lower Silesia, a richly historical area in southwestern Poland, the forests whispered with the sound of retreating armies and the distant, relentless thunder of artillery. The Russian Red Army was closing in, sweeping westward like an unstoppable tide, and with each mile gained, the Third Reich crumbled further into chaos.

At a secluded rail yard outside Wałbrzych, under the cold gaze of the moon, an extraordinary operation was underway. Hidden from prying eyes and shielded by layers of secrecy, an armored train sat idle on the tracks. Its blackened hull, slick with condensation, loomed like a specter in the dim light of torches. Around it, a feverish dance of men and machines played out, the air alive with shouts, the groan of steel crates, and the hiss of steam.

Inside the train, chaos reigned. The cars were packed with treasures—priceless artifacts looted from across Europe during the Nazi occupation. Masterpieces stolen from the Louvre Museum in Paris and the Uffizi Gallery in Florence leaned precariously against one another, their gilded frames jostled in the frenzy. Velvet-lined chests overflowed with jewels, their facets glinting like trapped starlight. Gold bars, stacked like bricks of a grotesque new cathedral, reflected the torchlight in ominous hues of yellow.

At the heart of the second car, crated in sections, lay the fabled Amber Room, its panels of translucent, honey-hued resin painstakingly dismantled and wrapped in silk. For centuries, it had adorned Catherine Palace near St. Petersburg, a symbol of opulence and power. Now, it sat like a relic of another world, bound for oblivion.

Generalfeldmarschall Hans Richter, a wiry man with hollow cheeks and piercing blue eyes, stood on the platform overlooking the operation. His SS uniform was immaculate, though it hung slightly loose after months of hardship on the Eastern Front. He watched impassively as soldiers and forced laborers struggled under the weight of the crates, their faces slick with sweat despite the chill.

"We are running out of time," Richter said, his voice cutting through the din. "The Russians will be here by dawn if we don't move."

"Yes, Herr General," snapped an officer at his side. "The last crates are being loaded now."

Richter's gaze shifted to the perimeter of the rail yard, where guards patrolled with machine guns. Beyond them lay the dark expanse of the Owl Mountains, their jagged peaks hiding secrets that few dared to imagine. The tunnels—part of the mysterious *Projekt Riese*—had been hastily expanded in recent weeks to accommodate this final act of the Reich's ambition.

Behind him, the chief engineer approached cautiously, clutching a map of the tunnel network. He was a civilian, his oil-stained overalls marking him as an outsider among the SS officers. "General," he began nervously, "the northbound tracks have been cut. There's no clear route to Berlin anymore."

Richter turned slowly, his expression cold. "We're not going to Berlin." He gestured toward the mountains. "The train will be hidden. Permanently."

"Hidden?" the engineer echoed, his brow furrowing.

Richter stepped closer, lowering his voice. "The Führer's orders are clear. This treasure cannot fall into enemy hands. The tunnels will serve as its tomb until the Reich rises again."

The engineer hesitated, then nodded reluctantly.

The last crate was hoisted aboard and the train hissed to life, its engine belching black smoke into the night sky. The prisoners who had loaded the train, their faces hollow with starvation, were herded to the edge of the forest. They didn't plead—they knew their fate. Gunfire cracked sharply, and the bodies were dragged into the darkness. No witnesses would be left to tell this story. Secrets demanded silence.

The train began to move, its iron wheels screeching against the rails. Richter climbed aboard the locomotive, standing beside the engineer as they rumbled into the night. The forest closed in around them, the towering pines swallowing the train like a predator devouring prey.

The journey was slow and deliberate, each curve of the tracks pulling them deeper into the mountains. Around them, the forest seemed to close in, an ancient and indifferent witness. Hours later, the train arrived at its final destination—a tunnel opening obscured by dense pines and disguised to the casual observer, a yawning black mouth carved into the mountainside. It had been hastily expanded in the past months by forced laborers—Jewish prisoners dragged from the Gross-Rosen concentration camp under inhuman conditions. The men who had dug it lay dead or dying in mass graves nearby, their suffering buried as deeply as the treasures soon would be.

The train crept forward into the tunnel, the sound of its engine echoing eerily off the damp stone walls. The air grew colder, denser, as the cars disappeared one by one into the earth. Farther in, SS troops prepared the mechanisms that would seal the tunnel. Explosives were set along the walls, enough to collapse the entrance and bury the train's access beneath tons of rock. The tunnels were serpentine by design, a deliberate maze intended to thwart discovery even if the Allies somehow learned of their existence.

The general and engineer left the train's engine, walking the train's length back out into the night air.

"Is everything secure?" Richter asked a subordinate, his voice low.

"*Jawohl,* Herr General," the man replied affirmatively. "The tunnel will be sealed within the hour."

Richter watched in silence as the charges were set, his breath visible in the frigid air. Once everyone had cleared out from the mountain's interior, a final command was given, and the explosives detonated with a deafening roar. The mountainside shuddered, and a cascade of rock and earth thundered down, burying the tunnel in an impenetrable wall of stone.

The dust settled and the entrance was gone, replaced by jagged rock and silence. Richter lit a cigarette, the flicker of the flame briefly illuminating his gaunt face. He exhaled slowly, watching the smoke drift upward into the freezing night.

"One day," he murmured to himself, "someone will come looking for it. And they'll wonder if it was ever real."

As he turned away, the distant sound of gunfire echoed through the mountains. The Red Army was closer than he had anticipated. He tossed the cigarette aside and stepped into his car, leaving behind the buried treasure and the ghosts of the men who died to protect it.

· · ·

IN THE DECADES THAT FOLLOWED, whispers of the hidden train refused to fade, gaining momentum with every retelling. Locals exchanged tales of strange happenings in the forest: flickering lights in the dead of night, distant metallic echoes, and the unsettling feeling of being watched by unseen eyes. The tunnels themselves became a source of fascination and fear, with some villagers claiming to have found hidden entrances only to encounter dead ends or barriers that seemed impossibly resistant to human effort. Explorers would emerge shaken, speaking of walls that felt unnaturally warm to the touch or of an inexplicable sense of dread that drove them back.

Treasure hunters from around the world descended on the Owl Mountains, armed with shovels, maps, and increasingly sophisticated technology. Ground-penetrating radar and seismic surveys offered tantalizing glimpses of hollow spaces deep below, yet no one could confirm their contents. Excavations often ended abruptly—either thwarted by the sheer impenetrability of the rock or by local authorities wary of disrupting the region's delicate balance between history and legend.

The train itself slipped further into myth, its story blending historical fact with wild speculation. Some claimed it carried unimaginable wealth: gold bars stamped with swastikas and the Nazi Imperial Eagle, crates of priceless art, and perhaps even experimental weapons or ancient relics. Others believed a curse protected it, supernatural forces guarded it, or explosives would punish anyone disturbing it. Yet through all the theories and countless failed expeditions, the treasures of a stolen world remained hidden, untouched in the dark and airless tunnels.

And so the mountains, ancient and watchful, kept their secrets. Time eroded memories, but the allure of the train endured, its legend whispering to a new generation of dreamers and seekers, all drawn to the timeless promise of unimaginable fortune and the tantalizing unknown.

CHAPTER
ONE

PRESENT DAY

T he marble floors of the Apostolic Palace were as cold as the winter air outside, their chill seeping up through Marcus Russo's shoes with each measured step. The Vatican's corridors, always steeped in quiet, seemed unnaturally still this morning, the usual murmurs of priests and scholars absent. Marcus, the Vatican's preeminent archaeologist, had been summoned to the Secretariat of State, an area he rarely visited. The terse message delivered by a young priest that morning still echoed in his mind: *Cardinal Severino requests your immediate presence. Do not delay.*

In his early fifties, Marcus Russo was a ruggedly handsome man with clear hazel eyes and salt-and-pepper hair that framed his lean, angular face. His tall, athletic frame reflected years of physical fieldwork, often clad in practical attire—dusty boots, rolled-up shirts, and a well-worn leather satchel. Today, he wore his one pair of pressed slacks and a shirt with a presentable tweed jacket he had hastily thrown on after the summons. He stuffed one of his calloused hands, equally skilled at unearthing delicate artifacts and solving mysteries, into his pocket, as the other held his ever-present satchel. Beneath his composed exterior lay a man deeply shaped by the weight of history, carrying the burden of both its treasures and its darkest secrets. Though not of the clergy himself, he was a man of at least some faith coupled with a deep reverence for history. For him, it was a high privilege to have been tapped as the Vatican's chief archeologist.

He reached the ornate double doors that marked the entrance to Severino's private office. Two Swiss Guards, their halberds gleaming in the light filtering through a high window, stood as sentinels. They acknowledged him with brief nods, their impassive expressions betraying nothing. With a slight creak, one guard pulled the heavy door open, and Marcus stepped inside.

The chamber beyond was unlike any other he had visited within the Vatican. The walls, lined with towering bookshelves, seemed to press inward with the weight of centuries. Scrolls, their edges frayed, lay in neat stacks alongside ancient codices bound in cracked leather. Maps, some framed and others rolled, filled every available space, their delicate lines hinting at long-forgotten journeys. The faint scent of beeswax candles mingled with the earthy aroma of aged parchment, creating an atmosphere of somber reverence.

At the center of the room sat Vatican Secretary of

State Cardinal Giovanni Severino, a figure who radiated authority even in stillness. He was a man of contradictions: his face bore the lines of age, but his keen, calculating eyes hinted at a mind that missed nothing. Severino gestured for Marcus to sit without rising, his gaze fixed on the younger man as if appraising him anew.

"Dr. Russo," Severino began, his voice low and deliberate. "Thank you for coming so promptly. What we are about to discuss is of the utmost sensitivity. You understand this, yes?"

Marcus nodded, the weight of the cardinal's words already pressing on him. "Of course, Your Eminence. I'm here to assist in whatever way I can." With a voice low and resonant, tinged by an Italian accent, Marcus exuded quiet charisma and often a sharp wit. But there was no masking his relentless drive to uncover the truth, no matter the cost.

Severino leaned back, his hands resting lightly on the edge of his desk. "Tell me, Marcus, what do you know of the fabled Nazi Gold Train?"

The question hung in the air, as unexpected as it was intriguing. Marcus frowned slightly, searching for the right words. "It's more legend than fact, as I understand it. A train said to have vanished in the final days of World War II, rumored to carry stolen treasures—gold, art, jewels. Historians have debated its existence for decades, but there's never been definitive proof."

Severino's lips pressed into a thin line, his expression unreadable. "So the world believes. Until now."

From beneath his desk, the cardinal retrieved a

leather-bound folio, its edges scuffed with age. He placed it on the desk with deliberate care, opening it to reveal a collection of documents. Marcus leaned forward instinctively, his trained eyes immediately drawn to the largest piece: a yellowed map fragment, its markings faint but legible.

"This," Severino said, tapping the map, "was unearthed two weeks ago in a section of the Vatican Secret Archives that has remained unexplored for decades. Alongside it was this." He lifted another sheet, this one covered in ciphered text, its margins adorned with the insignia of the Nazi regime and, shockingly, the Vatican crest.

Marcus inhaled sharply, his gaze flicking between the two items. "This... this is real?"

Severino's eyes narrowed. "Very much so. The map indicates a location in the Owl Mountains of Poland—a place long whispered to hold the train's final resting place. The document refers to something called Operation Iron Cross. It appears to have been a wartime agreement between a high-ranking Nazi officer and certain Vatican intermediaries. Among other things, its purpose was to obscure the train's location."

Marcus felt the room grow colder. "Why would the Vatican be involved in hiding the train?"

"The reasons are speculative," Severino admitted, his voice grave. "The correspondence found with these items hints at treasures aboard the train—riches stolen from across Europe, yes, but also sacred Christian relics. Among them, a fragment of the True Cross; an ancient reliquary believed to date back to the early Church; and

—of particular interest—a mysterious scroll with apocalyptic prophecies from the Knights Templar.

"The Vatican may have sought to prevent these relics from falling into enemy hands."

Marcus's mind raced, the implications staggering. Legends abounded of hidden caches, secret codes, and ancient manuscripts preserved by Templars who survived the fall of their Order in 1312. For nearly two hundred years, they had roamed all of Europe and the Mediterranean as they safeguarded travelers on perilous roads to Jerusalem. In the process, they had amassed untold secrets of cultures that had now vanished in time. Among the most whispered tales was that of a lost codex, an artifact said to contain the accumulated wisdom of the Order—maps to hidden treasures, rituals of initiation, and forbidden knowledge obtained during their time in the Holy Land. This codex would have been both a blessing and a curse, holding truths too dangerous for ordinary men to wield. Apocalyptic prophesies? Such revelations could be a blessing or a curse to the current-day Church.

The existence of such relics alone was monumental, but their connection to the Gold Train and the Vatican's involvement raised questions that could reshape historical understanding. The cardinal would know this, of course, yet something in Severino's eyes spoke of more. Marcus wondered if the man feared some documents might potentially scandalize the Church.

"And you want me to investigate this?" he asked, his voice measured but tinged with unease.

Severino nodded, his expression hardening. "You are

uniquely qualified, Marcus. As an archaeologist, you have the skills to verify the map and decipher the text. But more importantly, you are loyal to the Church. This is not just an academic matter—it is a test of faith and discretion."

Marcus leaned back, his gaze fixed on the map. "What exactly are you asking of me?"

"Be prepared to travel," Severino instructed. "You must retrace the steps of those who hid this train and determine whether it truly exists—and if so, what it contains. I will provide you with the necessary clearances and resources. But be warned: as you are no doubt aware, others continually search and have been for years. Governments, private collectors, even criminal syndicates. This is a race that the Church cannot afford to lose."

The cardinal's words settled heavily on Marcus. The Nazi Gold Train had always seemed like a distant myth, a story told to entertain or distract. Now, it loomed as a tangible, perilous reality. And he, Marcus Russo, stood at the center of it.

"I'll begin immediately," he said, his voice steady despite the maelstrom of thoughts swirling within him.

Severino's expression softened slightly, his voice low, almost confessional. "Be careful, Marcus. This path you are about to walk is fraught with danger—for yourself, I fear, and for the Church and history itself. But I believe you are the right man to walk it."

The cardinal leaned back in his chair, steepling his fingers as he observed Marcus carefully. The map fragment and ciphered letter lay between them like silent witnesses to the monumental task that had just been handed to the Vatican's chief archaeologist. Severino's intense gaze bore into Marcus, as though willing him to grasp the enormity of what lay ahead.

"I would not ask this of you, Marcus, if the stakes were not so high," Severino began, his voice low, almost confessional. "This mission is as perilous as it is vital—not just for the Church, but for history itself."

Marcus leaned forward, his hands clasped tightly. Already he felt his loyalty being tested between the truth of history and his connection to the Church. "I understand the gravity of the task, Your Eminence, but if the train is found, there could be consequences. Serious ones. The Vatican's involvement, no matter how well-intentioned, will be scrutinized—and likely condemned."

Severino's lips pressed together. "You are correct, of course. Should the world learn that certain members of the Church may have assisted in hiding the train, the resulting scandal could be devastating. Questions will arise—questions we may not be able to fully answer. And yet," he added, his tone hardening, "to ignore this discovery, to let it fall into the hands of others, would be an even greater risk."

Marcus squinted at the cardinal. "There's more to it than that, isn't there?"

Severino nodded grimly. "Yes. The treasures aboard the train are not merely material. Among them, if these documents are to be believed, are sacred Christian relics —items tied to the very foundation of our faith. Their recovery would reaffirm the Church's spiritual heritage in a way nothing else could. But"—he hesitated—"if they are discovered first by others less faithful, greedier..."

Marcus finished the thought, his voice steady but strained. "Such relics would be used like currency in the secular world. Centuries of faith built on their authenticity could be undermined as they pass through unbelievers' hands."

"Precisely," Severino said. "And the secular treasures —the gold, the art, the wealth stolen by the Nazis during their reign of terror—those present their own challenges. If recovered, they will not belong to the Church. Holocaust survivors, the descendants of those who lost everything, and the governments and museums of Europe will all stake claims. Handling this with fairness and integrity will be a task fraught with conflict."

Marcus shook his head slowly, the sheer complexity of the mission dawning on him. "So, what you're asking me to do is not just archaeological. It's political, theological, and deeply personal for anyone connected to this history."

Severino's eyes softened slightly, though his resolve remained firm. "Yes, but you need not worry yourself on those things. The discovery of the Gold Train will be your only task for now. You needed to be aware of the resulting complexities, however. You understand, then, why I have chosen you. You have the skills, the knowledge, and the loyalty to navigate these treacherous waters. I would trust no one else with this."

For a long moment, Marcus said nothing. The weight

of Severino's trust—and the enormity of the task—felt almost unbearable. But beneath the hesitation, a spark of determination ignited. This was more than a mission. It was a calling, one that could alter the course of history.

"I'll do it, of course," Marcus said finally, "but on one condition."

Severino arched an eyebrow. "Name it."

"I'll need a team. Trusted individuals with the skills and expertise to assist me. This is not something I can accomplish alone."

The cardinal considered this for a moment before nodding. "Agreed. But choose wisely. And remember—discretion is paramount. The fewer people who know of this mission, the better."

Marcus stood, the documents and map now tucked securely in his satchel. "I already have a few names in mind."

Severino rose as well, his presence as imposing as ever. "Then go, Marcus. Begin your preparations. Time is not on our side."

As Marcus left the office, his mind churned with plans. The names of his trusted colleagues surfaced quickly: Father Michael Dominic, the Prefect of the Secret Archives, whose knowledge of Vatican history and artifacts would be invaluable; Karl Dengler and Lukas Bischoff, the formidable Swiss Guards who had proven their loyalty and skill time and again; and perhaps even Hana Sinclair, the investigative journalist whose past resourcefulness had unraveled secrets others would have missed.

He would need them all for what lay ahead.

For as much as Marcus wanted to view this as an archaeological endeavor, he knew better. The Nazi Gold Train was no simple treasure hunt. It was a Pandora's box of history, faith, and morality, one that couldn't be opened without consequence.

And yet, it was a box he was now bound to open.

CHAPTER

TWO

T he sun dipped low over the tiled rooftops of Trastevere, the district of Rome where Marcus Russo lived. That district, known for its colorful flavor, held tight to its centuries-old structures while sprinkling in modern artisan shops, local craft beer pubs, and amazingly creative trattorias amid budget hotels. The sun cast the neighborhood's narrow cobblestone streets in a warm, golden glow as Marcus Russo made his way to Hana Sinclair's apartment. Hana resided nearby in a more upscale yet nonetheless picturesque area. The quiet hum of the bustling Roman evening provided a soothing backdrop, but Marcus's mind was anything but calm. He clutched a leather folder tightly under his arm, the contents of which had been plaguing him since he was entrusted with them by the Vatican's Secretary of State himself.

Hana responded almost immediately to his cryptic message: *"I have something that requires your expertise.*

Bring your cipher tools." She was known for her sharp-edged intellect and clever puzzling skills, and Marcus trusted her implicitly when it came to unraveling historical mysteries. Still, the gravity of what he carried made his pulse quicken.

When he arrived at her modest building, he paused briefly to collect himself before ringing the buzzer. Moments later, the door opened to reveal Hana Sinclair, a striking woman in her early thirties, her green eyes sparkling with curiosity. Her shoulder-length chestnut brown hair swept naturally inward, framing a smooth, tanned face. A graceful confidence in her bearing suggested years of boarding and prep schools, and she owed her fit, stalwart build to a privileged Swiss heritage. She wore a neatly tailored blouse and slacks, her professional demeanor matched by the warmth in her smile.

"Marcus," she said, stepping aside to let him in, "you've piqued my interest. What's so urgent it couldn't wait until morning?"

"Thanks for seeing me on such short notice, Hana," Marcus replied, stepping into her meticulously organized apartment. Shelves lined the walls, filled with books, maps, and carefully labeled binders. A sleek desk dominated one corner, its surface spotless except for a laptop, a small stack of notes, and a neatly arranged collection of pens and tools. The space exuded efficiency and intellect.

She gestured to the couch. "Sit. Tell me everything."

Marcus didn't waste time. He pulled the leather folder from under his arm and carefully removed a single sheet of yellowed paper. He handed it to Hana, who took it with the kind of reverence reserved for fragile relics. The document bore two unmistakable insignias—the Nazi regime's eagle and swastika on one corner and the Vatican crest on the other.

Hana's eyebrows shot up as she examined it. "This is... well, as first impressions go, this is extraordinary. Where did you get it?"

Marcus hesitated for a moment. "Let's just say it's from a rarely visited section of the Secret Archives, obtained directly from the Secretary of State," he replied. "I need your help to decipher it. Whatever this says, it's the key to a mission I've been tasked with. And time is critical."

Hana tilted her head, curiosity flaring in her expression. "A Vatican mystery involving Nazi insignias? You do know how to pick your puzzles, Marcus."

She moved to her desk, retrieving a notebook, a magnifying glass, and her trusted cipher tools: a cipher wheel—a tool used for encrypting and decrypting messages through a substitution cipher—and a set of reference charts for historical encryption methods. "Let's get to work."

For hours, the two of them worked side by side, the room illuminated by the warm glow of a desk lamp. Hana's fingers moved deftly as she analyzed the faded symbols and scribbled notes in her notebook. Marcus provided context where he could, detailing what little he knew about the document's origins from the letters that were found with it. As they worked, the air grew heavier with the realization that this was no ordinary historical artifact—it was something far more consequential.

"I've seen Nazi encryption methods like this before," Hana muttered, her brow furrowed as she spun the cipher wheel. "But this one is layered—there's a secondary code embedded beneath the surface text. They were trying to hide this from anyone who didn't know exactly what to look for."

Marcus leaned over her shoulder, watching as lines of text slowly emerged from the chaos of symbols. "Can you break it?"

Hana's keen eyes flicked to him, a hint of determination in her expression. "I can break anything."

Minutes turned into hours, the sounds of the city fading as the night deepened. Finally, Hana leaned back in her chair, her face pale but triumphant. She took a deep breath and turned to Marcus, holding up her notebook.

"I've got it."

Marcus sat forward, his heart pounding. "What does it say?"

Hana ran her finger over the decoded text. "It refers to something called *Operation Eisenkreuz*, or 'Iron Cross.' From what I've pieced together, it was a covert effort during the war to relocate artifacts—possibly Vatican treasures—out of Rome to protect them from Allied bombings. But here's the chilling part."

She pointed to a hastily scrawled section of the text. "This phrase repeats multiple times: '*Guardians who cannot be moved.*' It suggests that certain individuals, or perhaps something else, were tasked with protecting these artifacts. As for the 'cannot be moved' portion, it could mean they were steadfast in their duties or in a stationary location and they weren't relocated with the treasures."

Marcus frowned, leaning closer to examine the words. "Guardians? Why emphasize it so strongly? Who, or what, are these 'guardians'?"

Hana tapped her pen against her notebook, her expression thoughtful. "It could be symbolic. Or it could be literal. This document seems rushed, like someone was trying to record these details in a hurry. Whatever these guardians are, they were central to this operation."

Marcus ran a hand through his hair, his mind racing. "If the treasures were relocated, then there might be a record of where they went. But if these 'guardians' stayed behind, it raises a lot of questions. Why weren't they moved? And what exactly were they protecting?"

Hana's gaze sharpened. "Or who were they protecting it from? This wasn't just about hiding treasures from bombs, Marcus. This feels bigger. More deliberate."

The weight of her words settled between them like a heavy stone. Marcus knew she was right. The document was only the beginning of a much larger mystery, one that seemed to involve layers of deception, history, and danger.

"We need to find out more about *Operation Eisenkreuz*," Marcus said finally. "And we need to figure out who—or what—those guardians were."

Hana nodded, her curiosity now fully ignited.

"Agreed. But we'll need to tread carefully. If this operation was as secretive as it seems, then there's a reason it was buried—and someone may not want it uncovered."

Marcus nodded and handed her the accompanying map. In the hours that followed, Hana decoded the map as well. Finally, the two of them sat back and exchanged a look of quiet determination. This was no longer just an academic exercise. Whatever secrets *Operation Eisenkreuz* held, it was clear that they were stepping into a mystery that could have profound implications—not just for history, but for the present.

THE FOLLOWING MORNING, Marcus arrived early at the Vatican Secret Archives to meet with Father Dominic, his steps echoing through the quiet, hallowed corridors. The Pius XII Reading Room, their agreed meeting place, was an intimate chamber of oak paneling and leather chairs. The room, bathed in the warm glow of morning light filtering through high windows, featured shelves of ancient tomes and manuscripts, each radiating an aura of secrecy and the weight of history.

Michael was already there when he arrived, seated at a table with a small stack of carefully arranged documents. He looked up as Marcus entered, rising to greet him with a firm handshake.

These two friends had worked together many times, each well familiar with the fragility of the documents and artifacts entrusted to them. Michael served as the

Vatican's Prefect for the Secret Archives and Marcus as the Vatican's chief archeologist, which meant most of the time Michael worked in the dark recesses of the Vatican while Marcus toiled in the blazing sun, but their duties coalesced on many occasions.

"Good morning, Marcus," the priest said, his tone brisk but friendly. "I hear you've been busy. Cardinal Severino mentioned you might need access to some of our more restricted wartime records. Based on what he told me, I've pulled files that I think might help."

Marcus offered a nod of thanks, settling into the chair across from old friend. "You've saved me a lot of time, Michael. Thank you."

Michael gestured to the table. "We'll start with these. They're from the Vatican's correspondence during the early 1940s, including personal journals and meeting minutes. Handle them carefully—some are quite fragile."

Marcus slipped on the white cotton gloves Michael provided, and together, they began their work. The hours passed in concentrated silence, broken only by the faint rustle of aged paper and the occasional murmured observation. The documents painted a picture of a Vatican caught in a maelstrom of war—letters from bishops pleading for guidance, coded messages from Vatican envoys in occupied territories, and cryptic minutes from meetings held in secrecy.

"This," Marcus muttered, holding up a memo dated 1943, "talks about relocating Vatican artifacts to 'secure locations.' But it doesn't say where."

Michael scanned the page, nodding. "It matches

what we've seen before—hints of a coordinated effort, but never specifics. Whoever organized this operation didn't trust anyone with the full details."

They continued to sift through the records, piecing together fragments of a larger narrative. The table became crowded with documents, some bearing cryptic annotations, others detailing mundane logistical concerns. Marcus's eyes burned from the strain of reading, but he pressed on, driven by the tantalizing sense that they were closing in on something significant.

"Here," Michael said suddenly, holding up a faded sheet of paper. His tone shifted, carrying a note of urgency. "This might be relevant."

Marcus leaned closer as Michael laid the document between them. It was a journal entry written in Latin by a priest who had attended a clandestine meeting in 1944 between Vatican envoys and Nazi officers. The handwriting was hurried, the tone anguished.

The two men read in silence, their expressions growing grim. The priest described the meeting in vivid detail—heated arguments over the fate of "certain sacred relics," with the Vatican envoys fiercely resisting the Nazis' demands. Yet, there was an undercurrent of desperation in the account, a sense that the Vatican representatives were cornered.

"The phrase *'Blood will seal this Covenant'* appears multiple times," Michael said, his voice low, almost reverent. He pointed to the line, underlined by the priest himself, *"'It sounds almost ritualistic.'"*

Marcus's stomach tightened as he read further. The meeting ended abruptly, the Nazis storming out after failing to secure the artifacts. The priest wrote that as the officers left, one of them muttered ominously: *"We will take what is ours, with or without their blessing."* The final paragraph was even more chilling. The priest confessed his fear for his life, expressing doubts about the safety of the relics, even within the Vatican's walls.

"This changes things," Marcus said, sitting back in his chair and rubbing his temples. "It suggests there were divisions within the Vatican. Some were working with the Resistance, but others... it sounds like some were coerced—or worse, complicit."

Michael nodded, his expression grim. "This isn't just a simple case of hiding relics. The letters accompanying the document refer to the Covenant of the Iron Cross. Yet the document itself mentions only Operation Iron Cross. I'm thinking now that the Covenant refers to a pact that predates the Nazis, something the Nazis wanted. The use of 'Iron Cross' in the name of their operation implies that as well—although the Nazis used that as part of their own symbolism, I'm guessing they had some interest in or access to that original Covenant."

"I agree. So, we have an early pact involving the Vatican and likely the Templars, who used the Iron Cross as their symbol. And an agreement of sorts between the Vatican and the Nazis in Operation Iron Cross?"

"Yes. It's a tangled web of allegiances and betrayals. And if there was internal dissent once the Nazis got involved, it raises the possibility that the operation wasn't as secure as they intended."

Marcus picked up the document again, his eyes lingering on the priest's scrawled words. "What's more troubling is this language—'*Blood will seal this Covenant.*' If this wasn't just a figure of speech, it might point to something deeper. Something ritualistic or symbolic, just as the priest also speculated."

Michael leaned back, his brow furrowed in thought. "It could refer to the sanctity of the relics, but it could also hint at something darker. A pact, perhaps? Or an agreement that cost lives?"

Marcus shook his head slowly. "And the Nazi's parting words—they sound like more than just bravado. If they believed the relics belonged to them, it might mean they were part of some larger plan. Something beyond ordinary wartime looting."

They sat in silence for a moment, the enormity of what they had uncovered settling over them. The weight of the Vatican's wartime actions, combined with the Nazis' obsession with relics, hinted at a story far more complex than either of them had anticipated.

"This is only the beginning," Michael said finally, his voice steady but laced with unease. "We've opened a door, Marcus. But what's on the other side might be more dangerous than we realize."

Marcus nodded, carefully placing the document back in its folder. "We need to keep digging. Whatever this 'Operation Iron Cross' was, it didn't end in 1944. I can feel it—this is part of something much bigger."

Michael stood, crossing his arms as he gazed out the window at the distant spire of St. Peter's Basilica. "Then we keep searching. But we need to be cautious. If the answers we're looking for were hidden this carefully, there's a reason. And whoever buried them might not want us to uncover the truth."

The weight of history surrounded them, pressing in from every side as the two men returned to the documents. Whatever secrets *Operation Eisenkreuz* and this strange Covenant held, they were determined to uncover them—even if it meant stepping into the heart of a mystery that had lain dormant for over a half-century.

LATER THAT EVENING, Marcus Russo stood outside Cardinal Severino's office, the faint echo of his knock dissipating in the vast corridor. A muffled voice from within beckoned him to enter. The heavy oak door creaked open, revealing the cardinal seated at his desk, bathed in the warm glow of a single lamp, an amber Murano glass ashtray perched on the corner of the desk. The room, lined with tall shelves of theological texts and historical tomes, radiated an air of both authority and secrecy.

Severino looked up, and Marcus immediately noted the strain on the cardinal's face. His usual air of measured composure had frayed at the edges, his expression shadowed by something heavier than worry.

"Come in, Marcus," Severino said, gesturing to the chair across from him. His voice carried an uncharacteristic weight. "Please sit. There is another layer to this mystery that you must understand before proceeding."

Marcus obeyed, his curiosity sharpening with each passing second. The cardinal reached into a drawer—its lock requiring both a key and a code—and withdrew a tightly rolled scroll. The edges of the parchment were darkened with age, its surface creased and delicate.

"This," Severino began, unrolling the scroll with painstaking care, "is a reproduction. The original was stolen during the war. It is one of the few remaining Templar manuscripts we allowed to remain in the Vatican's possession after the dissolution of their order."

Marcus leaned forward, his eyes tracing the faded ink. The scroll was covered in intricate symbols, arcane markings, and Latin text. He recognized the unmistakable stylistic flourishes of the Templars, their cryptic blend of maps and ciphers designed to obscure as much as they revealed.

"Where did this come from?"

Severino sighed. "As you know, there are tens of thousands of documents and relics under our care. One of the older priests, entrusted with a cloistered area of the archives, found this as well as what I revealed to you yesterday."

"What does it say?" Marcus asked, his voice low, almost reverent.

Severino's eyes narrowed as he studied the manuscript. "It is a map, but not in the traditional sense. This document describes the locations of sacred Christian relics hidden across Europe, relics the Templars concealed centuries ago to protect them from invaders, looters, and even their own Church during turbulent times."

Marcus's brow furrowed as he took in the enormity of what he was hearing. The Pope at that time had established the Templars to escort pilgrims to Jerusalem, their distinctive white mantles adorned with a red cross striking fear into their enemies and awe into the hearts of Christendom. They were warriors of faith, soldiers of a divine mission, but they were also bankers and administrators, safeguarding the transfer of funds across continents. This wealth, combined with their legendary discipline and battlefield prowess, made them indispensable allies—and dangerous enemies. It was this fact that led to their fall.

In 1307, under the shadow of mounting debt and envy, King Philip IV of France orchestrated a brutal crackdown on the then wealthy Templars. On October 13, hundreds of members were arrested, tortured into confessions of heresy, and executed. By 1312, the once mighty Order was officially dissolved by Pope Clement V, their lands and assets scattered. But the questions lingered: what happened to the Templars' greatest treasures? Their sacred relics, their immense wealth, and, most tantalizingly, their knowledge? Was the copied document in Severino's hand a key to their location?

"And the Nazis—did they know about this?"

Severino nodded, his expression grim. "The Nazis were obsessed with relics, particularly those tied to the Christian faith. They believed in their symbolic—and potentially supernatural—power. This manuscript, we believe, was used by them to locate several of these hidden treasures during the war."

Marcus felt a chill settle over him. "And these treasures—are they aboard the train?"

Severino paused, as if weighing the gravity of his words. "We believe so. If the train truly exists, it is more than a repository of stolen wealth and the relics we already knew it could hold. It could hold relics of the Templars uncovered in their journeys and concealed. These could be relics of other faiths before the Church, of other cultures."

Marcus let the words sink in, the implications sending a jolt through his mind. The Nazi Gold Train, long dismissed by many as a myth, could hold relics of immeasurable value—not just monetarily, but spiritually. Objects that could redefine the Church's history and its role in the world.

Severino's gaze hardened. "The relics could reshape the legacy of the Church, perhaps even strengthen its place in a rapidly changing world. But if they contained relics of heathen religions, it could stimulate interest in them, undermine centuries of Christian faith."

Marcus felt the weight of Severino's words settle heavily on his shoulders. He realized another danger for the Church: What might be uncovered could hint at a web of secrets spanning centuries, threads that tied the remaining Templars (who were said to still exist in the shadows) to the rise of Nazi occultism and Operation Iron Cross's sinister agenda. Even though the Church had disbanded the Order, any connection to the Nazis would be harmful to the Church. The stakes were monumental—not just for the Vatican but for history itself. "So the train is more than just a treasure hunt. It's a test of history and legacy."

The room fell silent for a moment, the only sound the faint ticking of a clock on the cardinal's desk. Marcus felt a growing sense of urgency. "Do we have any leads from the Templars' manuscript? Anything that could point us in the right direction?"

Severino gestured to the scroll. "The symbols on this reproduction align with references in *Operation Eisenkreuz*."

"And something else might align," Marcus said. He informed the cardinal of what he had discovered in talking to both Hana and then Michael.

The cardinal nodded. "The guardians mentioned in the decoded letter are likely tied to the Templars' efforts to protect these more ancient relics. We know from history that some of the sites marked on this map were visited by the Nazis during the war. If they found something the Templars hid, it is possible they included it in their Operation Iron Cross."

Marcus stood, his mind racing as he tried to piece together the threads—*Operation Eisenkreuz*, the Templars, the Nazi obsession with relics, and the guardians mentioned in the priest's journal. "I'll need access to any additional records tied to this manuscript and to *Operation Eisenkreuz*."

"Everything you need will be made available," Severino said. "But you must proceed with care. If the map I gave you yesterday truly leads to the train, the consequences of its discovery could reverberate far beyond anything we've seen in recent history."

The cardinal stood as well, his expression stern. "Go, Marcus. Find the truth, whatever it may be. And prepare yourself for the consequences of what you might uncover. There are those who would do anything to control the power this train represents."

As Marcus stepped out into the quiet of the Vatican night, the pieces of the puzzle began slotting into place in his mind. The guardians, the priest's warning, the stolen Templar manuscript—it was all connected. But how? And who else was chasing the answers?

The air was cool, but the weight of the task ahead burned hot in his chest. The road before him was treacherous, but there was no turning back now. Whatever secrets the Nazi Gold Train held, he would uncover them. And he would face whatever dangers lay in wait.

CHAPTER

THREE

With the deciphered map and new clues in hand, the team embarked on their journey to Poland—their destination: the enigmatic Owl Mountains near Wałbrzych, a region steeped in legends of hidden Nazi treasures. The journey began in Rome, where Marcus Russo, Father Michael Dominic, Hana Sinclair, and the Swiss Guards Karl Dengler and Lukas Bischoff convened at Leonardo da Vinci International Airport. Their flight on Ryanair would take them directly to Wrocław, a city in western Poland close to the fabled mountains.

The team arrived at the airport in the early morning, the bustling terminal alive with travelers and the constant hum of announcements. Marcus carried the secured document case containing a reproduction of the map and a dossier of clues and sat by himself, while Father Michael, sitting next to Hana, carried his small, battered leather bag filled with books and notes. Hana, ever prepared, had her laptop and research materials neatly packed, ready to continue her analysis during the flight.

Once aboard the sleek Boeing 737, the group settled into their respective seats in the business class cabin, chosen for its privacy and quiet—a necessity for such a sensitive mission. Hana immediately opened her laptop, her fingers dancing across the keys as she continued to digitize and cross-reference portions of the decoded map with other historical data she had stored. Meanwhile, Marcus reviewed a set of old black-and-white photographs of the Owl Mountains, comparing them to the markings on the map.

Father Michael, more introspective, pulled out a well-worn prayer book, but his eyes often drifted toward Hana, a small smile showing. Michael and Hana had worked together on many missions involving his discoveries in the Vatican Archives. Her keen knowledge and insightfulness had been instrumental in solving clues they encountered on those journeys. But in time, his deep respect for her intellect was transcended by a love that defied a priest's vows. Eventually, they admitted their love for each other. Yet his commitment as a priest wore heavy on him, and even now he carried that mantle. As with all things involving the Church, his decision process would be lengthy, but both he and Hana knew their time together as a married couple grew closer. For now, he gazed at her with an appreciation of her intensity in her research.

He glanced at Marcus and saw his friend's mind clearly wrestled with the implications of their mission before returning to his prayer book for the strength they would need for this journey.

Seated nearby, Karl and Lukas, ever vigilant, exchanged quiet words in German while occasionally glancing at the cabin. Their presence was a constant reminder of the potential danger awaiting the team.

The flight crew served light meals and drinks, which the team accepted with varying levels of enthusiasm. Hana sipped on a cup of coffee, her focus unwavering as she continued to work. Marcus, however, leaned back after a meal of smoked salmon and a glass of sparkling water, staring out the window at the endless expanse of clouds, his brain working at a feverish pace, sorting through the possibilities. Michael remained contemplative, occasionally scribbling notes in the margins of his prayer book.

As the flight progressed, the group held a brief, hushed discussion. Hana summarized her findings, pointing out additional notations on the map that seemed to reference underground structures. Marcus speculated on the possible connections between those markings and the Nazis' suspected construction efforts in the Owl Mountains. Father Michael contributed a theological perspective, considering how the sacred relics hidden during *Operation Eisenkreuz* might have been tied to broader Church efforts to safeguard treasures from wartime destruction.

The mood was a mixture of excitement and tension. The deciphered map hinted at answers to decades-old questions, but the team knew they weren't alone in the hunt. Reports of treasure hunters and conspiracists scouring the Owl Mountains had been rampant for years. Their task would not only require uncovering hidden truths but also navigating the risks of being pursued by those with greedier motives.

As the plane began its descent into Wrocław, the sun was high in the sky, painting the landscape in hues of gold and orange. Marcus gazed out the window at the approaching city, its spires and modern buildings contrasting against the distant silhouette of the Owl Mountains. The next phase of their journey was about to begin, and the weight of history pressed heavily on their shoulders.

As their convoy of three cars crested the final rise of the forested hills, the Owl Mountains stretched out before them, a haunting blend of rugged wilderness and hushed history. The peaks, blanketed in a dense canopy of fir and spruce, appeared like a dark green ocean frozen in time. Low-lying mist wove through the trees like pale ribbons, masking the ground below and giving the area an almost ethereal air. In the distance, jagged granite outcrops pierced the shrouds of fog, their weathered surfaces bearing the marks of centuries of erosion and whispered secrets.

The narrow roads wound through sleepy villages with slate-roofed cottages, each seemingly untouched by modernity. Elderly residents watched from their porches, their eyes betraying suspicions about the passing convoy. Occasionally, the team passed dilapidated roadside shrines, their weathered crosses and saintly figures half-swallowed by creeping ivy, silent sentinels to human hope darkened by time.

The Owl Mountains had long been a region steeped in mystery. During World War II, the area became the focus of immense and enigmatic Nazi activity. Known as *Projekt Riese*—the Giant Project—this mountainous expanse saw the construction of vast underground complexes, purportedly designed to serve as secret bunkers, armament factories, and perhaps even a final redoubt for Adolf Hitler himself. Yet despite years of research and exploration, the true purpose of these maze-like tunnels remained unclear. Were they merely logistical hubs for the Reich, or something more sinister —vaults for stolen gold, religious relics, or even mythical treasures like the fabled Russian Amber Room?

The legends of hidden wealth ran deep. Locals spoke of freight trains laden with gold and priceless art, stolen from across occupied Europe, vanishing into mountain tunnels as the Third Reich began to crumble. Some whispered that the treasures were buried deliberately, a desperate attempt to keep them out of Allied hands. Others claimed they were booby-trapped, guarded by explosives and curses alike, to ensure their secrets died with the war.

And then there were the darker tales—stories of occult rituals and experiments. The Nazis' obsession with arcane knowledge was well documented, and many believed the Owl Mountains held remnants of this pursuit. From cryptic carvings etched into tunnel walls to rumors of hidden chambers where sacrifices were made, the area's reputation as a hotspot of supernatural activity had grown over decades.

As the team disembarked near a trailhead leading into the forest, the air grew heavier, laden with the pitch scent of pine and the metallic tang of earth. Drifts of snow dotted the otherwise bare forest floor, leftovers of earlier snowfalls.

Father Michael stood beside Marcus, his sharp eyes scanning the horizon. He could almost feel the mountain's weight pressing down, as if the secrets buried within were whispering to him, daring him to dig deeper. Nearby, Karl and Lukas checked their gear, their movements precise and methodical, yet even they seemed subdued by the oppressive stillness of the forest.

The two Swiss Guards enjoyed spelunking throughout Europe in their off-duty time and had coerced Michael into joining them a couple of times. Hana, too, had briefly explored caves in the past. Marcus, the oldest of the group, had faced more than his share of nature's barriers in his life's work on archeological expeditions, caves included. Today, the two guards had supplied the group from a shop near the airport with enough equipment to handle whatever the Owl Mountains brought them. Or so they hoped.

Hana stood studying the map in her hands. The deciphered map suggested that their destination lay within the labyrinthine complex beneath Włodarz Mountain, one of the most infamous sites of *Projekt Riese*. The tunnels there were said to extend for miles, a subterranean maze carved into solid rock. Local guides at the supply shop had offered their services to what they guessed was a simple expedition into the Owl Mountains. Marcus declined, and the guides then warned them of the dangers: unstable passages, hidden traps, and the ever-present risk of collapse. The locals asked again: were they certain they didn't need guides? Marcus assured them they did not, even as he avoided sharing their real purpose. But it wasn't the physical hazards that unnerved the team. It was the lingering energy of the place, the echoes of forced laborers who had died carving out the Reich's secrets, their cries trapped in the stone for eternity.

As they pushed deeper into the forest, the sunlight grew faint, filtered through the dense canopy overhead. The only sounds were the crunch of boots on the ground and the occasional call of a raven, its raspy caw like a warning from some unseen sentinel.

"This place," Hana finally said, breaking the silence, "feels alive. Like it's watching us."

Marcus nodded grimly. "The mountains have seen too much, Hana. They remember."

They veered from the path and trudged through woods, with Hana leading the way, map and compass in hand. Twice they backtracked a few steps, turning slightly to match the coordinates she called out. And suddenly, the mountain's stone wall rose in front of them.

Ahead, moss-covered rock and tangled vines covered the cold stone of the mountain. Without speaking, the team spread out along the wall, using flashlights to peer through foliage, pushing the tangles away as needed. Many minutes passed, with nothing said until Lukas called out, "Here!"

The team gathered behind him and witnessed the entrance to the Włodarz tunnels—an unassuming hole in the mountainside hidden by boulders, undergrowth, and the shadows of the trees. Yet it could be a gateway to another world, one filled with both promise and peril. Marcus used his flashlight, illuminating the darkness beyond. The light caught on something metallic embedded a meter or so farther in the wall—an ancient iron plate etched with runes that none of them recognized.

"Looks like our adventure is just beginning," Michael said softly, stepping forward. They all trudged over and through the natural barriers to stand in the small opening.

Marcus adjusted the beam of his flashlight, casting the stark white light deeper into the yawning void of the tunnel. The iron plate embedded in the wall was pitted and tarnished, its runes worn down by decades of damp air and neglect. He traced a finger over the strange symbols, feeling the grooves beneath his touch.

"These markings…" he began, his voice echoing softly in the enclosed space, "they're not German. Nor are they Slavic. This is something older."

Father Michael stepped closer, peering at the runes. "Older? How much older?"

Marcus shrugged, his brow furrowed in concentration. "Difficult to say. But they resemble some of the proto-European scripts I've seen—languages tied to the early Bronze Age. What they're doing here, in a tunnel constructed by the Nazis, is a mystery in itself."

Hana snapped a quick photograph, the flash momentarily illuminating the damp stone walls of the tunnel. "If this was part of *Projekt Riese*," she said, "maybe the Nazis found something they weren't supposed to. Something ancient. And they made use of this older tunnel for their own purposes."

Michael nodded, his mind turning over the implications. "If the Reich believed they were uncovering something of immense power or significance, it would explain their obsession with this region. We know their fixation on relics and arcane knowledge wasn't just propaganda."

Behind them, Karl and Lukas stood guard, their figures tense and alert in the dim light. The Swiss Guards had been in hazardous situations before, but the oppressive atmosphere of the tunnel seemed to gnaw at their usually unflappable composure.

"Let's move," Karl said, his voice intense but low. "I'd rather we not linger."

The group pressed onward, their footsteps muffled on the uneven stone floor. The air grew warmer as they ventured deeper, and the faint sound of dripping water echoed like a slow, ominous heartbeat. The walls were slick with moisture, and the scent of damp earth mingled with a faint metallic tang, like old blood.

As they advanced, the tunnel began to widen, revealing a larger chamber ahead. The beams of their flashlights danced across the rough-hewn walls, illuminating crude support beams that looked as though they might give way at any moment. At the center of the chamber stood an object that made them all stop short—a large stone altar, its surface scarred with strange markings and dark stains.

Marcus approached cautiously, his light playing over the altar's surface. "This isn't part of the Nazi construction," he said, his voice hushed. "This is much, much older."

Michael joined him, his gaze fixed on the altar. "You're saying the Nazis found this and decided to build their tunnel system around it?"

"Possibly," Marcus replied. "Or maybe they were looking for it. Either way, it's clear they saw some kind of significance here."

Hana stepped closer, snapping another photograph. "Those stains," she said, her voice tight. "Are we looking at evidence of… sacrifices?"

Marcus didn't answer immediately, but his silence spoke volumes. He leaned in, brushing away a layer of dirt from the surface of the altar. Beneath it, a faint carving became visible—a snake coiled around a tree, its fangs bared.

"A serpent," Michael murmured. "A symbol of wisdom, danger, and betrayal in so many cultures. And tied to ancient rites."

"And death," Marcus added grimly. "This was more than an altar. It was a place of ritual. And those rituals weren't peaceful."

Hana shivered, pulling her jacket tighter around her. "So what now? Do we keep going?"

Michael straightened, his jaw set. "We have to. If the

Nazis knew about this, which we can assume they did since their coordinates led us here, and if they were trying to use it for their own ends, then whatever lies deeper in this mountain might be what we're looking for."

Marcus nodded. "And it can mean more dangers as well."

Karl and Lukas exchanged a glance, their hands instinctively resting on their holstered weapons.

"We'll take point," Lukas said, stepping forward. "Stay close."

The team continued past the altar, the path narrowing once more. The oppressive weight of the mountain seemed to close in around them, and the silence was absolute, save for the occasional drip of water. As they walked, Marcus noticed faint carvings etched into the walls—more runes, spirals, and symbols that grew more intricate and unsettling the farther they went.

They rounded a corner and froze. Ahead, the tunnel opened into an enormous cavern, its ceiling lost in darkness. The light of their flashlights barely reached the far walls, but what they could see was staggering: rows of rusted rail tracks leading from the nearby wall, where boulders swallowed the tracks in that direction, to a massive, sealed iron door set into the cavern's far wall. The door was adorned with more runes, as well as the unmistakable emblem of the Third Reich—a swastika encircled by a wreath.

"Looks like we've found what the map was leading us to," Hana whispered.

Marcus stepped forward, his flashlight trained on the door. "The question now," he said, "is whether what's behind that door is treasure—or something we should never have disturbed."

Father Michael's eyes lingered on the swastika, a bitter reminder of the horrors tied to this place. "One thing is certain," he said quietly. "Whatever the Nazis sealed in here, they didn't intend for it to be found again." He motioned to what had obviously been a much larger opening before it was buried under a carefully set explosive charge. Just enough to block the space where the rails emerged, but not enough to collapse the cavern. Clearly, something large could have been moved in on the rails and through the massive iron door before the outside entrance had been concealed. The Gold Train?

The team exchanged uneasy but excited glances. The only sound was the distant drip of water echoing in the vast chamber. Michael took a deep breath and nodded. "Let's see what secrets the mountain is ready to reveal."

Marcus stepped closer to the massive iron door, his flashlight beam gliding over its surface. Rust had crept into the edges, but the sheer size of the door—and the craftsmanship of its intricate mechanisms—spoke of a deliberate and calculated effort to seal whatever lay beyond. As he reached out to touch the surface, the chill of the metal seeped into his fingertips, and for a moment, he swore he felt a faint vibration, as though the mountain itself were alive and breathing.

"Do you feel that?" he murmured, glancing back at the others.

Father Michael frowned and placed his hand on the door as well. His expression hardened. "It's... humming. Faint, but it's there."

Hana took a cautious step forward, camera in hand, her eyes darting around the cavern as though expecting something—or someone—to emerge from the shadows. "Humming? Are we sure it's not some kind of seismic activity? These tunnels are pretty old."

Marcus shook his head. "No, it's too localized. It's coming from behind this door."

Karl and Lukas exchanged a glance, their instincts kicking in. Lukas approached the edge of the doorframe, his flashlight scanning for any signs of hidden mechanisms or traps. "If this is some kind of security system, it's unlike anything I've seen before. The Nazis were meticulous, but this feels... unnatural."

Hana aimed her flashlight higher, illuminating faint symbols etched into the iron above the swastika. "More runes," she said, her voice imbued with unease. "But these are different from the ones we've seen so far."

Marcus stepped back and studied the symbols. "They're... Nordic. But not the usual kind associated with Nazi mythology. These predate even the Viking Age. *Elder Futhark*, perhaps?"

"Which means?" Michael prompted, his tone curious.

Marcus exhaled slowly. "Which means we're looking at something ancient. Something the Nazis didn't create but found. Considering their penchant for looting ancient relics of any kind, if they sealed it behind this door, it was to protect it—to save it for their reclamation later."

The air in the cavern seemed to grow colder, the silence heavier. A faint, rhythmic sound echoed through the cavern—soft at first, almost imperceptible, but growing louder with each passing second. A deep, resonant thudding, like a heartbeat amplified through the stone. The team froze, their flashlights scanning the darkness.

"That's not seismic activity," Karl said, his voice tight, his hand moving to the grip of his weapon.

"No," Marcus agreed, his voice barely audible. "That's coming from behind the door."

The sound deepened, resonating in their chests like the pulse of some ancient force. Marcus stepped back from the door, his arms spread out, his instincts screaming at him to put as much distance as possible between his team and whatever lay beyond. "We need to rethink this," he said. "We might not be equipped to deal with—"

Before he could finish, a sudden gust of icy wind tore through the cavern, their flashlights flickering as each of them staggered from the shock of it, their breaths visible in the freezing air. When they steadied the lights on the door again, it revealed a new detail they hadn't seen before: a faint glow emanating from a crack at the base of the iron door.

The glow was an eerie, pulsating green, like phosphorescence found in the deep ocean. Marcus crouched, staring at the crack. "This wasn't visible before," he said. "It's as if something... something on the other side is reacting to us."

"Reacting?" Michael said, his voice filled with alarm. "You mean it knows we're here?"

"Maybe," Marcus replied. "Or maybe we've triggered something that was dormant."

Karl and Lukas stepped forward, weapons drawn. "Whatever it is, we're not opening this door," Karl said firmly. "We need to regroup, assess the situation."

Hana nodded quickly, taking a step back. "Agreed. This isn't treasure hunting anymore. This is something else."

Before they could retreat further, the glowing crack widened slightly, and a faint mist began to seep through. It swirled at their feet, unnaturally cold and carrying a metallic scent that stung their nostrils. Marcus instinctively covered his mouth and nose with his sleeve, the others quickly following suit. "We need to leave. Now."

But just as they turned to retreat, the rhythmic thudding behind the door stopped. The cavern fell silent, the absence of sound almost deafening. The team paused, glancing at one another, their expressions a mixture of confusion and dread.

"What just happened?" Hana asked, her voice trembling as she snapped a picture of the misty glow at the base of the door.

The answer came almost immediately. From somewhere deep within the mountain—far beyond the iron door—a low, guttural groan reverberated, so deep it seemed to vibrate their very bones. It wasn't mechanical, nor was it human. It was something else entirely.

Michael crossed himself instinctively, his face pale. "We're not alone here," he said. "And whatever is in this mountain… it wasn't meant to be found."

The team hurriedly retraced their steps, the oppressive air of the cavern pressing down on them as they moved. The glowing mist lingered at the base of the door, pulsating softly like a heartbeat. As they emerged back into the forest, the faint sound of the groan followed them, echoing in their minds long after it had faded into the silence of the mountain.

The Owl Mountains had given them their first answer: whatever the Nazis had sealed away, they had done so for a reason. And now, Marcus and his team had disturbed it.

CHAPTER

FOUR

T he team rushed to exit the cavern and scrambled through the tunnel to plunge into the dense forest outside and its welcome but oppressive embrace. The afternoon light was weak, filtered through the ever-present mist that clung to the mountains like a veil as they escaped. No one spoke for several minutes, the group instinctively putting as much distance as possible between themselves and the eerie door buried in the mountain.

It was Karl who broke the silence, his voice steady but low. "I think we can all agree that whatever that was… it wasn't natural."

The five of them came to a stop now, eyes scanning the dark woods as they each caught their breath. Hana pulled out her camera, scrolling through the images she had captured in the cavern. Her fingers trembled as she stopped at the photograph of the glowing mist seeping through the crack. "Natural? Karl, it's like we just walked out of some nightmare. That… thing behind the door? It felt alive. Sentient."

Marcus, who had been silent, stopped abruptly and turned to face the group. His face was pale but resolute. "Not alive. But reactive to us being there. That mist, the blast of cold air, those vibrations… they weren't random. The door—it's not just a barrier. It's a threshold. And whatever lies beyond… is more than a train full of loot."

Michael frowned, folding his arms against the cold that seemed to cling to him even outside. "The question we need to answer isn't just what's behind that door, Marcus. It's why the Nazis sealed it. And why they left those symbols—the serpent, the runes—like warnings."

Marcus nodded, his thoughts racing. "There's no denying the precision of how this site was hidden. The map, the cryptic phrasing in the document we found in the archives, even the rumors about *Projekt Riese*. Everything points to deliberate obfuscation. Someone wanted this place forgotten."

"Or left as a trap," Lukas muttered grimly. He had kept his weapon drawn the entire time, and his posture radiated unease.

Marcus sighed and rubbed his temples. "We need more information. There's no point speculating when we don't even know what we're dealing with. Those runes—they're the key. I need time to study the photos and cross-reference them with what we know."

Hana glanced at Michael. "Can we trust the Vatican's Archives to have answers? Or are we just peeling back more layers of secrets?"

Michael hesitated, feeling the weight of the question. "The Vatican Archives have answers, yes. But whether they'll be complete or even accessible to us is another matter. What we found in the Pius XII Reading Room records was difficult enough to find. If there's more, it'll be buried even deeper."

A gust of wind rustled through the trees, and the group instinctively turned toward the sound. The forest seemed darker than before, the shadows stretching unnaturally. Karl motioned for them to keep moving. "Let's get back to the vehicles. We can't afford to stand here like sitting ducks."

They soon found the hiking path to the parking lot, and their walk back was brisk but tense, each step accompanied by the sensation of being watched. The oppressive atmosphere of the mountains hadn't lifted— it had followed them, its unseen presence like a heavy hand on their shoulders.

By the time they reached the small mountain inn serving as their base, dusk had settled, the orange glow of the setting sun barely visible through the thick mist. The Swiss Guards remained outside on guard. The innkeeper, an elderly woman with a weathered face and intense eyes, greeted the rest as they trundled in with her usual brusque nod but paused as she caught sight of their expressions.

"You've been to the tunnels," she said, her voice suffused with an edge of fear. It wasn't a question.

Michael stepped forward, forcing a calm smile. "Just some preliminary exploration."

The innkeeper's gaze flicked to Marcus, then to

Hana. "You won't find peace there. Those tunnels are cursed. Everyone around here knows it. What you're looking for—it should stay buried."

Before Michael could respond, the woman turned away, muttering under her breath as she disappeared into the kitchen.

"Well, that's comforting," Hana said dryly, collapsing into a chair by the fireplace. She pulled her laptop from her bag and began transferring the photos. "Let's see if we can make sense of what we found."

Marcus joined her, flipping through his notes and cross-referencing with a digital archive he had loaded onto his tablet. "The serpent symbol—it's not unique. It's appeared in various forms across ancient cultures. It could signify protection, but just as often, it's a warning. The runes, though, are what bother me."

He zoomed in on one of Hana's photos, pointing to a specific sequence etched above the door. "This one here—it's not a letter or a word. It's a cipher. A key, maybe."

Michael leaned over, frowning. "A key to what?"

"Maybe to whatever is behind that door," Marcus replied. "Or to understanding it."

Before they could delve further, Lukas entered the room, his face grim. "We have a problem. There's movement in the forest."

Karl was close behind, adjusting his earpiece. "It's not locals. Too coordinated. I think someone followed us from the tunnels. We need to secure this place."

Marcus closed his notebook, his jaw tight. "If someone else knows about this site, it means they've been watching us from the beginning. We've stirred up something much bigger than we thought."

Michael nodded, his mind already racing ahead. "Bigger—and possibly more dangerous."

Marcus motioned to the two Swiss Guards, who left again quickly to check out the situation. Then he turned to the others. "Our best course is to understand exactly what we're dealing with and what these others are looking for. Let's find the answers if we can before we take the next step."

Outside, the wind howled through the trees, carrying with it the faint, haunting echo of that guttural groan from deep within the mountain. The Owl Mountains weren't finished with them yet.

THE FAINT HOWL of the wind outside seemed to creep through the walls of the inn, curling into the corners of the room like a living thing. The team moved with a heightened sense of urgency, their unease palpable as they prepared for what could only be described as the unknown.

Lukas and Karl swept the outside perimeter of the inn, their training guiding their movements. The forest shadows encroached on the building like a silent army, the shifting forms of the trees appearing almost humanoid under the moonlight. Lukas motioned to Karl, pointing toward a disturbance in a plot of snow—a patch that had been recently disrupted.

"Tracks," Lukas murmured, crouching to inspect them. His gloved hand brushed the outline of boot prints, larger than any they had seen on the locals. "Military issue. Whoever it is, they're professionals."

Karl's jaw tightened. "We're not alone. Let's double back—we don't want to lead them right to the team."

INSIDE, Marcus had commandeered a corner of the room, books and printouts strewn around him as he compared Hana's photographs with ancient texts stored in his tablet. "Look at this," he said, beckoning Michael and Hana closer. He pointed to a runic sequence in the photograph from the iron door and held up an old illustration from a scanned manuscript.

"This sequence here is tied to an old Nordic myth about something called *Jörmungandr's Vault*. It's obscure, but there are references in apocryphal texts that suggest it's not just a myth. Some accounts tie it to artifacts or relics of great power—'the serpent's treasures.'"

Hana leaned in, her brow furrowing. "Artifacts of power? That sounds a little… fantastical."

"Fantastical, yes," Marcus admitted. "But the Nazis were obsessed with this kind of thing. We know they scoured the world for anything they thought might give them an edge—historical, religious, even mystical. If they believed they'd found something buried here that fit the bill, they'd have built an entire mountain complex to secure it. However, if it truly was a thing of power, I'd think the Nazis would have used it, weaponized it in some way."

Michael nodded thoughtfully. "Unless they didn't

have time to harness it yet, so they sealed it away rather than risk using it."

"Exactly," Marcus said. He hesitated, his eyes darting to the photos again. "And there's more that fits this concept. The carvings—especially the serpent coiled around the tree—suggest this might not be a treasure at all. It might be a warning. Something meant to be left undisturbed."

Hana leaned back, crossing her arms. "And now we've cracked open the metaphorical tomb."

Michael sighed, pinching the bridge of his nose. "If it's a warning, then what's behind that door could be far more dangerous than we anticipated."

Before Marcus could respond, Karl and Lukas burst into the room.

"We've got company," Karl said sharply. "There are at least three of them in the forest, maybe more. Armed and tracking us."

Hana's eyes widened. "Who are they?"

"Not locals," Lukas replied. "They're professionals. Military boots, coordinated movement. Someone's been watching us, and they waited until we were vulnerable."

Michael's mind raced. "If they've been watching us, then they know we've been inside the tunnels."

Marcus nodded. "In which case, if they were only hoping we'd lead them to the tunnel, they would already know the access to it. They wouldn't need to come after us. Maybe they want to stop us from revealing it because they want it only for themselves. Or... they know we still have something else they want." His eyes scanned the folder of documents and maps they had from the archives that had led them here in the first place. He added grimly, "This isn't a coincidence."

Hana grabbed her laptop, quickly shutting it and packing it into her bag. "Do we stay and fight, or do we move?"

"We move," Karl said decisively. "We can't risk a confrontation here. We'll retreat to the vehicles and regroup."

Michael nodded, his expression resolute. "We'll need to keep the map and photographs safe. If they're after the same thing we are, they'll try to take anything that gives them a lead."

The team moved swiftly, packing their gear and extinguishing any signs of their presence. Outside, the wind had picked up, obscuring any sound. Every shadow seemed to move, every creak of the forest magnified in the tense silence.

As they approached their vehicles, parked under the cover of a copse of trees, Lukas raised a hand, signaling for them to stop. He scanned the area with his night-vision scope and cursed under his breath. "They're ahead of us. Two figures near the vehicles."

"Options?" Michael whispered as he moved up to wrap an arm around Hana's shoulders.

"Flank them," Karl said. "Lukas and I can distract them while you head for the backup vehicle we stashed farther down the road."

Marcus glanced nervously at the forest, the weight of

the day's discoveries and dangers pressing heavily on him. "And if they're not the only ones?"

Karl's expression was grim. "Then we make sure they don't get what they came for."

Hana clutched her bag of precious documents and maps tightly, her knuckles white. She looked up at Michael beside her, and he gave her a comforting nod as his hand squeezed her shoulder. Marcus said, "Let's move."

The team split as planned, Karl and Lukas disappearing into the shadows like wraiths, their movements silent and precise. Michael, Hana, and Marcus hurried through the dense undergrowth, the cold biting at their faces as they navigated the uneven terrain.

Behind them, a faint commotion broke the quiet— shouted commands, the muffled crack of a silenced weapon. Lukas's voice crackled over the comms. "Go! We've got them pinned."

Michael quickened his pace, his heart pounding, pulling Hana behind him. The faint outline of the backup vehicle came into view, partially concealed by snow-dusted branches. They piled in, Hana sliding into the driver's seat and, with the key already in the ignition, started the engine.

As the vehicle roared to life, Marcus glanced back toward the forest, his gut twisting. For a split second, he thought he saw movement—something large and sinuous weaving through the trees, illuminated faintly by the moonlight.

"Did you see that?" Marcus asked, his voice barely

audible. But before he could say more, Hana hit the gas and they sped away into the night.

Michael turned to him, his expression grim. "See what?"

Marcus hesitated, his gaze lingering on the darkened forest. "Nothing. Let's just get out of here."

But he couldn't shake the feeling that the soldiers after them weren't the only thing stirring in the mountains.

CHAPTER
FIVE

The road out of the mountains was a jagged ribbon of ice and gravel, barely wide enough for their vehicle to pass without skidding dangerously close to the drop-offs that bordered it. The headlights carved thin, pale tunnels of light through the darkness, illuminating the dense forest that seemed to close in tighter with each passing kilometer. Inside the car, the tension was suffocating, the silence broken only by the hum of the engine and the occasional crunch of loose stones under the tires.

Marcus sat in the back, his fingers nervously flipping through the photographs Hana had transferred to a tablet before they fled. The glowing mist from the crack beneath the iron door seemed to pulse on the screen as if alive, even in still imagery. He kept glancing at it, a gnawing sense of unease tightening in his chest. Something about the light, the color, felt wrong— unnatural in a way that defied explanation.

Hana gripped the wheel with white-knuckled intensity, her eyes locked on the winding road ahead. "How far to the safe house?" she asked, her voice strained but steady.

"Another thirty minutes, give or take," Michael replied from the passenger seat, his gaze flicking between a map, the forest outside, and the side mirror. "Assuming we weren't tailed."

"We weren't," Marcus said absently, his attention still on the photos. "Karl and Lukas would've warned us if anyone got past them."

Michael didn't look convinced. "Unless whoever—or whatever—is following us isn't bound by normal rules."

Hana shot him a searing look. "Let's not go *there*, Michael."

But Marcus glanced up, his expression troubled. "What if he's right? What if this isn't just about treasure hunters or rival factions? What if it's something... older?"

Michael turned to face him fully, his tone firm. "Older doesn't mean supernatural, Marcus. You're the one who always insists on logic and evidence."

"Exactly," Marcus shot back, his voice rising slightly. "And the evidence we've seen so far doesn't fit into any logical framework. Those runes, that mist... even the vibrations we felt from the door. This isn't just history, Michael. It's something else."

The car hit a rough patch of road, jostling them violently and cutting off the conversation. Hana tightened her grip on the wheel, muttering a curse under her breath. "Focus, people. Let's argue about the impossible after we're somewhere safe."

The safe house Marcus had arranged through a Polish colleague was a dilapidated farmhouse tucked into a secluded hollow at the base of the mountains. Its weathered exterior and sagging roof gave the impression of abandonment, but the reinforced doors and security cameras hidden among the surrounding trees told a different story. Hana killed the engine and the three of them climbed out, shivering as the icy wind bit through their coats.

Marcus punched in a code on the keypad beside the front door, and the lock clicked open. They stepped inside, the warmth of the interior a stark contrast to the biting cold outside. The farmhouse was sparsely furnished but functional, its main room dominated by a large table cluttered with maps, documents, and survival gear provided by previous tenant operatives.

"We'll set up here," Marcus said, dropping his bag onto the table. "Michael, check the perimeter cameras. Hana, you go through those photos again. Look for anything we might've missed."

"And you?" Michael asked, already moving to the monitor bank in the corner.

"First, I'll set up our satellite dish so we have internet access; then I'm going to check in with Karl and Lukas. We need to be sure they made it out," Marcus replied. Reaching into his backpack, he withdrew a twenty-five by thirty-centimeter Starlink Mini satellite dish and set it, facing north, outside on a weathered picnic bench, enabling the built-in wireless Wi-Fi access point for their electronic gear. Then he pulled out his phone, his fingers moving quickly over the keypad as he sent a message to Karl.

The minutes stretched into what felt like hours as each of them worked. Michael cycled through the camera feeds, his eyes scanning the darkened forest for any sign of movement. Hana reviewed the photos on the tablet, cross-referencing the runes with every resource they had available. Marcus paced the room, his phone in hand, waiting for a reply that didn't come.

Finally, Michael broke the silence. "Nothing on the cameras. Either we're alone, or whoever's out there is good enough to avoid detection."

"Let's hope it's the former," Marcus muttered.

Hana straightened, her eyes locked on one of the photos. "I think I found something."

Michael and Marcus joined her at the table, leaning over the photo she had highlighted. It showed the runes above the iron door, but Hana had overlaid them with a digital enhancement that revealed faint, almost invisible etchings in the stone surrounding the symbols.

"These weren't visible in the cavern," Hana explained. "The light wasn't strong enough. But when I boosted the contrast, this popped up."

The faint etchings formed a circular design surrounding the runes, and within the circle, a sequence of smaller symbols repeated in a spiral pattern.

"It's a seal," Michael said, his voice quiet. "The door isn't just a physical barrier. It's part of a containment system."

"A containment system for what?" Hana asked, her voice low.

"That's the question," Marcus replied. "But whatever it is, the Nazis didn't just lock it away. They used ancient methods—runes, seals—because they believed those were the only things that could hold it."

Hana stared at the photo, a chill running down her spine. "You're saying they believed it was alive."

"I'm saying," Marcus said carefully, "that the Nazis didn't take chances. And neither should we."

Before anyone could respond, Marcus's phone buzzed. He snatched it up, reading the message that had just come through.

"It's from Lukas," he said. "They're alive but pinned down near the tunnels. They think reinforcements are coming."

Hana's expression hardened. "Reinforcements? For who?"

"Sadly, not for us. For whoever's after us," Marcus replied, his voice grim. "And likely they're not just after us—they're after what's behind that door."

Michael looked up from the photo, his expression resolute. "Then we need to decide. Do we stop them—or let them open the door and face whatever comes next?"

Hana countered, "How could we even stop them if we wanted to?"

The room fell silent as the weight of the decision settled over them. Outside, the wind howled, carrying with it the unshakable sense that time was running out.

CHAPTER
SIX

The dense forest around the tunnels was eerily quiet, the kind of silence that set Karl's nerves on edge. He crouched behind a fallen tree, his weapon raised, scanning the area through the night-vision scope. Beside him, Lukas was equally tense, his eyes flicking from one shadow to the next.

"They're moving in a standard pincer," Lukas whispered, his voice barely audible over the faint rustle of leaves. "Three on the left, two circling right. Tactical, but not flawless."

"Mercenaries," Karl muttered. "Too precise for amateurs, but not trained enough for elite operatives. Could be hired muscle."

Lukas nodded, his movements deliberate and methodical as he adjusted his position. "Whoever they are, they knew about the tunnels and now know its location, thanks to us—and I'd bet they're after the same thing we are. Only they don't realize what we actually found instead of treasure."

Karl glanced over his shoulder, his gaze drawn toward the faint glow of the cavern entrance in the distance. "If they get inside, we'll have a much bigger problem. We can't let that happen."

Lukas said faintly, checking his ammunition, "We won't."

The two Swiss Guards moved silently, their years of training in the alpine forests of Switzerland allowing them to blend seamlessly with the shadows. They flanked the advancing group, positioning themselves between the intruders and the cavern. Karl raised his fist, signaling a halt as they neared the edge of a clearing where the mercenaries had paused, regrouping.

Five figures moved through the darkness, their outlines barely visible against the trees. They wore black tactical gear, their faces obscured by masks. One of them carried a small device—some kind of scanner—its faint beeping the only sound in the stillness.

"Tech-savvy," Lukas murmured. "Probably tracking heat signatures."

Karl's jaw tightened. "Then they know we're here."

The leader of the mercenary group raised a hand, signaling the others to spread out. Two figures peeled off to the left, their movements careful but deliberate. The other three moved forward, heading directly toward the cavern entrance.

"We take out the scanner first," Karl whispered. "They lose their edge without it."

Lukas nodded, sighting down his weapon. "On your mark."

Karl exhaled slowly, his mind racing through the calculations. The trees provided cover, but the mercenaries were too close to the cavern for comfort. A single mistake could give away their position—or worse, draw the enemy closer to whatever lay behind the door.

"Now," Karl said, his voice a whisper of command.

Lukas fired, the silenced round cutting through the night and striking the mercenary holding the scanner. The man dropped silently, the device falling from his hands and skittering across the ground. The others froze, their heads snapping toward the sound.

Karl didn't hesitate. He shifted his aim and fired at the nearest figure, the shot catching the mercenary in the leg. The man crumpled with a muffled grunt, his weapon clattering to the ground.

The remaining three sprang into action, returning fire in the direction of Karl and Lukas. Bullets tore through the undergrowth, splintering branches and kicking up dirt. Karl ducked behind the fallen tree, his movements smooth and practiced.

"Two down," he murmured into his comms. "Three to go."

Lukas moved to a new position, circling wide to flank the remaining mercenaries. He fired again, taking out another figure with a precise shot to the shoulder. The man dropped his weapon, shouting in pain.

The two remaining mercenaries regrouped, their movements more frantic now. One of them barked a command, and Karl recognized the sharp tone of desperation. They hadn't expected resistance this skilled.

Lukas's voice crackled softly over the comms. "They're falling back. Should we let them?"

"No," Karl replied, his tone cold. "They'll regroup and come back with more firepower. We finish this now."

The two guards moved in tandem, their coordinated attack overwhelming the mercenaries. Within moments, the skirmish was over. The last of the intruders lay incapacitated or retreated into the shadows.

Karl and Lukas emerged from the cover of the trees, their weapons raised as they approached the fallen figures. One of the mercenaries, still conscious, glared up at Karl with defiance.

"You don't know what you're dealing with," the man growled, his accent unplaceable. "You think you're protecting something? You're not. You're keeping the world from what it needs."

Karl's expression didn't waver. "And who sent you to decide that?"

The mercenary smirked, blood staining his teeth. "You'll find out. Sooner than you think."

Before Karl could respond, the man's head slumped to the side, his breathing shallow but steady. Lukas crouched to check him, then looked up. "Unconscious. Should we call it in?"

"Not yet," Karl said, standing and scanning the forest. "There might be more out there."

The faint rustle of leaves drew their attention, but

when they turned, there was nothing but darkness. The forest was silent once more, but it didn't feel like victory.

It felt like a warning.

INSIDE THE SAFE HOUSE, the tension was substantial. The faint hum of the perimeter cameras and the occasional creak of the farmhouse's old wooden beams were the only sounds as Marcus, Michael, and Hana gathered around the table. The photographs, notes, and maps spread out before them seemed to radiate their own unease, a stark reminder of the mystery they had barely begun to unravel.

Marcus paced the room, his frustration mounting. "We're missing something," he said, running a hand through his hair. "Something obvious. Those runes, the seal—it's not just about locking something away. It's a message."

Michael leaned against the edge of the table, his arms crossed. "A message to whom? The people who built it? The Nazis? Or us?"

"All of the above," Marcus replied. He gestured to the spiral pattern etched around the runes. "This design —it's ancient, predating any known Nordic civilization. But the Nazis didn't just stumble upon it. They incorporated it into their plans. That means they understood at least part of what they were dealing with."

Sitting with her laptop open, Hana tapped a few keys and brought up a grainy archival image. It showed a Nazi officer standing in a cavernous room, holding what appeared to be an artifact—an ornate disc etched with similar symbols. "This was taken in 1944," she said. "Włodarz Mountain. Same location as the tunnels we just left. They were already excavating when they found... whatever this is."

Michael squinted at the image. "A disc? Could it be connected to the seal?"

"It's possible," Marcus said, leaning in for a closer look. "If it's part of the mechanism, it might be a key— or a trigger."

Hana shook her head. "The real question is: if the Nazis had this key, why didn't they use it? They could've opened the door."

"Or they did open it," Marcus said, his voice low. "And whatever they found scared them enough to seal it again."

The room fell silent, the weight of his words settling over them.

Michael rubbed his temples, his thoughts racing. "We need to contact Karl and Lukas. If they're dealing with whoever's after us, they might have intel we can use."

Hana nodded and switched the laptop to the secure communications channel. A crackle of static filled the room before Lukas's voice came through, strained but clear.

"We're secure for now," Lukas said. "Engaged with a hostile group near the tunnels. Five men, well-equipped, but not professional military. We took some of them down, others escaped."

"Casualties?" Michael asked.

"None on our end," Lukas replied. "One of theirs was still conscious. Said we don't know what we're protecting. Claims it's something the world 'needs.'"

Michael exchanged a glance with Marcus, who frowned deeply. "Did they say who sent them?"

"No," Lukas said. "But their gear suggests significant funding. Not your average treasure hunters."

Hana leaned forward, speaking into the microphone. "Did they mention the door? Or what might be behind it?"

There was a pause before Lukas answered. "No specifics, but the way they talked… it's not treasure. It's something else. Something they think is powerful."

Michael's voice hardened. "Can you hold your position? We may need to regroup."

"We'll hold," Lukas said. "But whatever you're doing, Father Michael, do it fast. We're not alone out here."

The line went dead, and Hana leaned back, her expression grim. "They're not wrong. If other people know about the door and are already after us to find it or stop us, we're out of time."

Marcus tapped the photograph of the disc. "This artifact—it might be the key to everything. If it's still in the tunnels or somewhere nearby, we need to find it. Otherwise, whoever's after us will. Hana, check the archives for anything on this artifact. Nazi documents, Vatican records, anything. Michael, cross-reference those runes with other ancient seals. There has to be a precedent."

Marcus's gaze was steady. "In the meantime, I'll contact Cardinal Severino. If the Vatican knows anything more about what the Nazis were doing in these mountains, we need to access it now."

Hana opened a new search program, her fingers flying over the keyboard. "Let's hope the Vatican hasn't buried this one too deep."

Michael spread out his notes, flipping through pages and muttering to himself. "If this seal is as old as I think it is, we're dealing with something pre-Christian. Maybe pre-civilization. That's not just history—it's mythology."

Marcus's phone buzzed before he could place his call to the cardinal, pulling his attention. He glanced at the screen, his brow furrowing. The message was short, but it made his heart sink.

YOU ARE NOT ALONE.

He looked up at Michael and Hana, his voice steady but grim. "We have to move faster. Someone's watching us."

He held up his phone, showing Michael and Hana the message. "It's untraceable. No sender, no number, nothing. Someone knows where we are—and they want us to know it."

Hana stared at the screen, her expression tightening. "Could it be from Lukas or Karl? A warning?"

Marcus shook his head. "No, they'd have identified themselves. This feels deliberate, calculated."

Michael closed his notebook with a heavy thud, his voice low. "Whoever's watching us, they're playing a psychological game. They want us rattled."

"Well, it's working," Hana muttered, standing

abruptly. She paced to the nearest window, pulling back the heavy curtain just enough to peer outside. The forest was a wall of darkness, impenetrable and silent, save for the occasional whisper of wind through the trees. "If they're out there, they're not making it easy to spot them."

Michael crossed to her side, pulling her away from the dark scene outside and held her close as his gaze scanned the shadows. "They're waiting for us to make a move. If we stay here too long, we'll be exposed."

"We're not leaving without a plan," Marcus interjected, his tone firm. He gestured to the photos and notes spread across the table. "This artifact, the disc— we must confirm it's real and locate it. If the Nazis left it behind, it's either in the tunnels or somewhere nearby."

Hana turned back from the window, her arms crossed. "You're assuming it wasn't left behind or, if it was, it wasn't then taken away decades ago."

Marcus met her gaze, his expression resolute. "If it is still here and if we don't find it first, we risk letting it fall into the wrong hands."

Hana tapped her fingers against her arm, her mind sharpened, sifting through facts at lightning speed. "So how do we split our efforts? You contact Cardinal Severino while Michael and I search the archives and keep scanning for leads?"

Marcus hesitated, his instincts warring with the need for haste. "No. If we're moving, we move together. We can't risk splitting up when we're being tracked."

"Agreed," Michael said. "But where do we go? Back

to the tunnel? It's too dangerous with those mercenaries in play."

Marcus turned to Hana, his brow furrowed in thought. "What do we have on the surrounding area? Any abandoned sites, secondary Nazi facilities, anything that might connect to the tunnels?"

Hana returned to her laptop, pulling up satellite maps and overlaying them with historical records. After a few moments, she pointed to a location a few kilometers from the tunnels. "Here. It's a smaller site, listed in some Nazi records as a 'support station' for *Projekt Riese*. If the artifact wasn't left in the main complex, it could've been stored there."

Marcus leaned over her shoulder, studying the map. "The terrain looks rough. If the facility's still intact, it'll be hidden—likely underground."

"Which means it could also be guarded," Michael said. "By whoever's watching us, or by something else."

Hana arched an eyebrow. "Something else? We're really going there, huh?"

Michael didn't answer immediately. Instead, he met her gaze, his expression steady. "We can't ignore the possibility. Not after what we've seen."

Hana sighed, shutting her laptop and packing it into her bag. "Fine. Let's go find this thing before someone else does."

Michael automatically crossed himself, as he muttered a prayer for guidance.

Marcus grabbed his gear, slinging his bag over his shoulder, glancing with respect at his priestly friend. He understood Michael's lifelong career in the Church had instilled in him a grasp of how things like faith and spirit, things beyond science, beyond logic, can not only exist but influence the world. But Marcus believed only in what he could see and prove. Still, Michael had a point: what they had seen contradicted anything Marcus could explain—for now anyway. And it opened new possibilities. "We'll need to move fast. If Karl and Lukas can hold off the mercenaries, we might have a small window to work with."

Marcos checked his phone again, the untraceable message still glowing ominously on the screen. He tapped a quick reply to Lukas, informing him of their plan and urging caution. Then, slipping the phone into his pocket, he turned to the others. "Let's move. The longer we wait, the more time we give them."

The trio stepped out into the cold night, the wind biting against their faces as they hurried to their vehicle. The forest loomed around them, the shadows seeming to shift and writhe in the dim moonlight. As Marcus slid into the back seat, his thoughts lingered on the door in the tunnels, the ancient runes, and the faint groan that had echoed through the mountain.

Whatever they were chasing, it wasn't just history. And it was waiting for them.

SEVEN

The forest road to the secondary site was narrower and more treacherous than the team had anticipated. Hana gripped the steering wheel tightly, her eyes fixed on the twisting path ahead, while Marcus juggled the maps and documents on his lap, cross-referencing their location. Michael sat in the passenger seat, scanning the darkened woods through the window, his thoughts a storm of questions and unease.

"Are we close?" Hana asked, her voice tight with concentration.

Marcus tilted the map, his flashlight casting a pale glow over its surface. "Almost. The site should be just ahead, near a bend in the road."

Michael shifted, his gaze still locked on the forest. "Do we have any indication of what's there? Any structures, access points?"

Marcus shook his head. "The records are vague. Just mentions of a storage facility tied to *Projekt Riese*. If the Nazis had stored something there, it would've been underground. A bunker, maybe."

"Perfect," Hana muttered, her voice laced with sarcasm. "Another hole in the ground. That's gone well for us so far."

The vehicle rounded the bend, and Marcus pointed to a narrow clearing ahead. "There. That's our turnoff."

Hana guided the car off the main road, the tires crunching over frozen gravel as they pulled into the clearing. The trees grew denser here, their skeletal branches forming a canopy that blocked out what little moonlight there was. She parked the car, cutting the engine, and the sudden silence was overpowering.

The three of them stepped out, the cold biting at their faces as they gathered their gear. Marcus consulted the map again, his breath visible in the frigid air. "The facility should be about a hundred meters north. There's an old service path we can follow."

Marcus adjusted the strap of his bag, his eyes scanning the shadows. "Stay alert. If the mercenaries know about this place, they might already be here."

The team moved in silence, their flashlights cutting narrow beams of light through the darkness. The forest seemed alive around them, the rustling of leaves and distant creaks of trees amplifying their every step. Marcus led the way, following the faint outline of the overgrown path, while Hana kept her hand near the compact firearm tucked into her jacket.

After several minutes, Marcus stopped abruptly, raising a hand. "There it is."

Ahead, partially hidden by a thicket of brambles, was the crumbling façade of what appeared to be a concrete bunker. The structure was small and unassuming, its entrance covered by a rusted metal door that hung slightly ajar. Snow and debris had piled up around the base, but the door itself showed signs of recent disturbance—scrapes in the dirt, boot prints, and broken branches.

"They've been here," Michael said, his voice low.

Marcus nodded grimly. "Recently, by the looks of it."

Hana approached the door cautiously, her flashlight sweeping over the entrance. "This doesn't look like much," she said, nudging the door with her foot. It creaked loudly, swinging inward to reveal a dark, narrow corridor descending into the ground.

Michael stepped forward, peering into the darkness. "Looks can be deceiving. Let's see what they left behind."

The trio entered the bunker, the temperature increasing slightly as they descended the staircase. The air was thick with dampness and the metallic tang of rust, and their footsteps echoed faintly in the confined space. The corridor led to a small, rectangular room, its walls lined with rusted shelves and overturned crates.

Marcus knelt beside one of the crates, brushing away a layer of dust and debris. Inside were fragments of old documents, their edges yellowed and brittle. He picked one up carefully, his eyes scanning the faded text.

"These are Nazi inventory records. Dates, serial numbers... but no description of what they were storing."

Hana moved to another corner, where a pile of broken equipment lay scattered. "Whatever it was, whoever came before us stripped this place clean."

Michael's flashlight landed on a metal box tucked into a recess in the wall. He stepped closer, inspecting the box carefully before opening it. Inside was a single object—a cylindrical artifact, with a lid at one end, like a case, its surface engraved with the same runic patterns they had seen on the door in the tunnels.

"Marcus," Michael said, holding up the container. "Does this look familiar?"

Marcus approached, his eyes widening as he studied the runes. "It's the same pattern. The seal design."

Hana joined them, her expression wary. "What's inside?"

Michael carefully unscrewed the top of the cylinder. A faint hiss escaped as the seal broke, and he tilted it to reveal its contents: a rolled piece of parchment, brittle but intact. The paper was covered in symbols and text written in an archaic script.

Marcus took the parchment gingerly, his excitement tempered by caution. "This is incredible," he said, his voice hushed. "It's a blueprint—schematic instructions for the seal. This might explain how the door works."

Michael frowned, his unease deepening. "Or how to open it."

Hana glanced toward the entrance, her hand tightening on her weapon. A faint sound echoed from the corridor—soft, distant footsteps. The three of them froze, their flashlights snapping toward the doorway.

Michael's voice was barely above a whisper. "We've got company."

THE FAINT FOOTSTEPS GREW LOUDER, accompanied by the subtle scrape of boots against stone. Marcus motioned for Michael and Hana to move back, pressing himself against the wall beside the doorway. He slipped the parchment into his jacket, careful not to crumple it.

The steps slowed, the intruder clearly aware of the group's presence. A shadow stretched into the room as a figure approached, the beam of a flashlight cutting through the dim corridor. Marcus tensed, his instincts screaming at him to act before they were discovered.

The figure stepped into the room, his face hidden beneath a black tactical hood. He paused, his light sweeping over the overturned crates and shelves before landing on the three waiting figures. Before the intruder could react, Marcus lunged, slamming his shoulder into him and knocking him off balance. The assailant's flashlight clattered to the ground, its beam spinning wildly as the two struggled.

Hana moved quickly, training her weapon on the fallen figure. "Don't move!" she barked, her voice sharp and commanding. Michael squatted to press his knee into the intruder's back, keeping him pinned.

The intruder froze, one hand raised in a gesture of surrender while the other hovered near his belt. Marcus knelt, snatching away a knife the intruder had been reaching for and tossing it aside. Then he grabbed the flashlight to train on the assailant.

"Who are you?"

The intruder didn't respond immediately, but the subtle rise and fall of his chest betrayed a steady, controlled breath. This wasn't panic—it was calculation.

"I'm not your enemy," the figure finally said, his voice muffled by the hood. The accent was subtle, European, but hard to place.

"Funny," Michael said sharply. "You don't look like a friend."

The intruder shifted slightly, testing Michael's weight still on his back. "You're after the same thing we are. Let me go, and I'll tell you what you're really dealing with."

Hana stepped closer, her weapon unwavering. "You're not in a position to negotiate."

Marcus crouched, his gaze keen as he studied the figure. "You're not with the mercenaries outside, are you? You're something else."

The intruder tilted his head slightly, the faintest smirk visible beneath the edge of the hood. "You could say that."

Michael pressed harder on the man. "Start talking. Who are you, and why are you here?"

The figure hesitated for a moment, then spoke. "My name doesn't matter. What matters is that you're poking at something far bigger than you understand. That door in the tunnels? It wasn't sealed to protect the Nazis' secrets. It was sealed to keep the rest of us safe."

Marcus exchanged a glance with Michael. "Safe from what?"

The intruder let out a low laugh. "You think this is about treasure? About history? No. That door is a prison. And you don't want to find out what happens if it opens."

Michael's grip didn't waver, but his voice softened slightly. "Then why are you here?"

"To make sure it stays closed," the intruder said, his tone deadly serious. "And if you're smart, you'll stop digging before you let something out that can't be put back."

Hana frowned, her weapon lowering slightly. "If that's true, why not work with us? Why the cloak-and-dagger routine?"

The intruder didn't answer immediately. Instead, he shifted again, clearly testing his chances of escape. "Because I don't trust anyone who's still asking questions instead of running."

Marcus leaned forward, his tone firm. "We're not running. So unless you want to spend the rest of the night pinned to this floor, you'd better start giving us something we can use."

The figure sighed, his resistance fading slightly. "Fine. You want the truth? That door is one of seven. Each one was built to contain something powerful, something ancient. The Nazis didn't create it—they found it, and apparently it's something they needed. And they barely understood what they were dealing with."

Michael's stomach tightened. "Something ancient? Like what?"

The figure's voice dropped, his tone grim. "Something older than your gods. Older than history. You've seen the runes, the seals. Those weren't made to keep people out—they were made to keep it in."

Hana's grip on her weapon tightened again. "And you're saying it's still alive?"

The intruder met her gaze, his eyes glinting in the dim light. "Alive? No. But awake? Maybe. And if it's awake, then we're already too late."

Before anyone could respond, a sudden noise from the corridor drew their attention—a sharp, metallic clang, followed by the unmistakable echo of approaching footsteps. More intruders.

The pinned figure seized the distraction, twisting and breaking free of Michael's hold. He sprang to his feet, retrieving his knife from the ground with a fluid motion.

"We're out of time," he said. "You want to survive? Leave. Now."

He darted toward the shadows of the corridor, disappearing before anyone could stop him. Michael stood, his chest heaving, and turned to the others. "Move. Now!"

The team scrambled, gathering the cylinder and Marcus's notes before retreating toward the bunker's exit. The approaching footsteps grew louder, voices echoing in a language none of them recognized. As they reached the staircase, Hana glanced back, her face pale.

"Do you think he was telling the truth?" she asked.

Marcus didn't answer immediately. He looked back into the darkened bunker, the weight of the intruder's words heavy in his chest. Finally, he shook his head.

"I don't know. But we can't afford to wait around and find out."

~

IN A MAKESHIFT COMMAND center deep within the Owl Mountains, the air was heavy with the scent of damp stone and machinery. A series of monitors cast pale, flickering light across the cavernous room, displaying feeds from drones, thermal imaging, and satellite overlays of the surrounding terrain. At the center of it all stood a man in a tailored black coat, his silhouette outlined against the glow of the screens.

He was tall, with angular features and a precision to his movements that suggested military discipline. His name was Anton Lenk, a name whispered in intelligence circles as a master of covert operations with questionable loyalties. A dossier on the table beside him labeled him as "Non-State Operative – High Threat."

Lenk's gloved fingers traced a red line on the map projected onto the main monitor—the tunnels beneath Włodarz Mountain. "They're getting too close," he said, his voice calm but edged with steel. "They've already accessed the secondary site and retrieved the schematics."

Behind him, another figure stepped forward—a woman with auburn hair tied back in a tight bun and piercing green eyes. Her name was Clara Weiss, an academic-turned-operative for a shadowy international organization with a vested interest in forbidden knowledge. Her expertise in ancient languages and myths made her indispensable to Lenk's operation, though her motives often seemed to extend beyond loyalty to the group. She had already done background investigations on Marcus and his team.

"They're not fools," Clara said, glancing at another monitor showing infrared images of Michael, Marcus, and Hana retreating from the bunker. "They've likely connected the artifact to the door. If they decipher those schematics on it and the parchment, they'll know how to access the prison."

"And do you believe they'll open it?" Lenk asked, his gaze flicking to her.

Clara hesitated. "Father Dominic? No. He'll resist. But Marcus Russo? He's different. Curious. Ambitious. He's the one leading their effort and might take the risk."

Lenk allowed himself a thin smile. "Good. We can use that."

Clara frowned, shifting uncomfortably. "If they're this close, why not intercept them directly? We've already deployed assets in the forest."

"Because the longer they dig, the more they reveal to us," Lenk replied. He gestured to the artifact schematics on another screen. "Every move they make brings us closer to the final piece of the puzzle. Let them do the hard work. We'll take what we need when the time comes."

COVENANT OF THE IRON CROSS

"And the door?" Clara pressed. "You know what's behind it."

Lenk's smile vanished, his tone turning serious. "I know what the myths say. That it's not a relic but a remnant. A force that shaped early humanity, feared and revered across cultures. The serpent. Chaos. Forbidden knowledge. Call it what you like, but it's power. If we control it—"

"We can't control it," Clara interrupted. "The Nazis tried and failed. They sealed it away for a reason."

"That was their mistake," Lenk said coldly. "They didn't have the means to harness it. We do. We just need these outsiders to unravel what you've failed to understand." He shot a critical look at his so-called expert semiotician.

Clara's lips tightened into a thin line. She had gotten them this far, closer than they had ever gotten to their prize. But Lenk failed to give her any credit for what she had interpreted from the artifact. She swallowed back her preferred retort, aware of the dangers of crossing this man. She had seen the lengths this group was willing to go to in pursuit of power, and while she didn't share their blind ambition, she was too far in to turn back now.

"What about the other two? The operatives guarding Father Dominic's team?" she asked.

"The Swiss Guards?" Lenk's smug smile returned. "They're well trained. Dangerous, even. But they're not infallible. If they rejoin the team, we'll deal with them."

"And if the team retreats?" Clara asked.

Lenk turned back to the monitors, his eyes

narrowing. "Then we give them a reason to stay. Contact the field unit. Force them toward the tunnels. The closer they are to the door, the closer we are to opening it."

Clara hesitated, her stomach twisting at the implications. "And if the entity wakes? Before you can 'harness' it, as you claim?"

Lenk's voice was quiet but resolute. "Then we'll find out if the stories are true."

CHAPTER
EIGHT

K arl and Lukas trudged through the dense forest, the snow crunching beneath their boots as they moved swiftly but cautiously. They had evaded the remaining mercenaries after their earlier skirmish, but the danger hadn't passed. Both men knew that the forces hunting them were part of something larger.

"Do you think they've reached the secondary site?" Lukas asked, his breath visible in the icy air.

"They'd better have," Karl replied, scanning the treetops for any sign of drones. "If we're being tracked, they're targets as well. I only hope they weren't detected getting there."

The two men quickened their pace, following the coordinates Marcus had sent them earlier. After nearly an hour, they heard the sound of hushed voices carried through the trees.

Michael, Marcus, and Hana turned sharply as the

two guards stepped into view, weapons drawn. Relief flashed across Michael's face as he lowered his flashlight.

"Karl, Lukas!" he said, exhaling. "We thought we'd lost you."

"You almost did," Karl replied, his voice grim. "The mercenaries aren't the only problem. Whoever's running this operation has resources. They're tracking you."

"We know," Marcus said, his expression dark. "They followed us to the bunker. Well, one of them did. Apparently, there are two groups after this same thing besides us."

Lukas's gaze swept over the group as they all headed for the vehicle the trio had driven here. "What did he say?"

"He thinks the door holds something that shouldn't be released and that the others after it want it no matter the consequences," Michael said. "And if he's right, this is far worse than we imagined."

Karl asked, "Did you find anything there?"

Marcus nodded, holding up the cylindrical artifact. "This. It's a schematic. A guide to the door. These runic buttons on it must relate to the symbols we found on the door."

Karl exchanged a glance with Lukas. "Then we need to move. Now."

Michael shook his head. "No. We need to figure out how to stop this before they get to the door."

Hana glanced nervously at the surrounding trees.

"And what if stopping it means opening the door ourselves?"

The silence hung heavy as Hana's question reverberated in their minds.

Marcus exhaled slowly, his gaze sweeping over the group. "We won't open the door," he said firmly. "Not unless there's absolutely no other choice."

"And if there's no other choice?" Michael pressed, his tone skeptical.

Marcus hesitated, his jaw tightening. "Then we make sure we're prepared for whatever comes next. But right now, our focus is keeping it sealed."

Karl stepped closer, his voice low but commanding. "We can't stay out here debating. Whoever these people are, they'll likely have reinforcements soon. We need to regroup somewhere more secure."

Marcus gestured toward the cylindrical artifact. "If we want answers, we need to decipher this fully. The schematics might not just tell us how the door works—they might reveal why it was built in the first place."

"And where exactly do we do that?" Hana asked, glancing nervously at the dark forest around them. "We're running out of safe places."

"There's one option," Michael said after a pause. He pulled a folded map from his jacket and spread it on the hood of the vehicle. He pointed to a location not far from their current position. "An old monastery. Abandoned for decades, but it's solid and defensible."

Marcus frowned, studying the map. "Are you sure it's abandoned?"

Michael nodded. "I checked its status on my phone

earlier. The Vatican stripped it of all assets years ago. It's been left to the elements ever since."

Lukas leaned in, examining the terrain. "Looks like a good fallback point. High ground, limited access routes."

Karl nodded in agreement. "We can hold it if we're tracked."

Hana crossed her arms. "And if we're walking into a trap?"

Michael met her gaze evenly. "We don't have many options. If we stay here, we're easy pickings. The monastery gives us a chance to regroup and figure out our next move."

Reluctantly, Hana nodded. "Fine. But if this goes south, I'm holding you personally responsible, Michael."

The priest managed a faint smile as he grabbed her hand and gave it a squeeze. "I wouldn't expect anything less."

THE DRIVE to the monastery was tense, the vehicle crawling over snow-laden roads that wound ever higher into the mountains. The forest thinned as they ascended, replaced by jagged rock formations and sheer cliffs that dropped into shadowy ravines. The higher they climbed, the colder the air became, their breaths fogging the windows as silence settled over the group.

Hana broke the quiet, her hands gripping the wheel tightly. "You think this monastery has some connection to the door?"

"It's possible," Michael said, watching the road ahead. "The Vatican often built over sites of historical or spiritual significance. If the monastery was placed here, it might not be a coincidence."

Marcus, seated in the back between the guards, flipped through his notes. "If that's true, there might be records—or symbols—hidden in the monastery itself. Something the Vatican didn't know about or chose to overlook before abandoning it."

Karl's voice cut in, "Or something they deliberately left behind."

The thought sent a chill through the group, though none of them voiced their agreement. The Vatican's history of secrecy was both an asset and a curse in their current predicament. Sadly, they had all witnessed that before during their various associations with the Vatican.

As the monastery came into view, it loomed like a shadow against the starless night. The stone structure was imposing, its walls weathered but still standing strong against the elements. Narrow windows stared out like empty eye sockets, and the arched entryway was flanked by crumbling statues of saints whose faces had been eroded by time.

"Home sweet home," Hana muttered, parking the vehicle near the entrance. She killed the engine, and the silence rushed in, oppressive and thick.

The group exited cautiously, weapons drawn and flashlights cutting through the dark. The wind howled through the mountain pass, carrying with it faint, eerie whispers that might have been nothing more than tricks of the mind.

Karl took point, his weapon at the ready as he approached the monastery's heavy wooden door. He tested it, and it creaked open with an ominous groan. "It's clear. For now."

Inside, the monastery was cold and dark, its air thick with the scent of damp stone and decay. The main hall stretched before them, its vaulted ceiling disappearing into shadows. Broken pews littered the floor and the faint outlines of faded frescoes clung to the walls, their religious imagery barely discernible.

Marcus stepped inside, his breath visible in the frigid air. "We'll set up here. Lukas, secure the entrances. Karl, sweep the perimeter."

The two Swiss Guards nodded and moved off silently. Hana and Michael followed Marcus deeper into the hall, their footsteps echoing off the stone walls.

"We'll need light," Marcus said, setting his bag down and reaching in for a portable lantern. Its glow cast long shadows across the room, illuminating the faded symbols on the walls. He frowned, stepping closer to one of the frescoes. "Michael. Look at this."

Michael joined him, his flashlight revealing a serpent coiled around a tree at the center of the fresco. The imagery was strikingly similar to the carvings they had seen on the iron door in the tunnels.

"It's the same symbol," Michael murmured, his voice barely audible. "The serpent."

Hana stepped closer, her expression tense. "So the monastery is connected. What does that mean for us?"

"It means," Marcus said, his tone grim, "that the Vatican knew more about this than they've ever admitted. And whatever's behind that door—it's tied to this place."

A sudden sound from the entrance froze them in place. A faint, rhythmic scraping, like metal on stone, echoed through the hall.

Karl's voice came through the comms, brusque and urgent, as he strode through the entrance. "We've got movement outside."

Michael's pulse quickened as he exchanged a glance with Hana and Marcus. "How many?"

"Too many," Karl replied. The two Swiss Guards lowered a heavy beam across the door, an old but effective method of securing the monastery. Or so they hoped. "Get ready. They're coming."

MARCUS STEPPED toward the table in the monastery's main hall, the artifact and parchment still laid out before him.

"Whatever happens," Marcus said, his voice calm but commanding, "we can't let them take this. It's the key to understanding what we're dealing with—and keeping it contained."

Karl, now positioned near the door with Lukas, gave a curt nod. "We'll hold them off, but it won't be for long. If they've got reinforcements nearby, we're outnumbered."

Marcus turned to Hana, who was scanning the walls of the monastery with a flashlight. "Anything? Symbols, hidden compartments, anything that could help us understand why this place is connected to the door?"

Hana shook her head, frustration etched across her face. "Just these frescoes. The serpent, the tree—it's all the same imagery we've seen before. Nothing new."

Michael stepped closer to Marcus, his expression serious. "You need to decide, Marcus. Do we fight them here, or do we fall back? If they breach this monastery, we lose the high ground—and the artifact that might be the key to it all."

Marcus hesitated, the weight of leadership pressing heavily on his shoulders. He glanced at the frescoes, the serpent coiled tightly around the tree. The Vatican knew something about this place, about the connection to the ancient seals and the danger they represented. But how much? How many layers of truth were buried beneath the myths?

"We stay," he said finally. "This is defensible, and we have the artifact. If we run, they'll follow us, and we'll lose any chance of understanding what we're up against."

Hana shot him a wary glance. "And if we can't hold them off?"

"Then we make sure they don't leave with anything," Marcus said firmly. He turned to Michael. "Get ready. We'll need to destroy the artifact if it comes to that."

Michael hesitated but nodded. "Understood."

The distant sound of boots crunching over frozen ground grew louder, accompanied by faint voices issuing clipped commands in an unrecognizable language. Karl motioned for the group to take cover, his weapon raised. "They're closing in."

Marcus grabbed the cylindrical artifact and parchment, stuffing them into his satchel. "Lukas, get to the upper levels. Find a vantage point and cover the entryway from the outside. Karl, you're with me at the door in here."

Hana moved to the far side of the hall, taking a position behind an overturned pew. Her hands shook slightly as she gripped her weapon, but her voice was steady. "Let's hope they're not packing more than we are."

Michael stayed near Marcus, his hand on his crucifix. "If they breach, we can't let this escalate into a bloodbath. There has to be another way."

"Right now," Marcus said, his tone intense, "the only way is survival. If you've got a miracle up your sleeve, Father, now's the time."

The door shuddered suddenly, a loud crack echoing through the hall as something heavy slammed against it. Karl braced himself, glancing back at Marcus. "They've got a battering ram."

Marcus's mind raced. "We need to funnel them. Limit how many can get in at once." He turned to Hana. "Can you shoot out the supports on that balcony? Block their path if they breach?"

Hana peered at the crumbling stone balcony above the door and nodded. "It'll buy us time. Just say the word."

The battering ram struck again, splintering the door slightly.

Marcus stepped back, his grip tightening on his satchel. "Everyone, get ready. If they get past us, we might not get another chance to stop them from getting to whatever is behind that tunnel door."

The next impact sent shards of wood flying into the hall. The door groaned under the strain, the ancient hinges threatening to give way.

Karl glanced at Marcus, his expression grim. "They're here."

NINE

T he ancient door exploded inward with a deafening crack as the beam securing it broke, scattering fragments of wood and iron across the monastery's stone floor.

"Hold your fire!" Marcus shouted, motioning to Karl. "Wait until they're bottlenecked!"

The first wave of intruders surged forward, silhouetted against the pale moonlight streaming through the broken doorway. They moved with precision, tactical gear gleaming and weapons raised, their movements tense and calculated.

Karl and Lukas had flanked the door, taking cover behind the thick stone walls. The mercenaries hesitated for a fraction of a second, realizing the vulnerability of the narrow entryway. That hesitation was all Karl needed. He opened fire, the sharp crack of his weapon echoing through the hall. The first intruder crumpled, and the others scrambled for cover, their carefully orchestrated assault disrupted.

From her position near the overturned pews, Hana aimed upward and fired at the weak wooden supports of the crumbling balcony above the doorway. The bullets struck true, and with a thunderous crash, the balcony collapsed, sending a cascade of stone and debris into the entryway. A cloud of dust billowed outward, obscuring the view and forcing the intruders to retreat temporarily.

"That'll slow them down!" Hana called out, reloading quickly.

Marcus moved to the center of the hall, his satchel clutched tightly. He could feel the weight of the artifact pressing against his side, a constant reminder of what was at stake. "Michael, check the other entrances. Make sure they're secure."

Michael nodded, disappearing into the shadows with a flashlight in hand.

Lukas, perched on the upper level of the monastery, called out over the comms. "More movement outside. They're regrouping!"

Karl glanced at Marcus, his jaw tight. "They might bring explosives next. This place won't hold forever."

Marcus's mind raced. They needed a way to neutralize the threat without risking the artifact falling into enemy hands. He turned to Hana, who was already scanning the room for their next move.

"Hana," he said, his voice urgent, "is there another way out of here? Anything in the Vatican records about an escape route?"

Hana bit her lip, her thoughts churning. Michael had known about this monastery; she hadn't. "Many monasteries have hidden passages, especially ones this old."

"Then find one," Marcus said. "If we can't hold them off, we'll need a way out."

As Hana moved toward the far end of the hall, scanning the walls for hidden seams or symbols, the mercenaries regrouped outside. Through the dust and debris, Marcus could hear their leader shouting orders, his voice fierce and authoritative.

"They're coming again," Lukas called from above. "Looks like they've got something else this time."

"Grenades or a ram?" Karl asked, his tone grim.

"Neither," Lukas said. "It's a cutting torch. They're widening the opening."

Marcus cursed under his breath. They couldn't let the enemy gain a foothold inside. He turned to Karl. "We need to keep them pinned down. Lukas, focus your fire on anyone near the entrance. Don't let them advance."

"On it," Lukas replied, his shots ringing out moments later.

Karl glanced at Marcus. "And then?"

"I'm buying us time," Marcus said, feeling the bulge of the artifact in the satchel at his side. "If they get in, this is what they'll be after. I'm going to make sure they don't get it."

Karl's eyes narrowed. "Don't do anything stupid."

Marcus smirked faintly. "Stupid's relative right now."

. . .

HANA'S FLASHLIGHT beam swept across the faded frescoes at the back of the monastery. The serpent imagery loomed large, its coiled body almost alive in the flickering light. She ran her hands along the cold stone, feeling for any irregularities.

Her fingers caught on a groove and she paused. "Got something," she murmured to herself. She pressed harder, and with a low, grinding sound, a section of the wall shifted inward, revealing a narrow, descending passage.

Hana leaned into her comm. "Marcus, I found it. There's a hidden passage behind the frescoes."

"Where does it lead?" Marcus's voice came through, edged with gravity.

"Not sure yet," Hana replied, "but it looks like it goes underground. I'll need to check."

"Do it," Marcus said. "But don't go too far. We may need to fall back quickly."

Hana gripped her flashlight tightly as she stepped into the dark passage. The air inside was warmer, overlaid with the faint scent of earth and decay. The walls were rough-hewn, the kind of work that spoke of centuries-old workmanship. Her footsteps echoed faintly as she descended, the passage sloping deeper into the mountain.

Suddenly, her light caught on something glinting faintly in the darkness—an ancient metal gate, its surface covered in runes nearly identical to those on the artifact. Her heart raced as she approached, her fingers brushing over the carvings.

"Marcus," she said, her voice steady despite the adrenaline surging through her veins. "You're going to want to see this."

MARCUS CROUCHED as he heard the sounds of the mercenaries' cutting torch grow louder, the glow of molten metal visible through the debris at the door.

Karl fired another round, keeping their attackers pinned. "They're pushing harder! Whatever they're after, they're not giving up."

Marcus's comm crackled. It was Hana. "Marcus, there's a gate down here—ancient, like the door in the tunnels. It's covered in runes. I think it's connected."

Marcus's pulse quickened. "Is it another seal?"

"Maybe," Hana said. "But it's intact—and it looks like it's been untouched for centuries."

Marcus's mind raced. The gate could be their answer —or their doom. Either way, it was their only chance to shift the odds. "Stay there. I'm coming to you."

He turned to Lukas. "Hold them off as long as you can. We might have a way out—or something to end this."

Karl gave him a curt nod. "Go. We'll buy you time."

Marcus bolted toward the passage Hana had found, his heart pounding as he plunged into the unknown.

He hurried down the narrow passageway, the weight of the artifact and parchment in his satchel pressing against him with each step. The air grew warmer and damper as he descended, the faint light of his flashlight catching on jagged rock walls and uneven steps. Hana's voice had been steady, but he could sense her urgency—whatever she had found wasn't ordinary.

When he reached the bottom, Hana was standing in front of an ancient metal gate. Rubble obscured a portion of it, from ceiling rock fallen over decades and leftover excavation when the gate was first placed. Her flashlight beam illuminated the gate's visible intricate carvings, the runes etched deep into the corroded surface. The gate was imposing, taller than either of them, and set into the stone as if it had grown there over centuries.

"This is it," Hana said, not looking away from the gate. "It's not just another seal. This is something bigger."

Marcus stepped closer, running his fingers over the runes. They were unmistakably similar to those on the artifact and the door in the tunnels, but the craftsmanship was older, more primal. His academic instincts kicked in, his mind sharpened to piece together what he was seeing.

"The gate isn't just a barrier," Marcus murmured. "It's part of the same system as the door in the tunnels. A secondary containment—or maybe a backup if the first fails."

Hana shot him a wary glance. "You think whatever's behind that door could reach this far?"

"It's possible," Marcus said, his voice tight. "If the entity—or force—behind the door isn't fully contained, it might be able to project itself. These seals could be stopping it from spreading."

Hana squinted in thought, her hand on the cold metal. "So what happens if this gate fails?"

Marcus didn't answer immediately. He pulled the artifact from his satchel, holding it up to the light. The cylindrical object seemed to resonate faintly, as though reacting to its proximity to the gate. He carefully unrolled the parchment, his eyes scanning the ancient script.

"These instructions," Marcus said, pointing to a section of the text, "describe a ritual. A way to strengthen the seal—or deactivate it."

"Deactivate it?" Hana took a step back, her voice rising. "Why would we ever do that?"

"We wouldn't," Marcus said firmly. "But if that other team figures this out, they might. They won't care about the consequences—they're likely after power, not preservation."

Hana stared at the gate, the weight of their situation sinking in. "So, what do we do? Strengthen the seal? Use the artifact?"

Marcus shook his head, his jaw tight. "Not yet. We don't know enough. Strengthening the seal might trigger something, and deactivating it is out of the question. First, we need to figure out why the Nazis stopped here. If they sealed this gate, they must have known what it was protecting."

· · ·

IN THE MONASTERY HALL, the mercenaries breached the entryway. The debris from the collapsed balcony slowed their advance, forcing them into a narrow choke point.

Karl fired another shot, taking down the first intruder who tried to climb over the rubble.

"They're regrouping," he said, his voice steady but strained. "Lukas, keep their flank pinned!"

Lukas, stationed on the upper level, picked off another attacker with a precision shot. "They're bringing in heavy gear," he called down. "We can't hold this much longer."

Karl grimaced, glancing back toward the passage Marcus and Hana had disappeared into. "We just need to buy them time."

Another explosion rocked the monastery, this one closer. A section of the wall near the doorway crumbled, creating another entry point. More mercenaries poured in, their tactical gear glinting in the dim light.

"Fall back to the inner hall!" Karl shouted, his voice cutting through the chaos.

Lukas scrambled down to the main hall and they retreated, using overturned pews and rubble as cover. The mercenaries advanced methodically, their leader barking orders in clipped tones.

As Karl reloaded, a thought struck him. *They're not shooting to kill.*

Lukas fired another shot, his voice tight with focus. "What are you thinking?"

"They're trying to capture us—or Marcus and the others," Karl said grimly. "They need us alive."

"Good luck with that," Lukas muttered, firing another round.

MARCUS AND HANA were still studying the gate when they felt the faint tremor of the explosion above. Dust shook loose from the ceiling, and the air grew heavier as though the mountain itself were reacting to the disturbance.

"They're breaching the monastery," Hana said, her voice tense. "We don't have much time."

Marcus stepped back from the gate, adrenaline-fueled ideas firing through his brain. The artifact's faint resonance was growing stronger, the runes on its surface glowing faintly in response to its proximity to the gate.

"This artifact has an energy source or pulls it from" —Marcus glanced at the gate—"some source nearby. It isn't just about sealing the entity," he said, his voice low. "This gate—it's a connection point. And the artifact is part of it. This all might lead to something deeper. Something tied to the serpent myths. If this thing is as old as the myths suggest, it could be tied to something our ancestors barely understood. The serpent—chaos, forbidden knowledge—it's all symbolic. But the danger? That's real."

Hana gestured toward the artifact. "And this? What does it actually do?"

"It's the key," Marcus said, his tone grim, "to unlocking—or reinforcing—the connection. It responds when near another segment of the same system."

Before Hana could respond, the sound of footsteps

echoed down the passage. Both of them turned, their flashlights snapping toward the noise.

It was Karl and Lukas, their faces pale and drawn from the battle above. Karl spoke first, his voice urgent. "We're out of time. They're breaching the monastery, and there's too many of them."

Lukas glanced at the gate, his eyes narrowing. "What the hell is that?"

"The reason we're here," Marcus said. He looked back at the gate, the weight of the moment pressing down on him. "And the reason we can't let them win."

Karl raised his weapon, his aim on the passageway where they had entered, his voice steady. "What's the plan?"

Marcus turned to the group, his expression adamant. "We hold this position. Whatever's behind that gate stays there—no matter the cost."

The gate groaned, the deep, resonant sound reverberating through the chamber, through the floor, and up through their bodies. Marcus froze, the artifact in his hand vibrating faintly, its glow brighter than before. The tremors beneath their feet intensified, and the air grew heavy with the unmistakable tang of metallic ions, like the charge of an impending storm.

"What's happening?" Hana asked, her voice tense as she backed away from the gate.

Marcus's brow wrinkled as he studied the artifact and the runes on the gate. "It's reacting. The artifact is connected to something beneath us—some kind of mechanism."

Karl, still standing by the corridor entrance with his

weapon raised, glanced back. "We've got company closing in." He aimed, braced himself and—

Michael rushed into the room, his hands raised. "It's me!"

Karl lowered his weapon and pulled Michael farther into the room, shaking his head as he took aim again at the entryway.

Michael started, "I didn't find another exit when I heard you..." He stopped, staring at the gate. "What's —?" The floor moved yet again, and he stumbled into Hana.

Lukas scanned the chamber with keen eyes. "The vibrations are getting worse. The whole place feels unstable."

The tremors culminated in a sudden jolt, throwing Marcus against the gate. His hand slammed into one of the engraved symbols, and the vibration from the artifact surged into the metal. The entire gate began to hum, not with mystical energy but with the unmistakable resonance of machinery, stirring to life after decades of dormancy.

"This isn't just a seal," Marcus said, stepping back as the gate began to shift. "It's a control system. A pressure valve."

"A valve?" Hana asked, panic creeping into her voice. "A valve for what?"

Marcus's eyes widened as the floor beneath them cracked slightly, revealing a faint orange glow. "Thermal vents. The mountain—this entire region—it's volcanic. The Nazis must have discovered the vents and built this system to harness or contain them. It also must be what powers the entire mechanism throughout this mountain."

Michael stepped forward, his face pale. "Are you saying this place is sitting on an active volcanic fault line?"

Marcus nodded, his nerves buzzing with the weight of realization. "Exactly. The gate controls the release of pressure from deep underground. The vibrations—the heat—it's not some supernatural force. It's geothermal energy. If we don't secure this, we could trigger an eruption."

Hana's breath caught. "And if our visitors force it open?"

Marcus looked back at the artifact. "They'll destabilize the entire system. It's not just this chamber—it's the entire mountain range. The Nazis probably built this to either weaponize or suppress the energy. Either way, the consequences could be catastrophic."

Another tremor rocked the chamber, followed by the distant echo of explosions from above.

Karl shouted from the corridor, "They're breaching the monastery! We need to move, Marcus!"

"No," Marcus said, his voice determined. "We stay here. If we leave this unchecked, we might not get another chance to stop it."

He grabbed the artifact and pressed it against the gate again, this time deliberately aligning it with the runic patterns. The artifact clicked into place, and a low, mechanical hum filled the chamber. The gate began to shift, revealing ancient gears and pistons hidden beneath its surface.

"What are you doing?" Hana demanded.

"Reinforcing the system," Marcus said. "If I can align the artifact with the gate's mechanism, it might stabilize the pressure and prevent an eruption."

"And if you're wrong?" Lukas asked, glancing nervously at the glowing cracks in the floor.

"Then we all go up with the mountain," Marcus said, not looking up.

ABOVE, the mercenaries advanced through the shattered remains of the monastery's main hall. Debris and dust filled the air as their cutting torches and explosive charges widened the entry points. Anton Lenk stood at the center of the chaos, his penetrating eyes fixed on a handheld device displaying seismic readings.

"Keep moving," Lenk ordered, his voice calm despite the tremors beneath his feet. "They're in the lower chambers. Secure the artifact at all costs."

Clara Weiss, standing beside him, hesitated as she watched the seismic readings spike. "This isn't just about the artifact, is it?" she asked. "You're trying to activate the system."

Lenk smiled faintly. "The Nazis were ahead of their time. They built this as a fail-safe. A weapon of last resort. If we can control the geothermal energy under this mountain, we'll have a power source unlike anything the world has ever seen."

Clara's expression darkened. "Or you'll destroy everything in the process."

Lenk's smile didn't falter. "Progress always comes with risks."

THE GATE GROANED AGAIN, this time louder, as the artifact clicked into place and the vibrations intensified. Marcus worked furiously, aligning the symbols on the artifact with the runes on the gate.

"I think I've got it!" Marcus shouted. "The system is stabilizing, but it's fragile. We can't let them force the gate open until this is complete."

Karl fired a shot into the corridor, slowing the advancing mercenaries. "They're almost here! Whatever you're doing, finish it!"

Hana crouched beside Marcus, her voice urgent. "Are you sure this will work?"

Marcus didn't look up. "No. But it's better than doing nothing."

Another explosion rocked the chamber, followed by the sound of footsteps closing in. Karl and Lukas retreated toward the gate, their weapons trained on the dark corridor.

Lukas warned, "We can't hold this much longer."

Suddenly, the vibrations ceased, and the gate clicked into place with a resounding thud. The faint orange glow from the cracks in the floor dimmed, and the air grew still.

Marcus stepped back, his chest heaving. "I think we did it," he said.

But before anyone could respond, a voice echoed from the corridor, calm and controlled.

"Congratulations, Dr. Russo. You've stabilized the system—for now."

Marcus turned, his heart sinking as a tall man stepped into the chamber, flanked by heavily armed mercenaries.

"Allow me to introduce myself," he said, his smile cold. "My name is Anton Lenk."

CHAPTER

TEN

"I must admit, I wasn't sure you had the skill," Lenk said, his voice still calm but edged with menace.

Karl and Lukas raised their weapons, positioning themselves protectively in front of Marcus and Hana. "Don't take another step," Karl warned, his voice a low growl.

Lenk smiled smugly, motioning subtly to his men. "Please, let's not waste time with theatrics. It's clear to everyone you're vastly outnumbered." Ten men, flanking Lenk, all had their weapons aimed at the team.

Hana's hand hovered near her weapon, her eyes darting between Lenk and his men. "What do you want, Lenk? The system? The artifact? Or are you just here to kill us?"

Lenk's smirk widened. "Kill you? No. Not yet. You're far too useful. You've already done most of the hard work." He gestured to the artifact. "That little trinket of yours is the key to something far more valuable than this geothermal system."

Marcus's heart pounded as he tightened his grip on the artifact. "You're talking about the train."

Lenk's expression didn't falter. "Ah, so you've pieced it together. Yes, the train. A legend, but one rooted in truth. The Nazis buried it somewhere deep within this mountain, using systems like this one to shield it. But they were far more ambitious than anyone realized."

Michael, who had been standing silently near the back, stepped forward, his voice steady. "If you destabilize this system to get to the train, you'll destroy everything. The mountain will collapse."

"Not if we do it carefully," Lenk said, his tone almost amused. "Which is why I need you, Dr. Russo. Your knowledge. Your skill. You've already proven you're capable."

"That's a pity, because I won't help you," Marcus said firmly, his gaze locked on Lenk.

Lenk's smile faded, replaced by a cold, calculating look. "You misunderstand, Doctor. This isn't a request."

With a quick motion, he signaled his men. Two of them stepped forward, rifles trained on Marcus and Hana. Another approached Michael, forcing him to step back. Karl and Lukas tensed, their stance firm, their fingers on their triggers.

"I'm giving you a choice," Lenk said, his voice lowering. "Help me uncover the train—or watch as your friends pay the price."

Marcus's mind raced, weighing his options. They

were cornered, outgunned, and outmaneuvered. But he knew one thing: the artifact and its connection to the gate held the only leverage they had.

"All right," he said, raising a hand. "I'll help."

"Marcus, no!" Hana snapped, her voice filled with both anger and fear.

Marcus shot her a look, his expression steadfast, then faced Lenk. "I'll help you—but only if my team stays safe."

Lenk raised an eyebrow, clearly amused by Marcus's attempt at negotiation. "Agreed. As long as you cooperate, your friends remain unharmed."

Marcus stepped forward, gripping the artifact tightly. "What's your plan?"

Lenk gestured toward the gate. "This gated system serves a purpose beyond containment of geothermal power. It functions as a marker as well. The key to the train's location lies beneath us—accessible only through this system. You've stabilized it, and now you'll help me unlock it."

Marcus glanced at the gate, then back at Lenk. "If I'm going to do this, I need access to the schematics. The artifact alone isn't enough."

Lenk nodded to one of his men, who produced a tablet displaying digital scans of Nazi documents. Marcus took it, his heart sinking as he realized the depth of Lenk's preparation.

As Marcus studied the schematics, Lenk stepped toward him, then leaned closer, his voice low. "Do you know why the Nazis hid the train here, Dr. Russo? It wasn't simply a matter of gold and art. There's something aboard that's far more valuable."

Marcus's gaze snapped to Lenk. "What are you talking about?"

Lenk smiled faintly, his eyes glinting. "Ah, so you don't know? Records. Research. Projects they couldn't risk falling into Allied hands. Imagine the secrets buried with that train. Weapons, technology, even truths about the war that could rewrite history."

Michael stepped forward, his voice accusing. "Or secrets that were meant to stay buried. The Nazis didn't abandon that train out of strategy. They left it here because it was too dangerous."

Lenk turned to Michael, his slight smile returning. "That's where you and I differ, Father Dominic. I see danger as opportunity."

Before anyone could respond, the ground trembled faintly again, the vibrations echoing through the chamber. Marcus frowned, staring at the gate and then back at the tablet. "If you push this system too far, the entire structure will collapse. The train will be lost forever."

"Then you'd better not fail," Lenk said smoothly.

A shared glance between Marcus, Hana, Karl, and Lukas communicated a silent understanding: survival wasn't the only issue. It was about stopping Lenk—no matter the cost.

Marcus crouched near the gate, the artifact still in his hand and Lenk's mercenaries looming over him. His flashlight cast a tight beam onto the runes and gears hidden within the metal. The hum of the geothermal system was faint but constant, like the ticking of a clock counting down to an inevitable disaster.

Lenk stood behind him, arms crossed, his cold gaze fixed on Marcus. "You'll need to work quickly, Dr. Russo. The longer we delay, the greater the chance the system destabilizes."

Marcus didn't respond immediately, his eyes scanning the Nazi schematics on the tablet he had been handed. He could feel the weight of Hana's, Michael's, and the guards' stares, their silent trust in him to find a way out of this alive.

"This system is more complex than you realize," Marcus said finally, his voice steady but calculated. "If you push it too hard, it won't just collapse the chamber —it'll seal off any access to the train permanently."

"Which is why you're here. I trust you'll avoid any such... complications."

Marcus forced himself to nod, though inside his mind churned with possible ways to turn this situation around. "I'll need full access to the mechanism. That means clearing out any obstructions and recalibrating the artifact."

Lenk gestured to his men. "You heard the doctor. Assist him."

The mercenaries moved to clear debris from around the gate and the chamber floor. Marcus handed the tablet to Hana to hold so he could refer to the schematics on it as he held the artifact in both hands. This gave him the opportunity to speak softly to Hana, who had inched closer under the pretense of helping.

"Whatever I do," Marcus murmured, his voice barely audible, "be ready to act. I'll buy us time, but we'll need a plan to take back control."

Hana nodded, her expression tight. "I'll signal Karl and Lukas. If we get an opening, we'll take it."

Michael, who stood nearby with two mercenaries guarding him, spoke suddenly, his voice cutting through the tension. "Lenk, you think you're in control here, but you're tampering with forces you don't understand."

Lenk chuckled, turning toward Michael. "Forces I don't understand? Father, I'm simply continuing what your precious Vatican chose to bury. The Nazis were innovators. Their methods may have been crude, but their vision was unparalleled."

Michael's eyes narrowed. "Their vision led to death and destruction on an unimaginable scale. You're walking the same path."

Lenk shrugged. "Perhaps. But history remembers those who take risks."

As Lenk and Michael argued, Marcus examined the artifact and the gate's mechanism more closely. He found the artifact controlled the system, but it was a stabilizer, not merely a seal. If the artifact was removed or its configuration altered, the system would default to an emergency state, sealing off the chamber entirely.

It was risky, but it could work.

Marcus called out, his voice steady. "Lenk, I've made progress. I'll need the artifact aligned with the mechanism for a controlled release."

Lenk approached, nodding to the men guarding Marcus to allow him closer to the gate. "Proceed."

Marcus stepped forward and carefully adjusted the artifact, aligning its glowing runes with the gate. He moved with deliberate slowness, buying time as he studied the schematics further. Beneath the gate, he spotted a hidden panel still partially obscured by dust and debris.

"Hana," Marcus whispered, tilting his head subtly toward the panel. "That panel. It might be a manual override. If I distract them, see if you can access it."

Hana glanced toward the panel, then gave the slightest nod.

Marcus took the tablet from her hands and stepped back from the gate, gesturing toward the artifact now affixed to the gate. "It's set. The mechanism is stabilizing. But I'll need to monitor the output—otherwise, we could lose control."

The artifact began to emit a faint vibration, and everyone's attention shifted to the gate. Lenk's eyes gleamed. "Impressive work, Dr. Russo."

Hana used the moment of distraction to slip toward the panel. She glanced at Michael, who quickly stepped between her and the others, blocking their view of her as he pointed forcefully at Marcus. "Traitor! How could you hand such power to this man?"

As Michael and Marcus argued, the soldiers focused on the two men. And Hana crouched, using her flashlight to illuminate the hidden compartment. Inside, she found a series of levers and dials labeled in faded

German. Her heart pounded as she studied them, trying to decipher their purpose.

"Enough!" Lenk finally poked a finger in Michael's chest and turned to Marcus. "Get on with it."

Marcus stepped closer to Lenk, his voice calm but firm. "You should know—this isn't just about opening a passage. The pressure system beneath the mountain is volatile. If it's not managed correctly, it could destabilize the entire structure."

Lenk arched an eyebrow, clearly intrigued. "And how do you propose we avoid that?"

Marcus glanced toward Hana, who gave him a small, almost imperceptible nod. "By not rushing the process."

Hana yanked one of the levers in the panel, and a deep, mechanical groan filled the chamber. The gate's glow flickered, and a series of vents along the walls opened, releasing a rush of hot air and steam.

"Move!" Marcus shouted, grabbing Michael and pulling him toward the far side of the chamber.

Chaos erupted as the mercenaries scrambled to maintain their positions. Karl and Lukas opened fire, taking down two of the guards, while Hana used the steam as cover to disable another, striking his head with the butt of her pistol. Lenk, caught off guard, retreated toward the entrance, shouting orders to his men.

The ground trembled violently, and Marcus realized the system was teetering on collapse. "Hana, shut it down!" he yelled.

"I'm trying!" Hana shouted back, frantically adjusting the controls in the panel.

Lenk's voice cut through the chaos. "Stop them! Take the artifact!"

Marcus turned, his eyes locking on Lenk. For a split second, everything seemed to freeze—their goals, their stakes, and the precarious balance of the moment hanging in the air.

And then the mountain roared—a deep, guttural sound, as though the earth itself cursed their intrusion.

CHAPTER
ELEVEN

The hiss of steam and the faint smell of sulfur hung in the air as the chaos subsided. The ground beneath the chamber still trembled intermittently, but the violent shaking had diminished. Marcus leaned against the wall, his breathing labored and his mind accelerating as he tried to assess the situation.

Karl and Lukas moved swiftly through the chamber, securing the weapons left behind by Lenk's retreating mercenaries. A few injured soldiers groaned nearby, disarmed but alive. The remaining men had fled, regrouping with Lenk deeper in the tunnels.

"We bought some time," Karl said, his voice grim as he checked the ammunition in his rifle. "But they'll be back. Lenk doesn't strike me as the kind to give up easily."

Marcus glanced at the gate, the artifact still faintly glowing in its center. The vibrations had steadied, but the system was far from stable. "He won't stop," he said, his tone heavy with certainty. "The artifact is the key, and as long as we have it, he'll keep coming."

Hana emerged from the hidden panel, her face streaked with grime but her eyes clear and determined. "The override worked, but barely. This system is hanging on by a thread. One more push and it'll collapse completely."

Michael, holding tight to a small wound on his arm, stepped closer. "What's the damage? Can we still use this mechanism to find the train?"

Marcus nodded, though his expression was tense. "The system is intact enough to give us what we need. The artifact isn't just a key—it's also a map. The runes correspond to coordinates embedded in the mechanism."

Hana looked puzzled as she stepped up to examine Michael's arm. "Coordinates? To where?"

"It must be to the train," Marcus said, turning to the artifact. "The Nazis didn't just bury it—they hid it behind layers of defense. This system was the first line, meant to protect the train by making it nearly impossible to reach without triggering a collapse."

Karl crossed his arms, his curious gaze on Marcus. "And now that we've stabilized it?"

"We've unlocked part of the puzzle," Marcus replied. "But there's more to decipher."

Lukas gestured toward the darkened corridor where Lenk had disappeared. "And less time to do it. He'll regroup, and next time, he'll come at us harder."

Michael sighed, his expression grave. Hana had

wrapped a bandana around his wound and the two stood together, arms protectively around each other. "Then we can't wait here. If Marcus can decipher the coordinates, we need to move before Lenk does."

Marcus set the artifact on the floor, pulling the parchment from his satchel and spreading it out on the dusty floor. The glow of the artifact illuminated the runes on the parchment, revealing a faint overlay of patterns he hadn't noticed before.

"These aren't just runes—they're part of a larger grid," Marcus said, tracing the lines with his finger. "The artifact is reacting to the gate, but it's also pointing to another location nearby. It's giving us the next step."

Hana crouched beside him, her flashlight steady. "What kind of location? Another gate? Another system?"

Marcus shook his head. "No. Something more refined. The Nazis must have built layers of protection —false paths, dead ends. I'm sure this is the real one, the final entry point to the train's chamber."

Karl and Lukas exchanged a glance, their expressions grim but resolute. "How far?" Karl asked.

Marcus studied the parchment and the artifact, his mind piecing together the fragments. "A few kilometers, maybe less. But it won't be easy to get there. The terrain will be rough, and we'll have to assume Lenk knows the general direction."

Hana stood, brushing dust from her knees. "Then we need to move. The longer we stay here, the more ground they'll cover."

Lukas looked toward the injured mercenaries still

groaning on the floor. "What about them? If Lenk catches up, they'll talk."

Karl stepped forward, his expression cold. "Then we deal with them now."

"No," Michael said quickly, standing to face Marcus. "They're out of the fight. Leave them here. They won't be able to follow us."

Marcus nodded his agreement with Michael to the Swiss Guards. Karl hesitated, his jaw tightening, but he said, "Fine. But if they come back to haunt us, it's on you."

Marcus turned back to the artifact, his determination growing. "Let's pack up and move. This is our chance to get ahead of Lenk—and find the train before he does."

The team worked quickly, gathering their gear and securing the artifact. Marcus carefully rewrapped the parchment and slipped it into his satchel, his mind still racing with possibilities and dangers.

As they exited the chamber, the air outside felt colder, more intense, as if the mountain itself were warning them. The distant sound of falling rocks echoed through the tunnels, a reminder of the fragile balance they were walking.

Hana fell into step beside Marcus as they climbed toward the surface. "You sure about this? That we'll find the train before Lenk?"

"No," Marcus admitted, his voice low. "But it's our best shot. If we don't, he'll turn that train into a weapon —or worse, destroy everything in the process."

Hana nodded, her jaw set. "Then let's make sure we do."

. . .

IN THE SHADOWED depths of the forest, Lenk marched with purpose, his men trailing him in tight formation. The faint smell of smoke lingered in the air from their earlier skirmish at the geothermal system, but Lenk's focus was razor-sharp. His handheld device flickered with data—thermal readings, seismic scans, and a crude digital map of the Owl Mountains, overlaid with the Nazi schematics his team had decoded.

Clara Weiss kept pace beside him, her jaw tight. Lenk had explained what had happened inside the monastery. He had ordered her to remain outside, to contact Base on their progress, and now she wondered if he had really explained to her everything that happened in there. Lenk had agendas beyond what he had admitted to her. She studied the readings on her own device and reported, "They're ahead of us. See the artifact's vibrations? Marcus must be using it to guide them."

Lenk didn't break stride, his voice calm and measured. "Good. Let him. He's clearing the path for us."

Clara glanced at him, her unease evident. "You're assuming he won't sabotage the system. Russo's not stupid—he knows what's at stake."

Lenk smiled faintly, his eyes scanning the terrain. "He's pragmatic. As long as his team survives, he'll keep moving forward. And when he reaches the train, we'll be there to collect the prize."

One of the mercenaries approached, his face grim.

"Sir, tracks ahead. They passed this way within the hour."

Lenk paused, crouching to examine the faint impressions in the dirt. The uneven tread of boots and broken branches painted a clear picture of Marcus's route. He glanced up at the ridge ahead, the jagged peaks outlined against the sky.

"They're heading for the old bunker," he said, his tone confident. "It's the next logical step. If they plan to use the artifact to triangulate the train's location, they'll need the bunker's schematics."

Clara frowned. "And if they find the train before we catch them?"

Lenk rose, his expression hardening. "Then we take it by force. The train isn't going anywhere, and neither are they."

As THE TEAM continued their ascent, Lenk motioned for his men to halt. They had reached a narrow pass, the trail ahead winding upward toward the plateau where the bunker lay hidden. The steep cliffs and dense forest provided ample cover for an ambush.

Lenk turned to his second-in-command, a grizzled veteran named Viktor. "Position the snipers here and here," he ordered, pointing to two elevated outcroppings overlooking the trail. "We'll force them into the open."

Viktor nodded, signaling the snipers to move into position. The rest of the mercenaries began setting up along the pass, their movements efficient and practiced.

Lenk turned to Clara. "Contact Base. Give them our coordinates."

"I told you, communications aren't working from this close to the mountain. These cliffs aren't helping matters. The geography here, or maybe the energy this mountain emits, something, scrambles the signals. I'll need to go back to our earlier camp to get anything—"

"Then do it," he snapped, his gaze on his men, long-range rifles in their hands. "At least you can accomplish that much."

Clara hesitated, her voice low, looking over the scene. "If you trap them here, you risk damaging the artifact—or worse, the schematics in the bunker."

Lenk gave her a harsh look. "If Russo is as resourceful as you believe, he'll protect the artifact at all costs. The schematics are secondary. The train is what matters."

"And if they fight back?" Clara asked, her tone skeptical.

"They will," Lenk said, his smile cold. "But they're outnumbered and outgunned. This ends here."

As Marcus and his team exited the forest onto the rocky plateau, everyone felt tense. The bunker loomed ahead, its concrete walls blending into the craggy mountainside, but the oppressive silence of the trail set Marcus's nerves on edge.

Karl, scanning the ridges with his binoculars, muttered under his breath, "We're being watched."

"Where?" Hana asked, her hand hovering near her weapon.

Karl pointed subtly toward a rocky outcrop. "There. And there." He gestured to another position on the opposite ridge. "Snipers."

Lukas moved closer, his voice low. "We can't go back. They'll pin us down."

Marcus's mind raced. The bunker was so close, but the ambush had tightened the noose around them. He glanced at the artifact in his hand, its vibrations steady but urgent.

"Keep moving," he said, his voice calm but firm. "If we stop, we're soft targets. The bunker is the only cover."

A shot rang out, the crack echoing across the plateau. The bullet hit the ground near Karl, kicking up dirt and rock. The team dropped to the ground, taking cover behind boulders and fallen trees.

"Snipers have us pinned!" Karl shouted. "We need to move!"

Hana pulled Marcus behind a large rock, her breathing heavy. "They've got the high ground. What's the plan?"

Marcus glanced toward the bunker, calculating the distance. "We need to create a distraction. If we can draw their fire, the rest of us can make a run for the bunker."

Karl nodded, his jaw tight. "I'll take Lukas. We'll draw their attention. You and the others head for the door."

"No," Marcus said quickly. "It's too dangerous."

Karl met his gaze, his voice steady. "It's the only way. If we don't, they'll pick us off one by one."

Before Marcus could argue, Karl and Lukas sprinted toward a cluster of rocks, firing their weapons as they moved. The snipers' attention shifted, their shots following the two guards as they zigzagged across the plateau.

"Now!" Hana shouted.

The three of them sprinted toward the bunker, bullets whizzing past them. Michael stumbled but caught himself, keeping pace as they reached the door and ducked inside.

Marcus turned, his heart pounding. "Karl! Lukas!"

"We're good!" Karl's voice came through the comms, strained but steady. "We've got their attention—get what you need and get out!"

Inside the bunker, the air was cold and musty, the walls lined with rusted equipment and faded Nazi insignia. Marcus knelt near the central desk, pulling out the parchment and artifact.

"This is it," he said, his voice trembling with both adrenaline and determination. "The final piece."

CHAPTER

TWELVE

The dim beams of their flashlights swept across the room, revealing a chaotic scene of overturned furniture, rusted filing cabinets, and faded maps pinned to the walls. The Nazi insignias were barely visible beneath decades of grime, but the room's purpose was clear: this had been a command post, the nerve center of operations for whatever the Nazis had hidden in the Owl Mountains.

Marcus didn't waste a second. He set the artifact on the central desk, its faint glow illuminating the scattered papers and faded blueprints, its light indicating its connection to this area. He carefully unrolled the parchment, aligning it with the artifact's runes.

"Start looking," Marcus said, his voice tense but focused. "Anything that mentions the train, coordinates, or schematics."

Hana moved to the filing cabinets, yanking open drawers that groaned with age. Michael began scanning the walls, his fingers tracing the edges of maps, searching for hidden compartments or annotations.

"This place looks ransacked," Hana muttered, tossing aside a stack of brittle papers. "Someone's already been through it."

"Not everything," Marcus replied, flipping through a bound logbook. The pages were fragile but intact, the handwriting meticulous. "This is a manifest. Supplies, personnel... notes about the geothermal system. This bunker was more than a checkpoint—it was an operations hub."

Michael turned from the wall, his flashlight illuminating a large map pinned to a board. "Here," he said, his voice determined. "This map is marked. Coordinates—look."

Marcus hurried over, his eyes scanning the faded markings. The map showed the mountain range, with several locations circled in red. Each was labeled with a site number. Marcus pointed to additional notes scrawled in the margins. "Each of these sites include defenses—they're layered. So every site is defended, and there is no way of knowing which is the real train's site and which are the decoys. They wanted anyone following to think they'd found the train and likely set off the defenses of a decoy first, thwarting their efforts."

Michael leaned closer, his expression darkening. "And if these decoys are heavily defended, the actual site will be nearly impossible to breach."

"We'll figure it out," Marcus said, his voice firm. He glanced back at the artifact, which was vibrating slightly as though reacting to the map. "The artifact confirms we are at least on the right track. That the train is nearby, here in the mountains."

Hana furrowed her brow. "Energy signature? I thought this thing was just a key."

"It is a key, yes," Marcus said, his mind abuzz with alternatives, "but it's also a beacon. The Nazis must have designed it to resonate with specific sites. That's how they ensured only someone with the artifact could access the train. We might be able to follow it, something like a metal detector, but it would take some time. Time we don't have."

As Marcus examined the map, Hana's flashlight swept across the room, catching on a cabinet less rusted than the rest of the metal furniture. She moved toward it, crouching to inspect the lock.

"This doesn't fit," she said. "Everything else in here looks like it's been here since the war, but this cabinet... it's different. Maybe newer?"

Marcus joined her, his flashlight illuminating the cabinet's surface. "Not newer. It's better steel, reinforced. Definitely not standard issue."

Hana pulled out a multitool from her pack and began working on the lock. After a few moments of effort, there was a satisfying click, and the door swung open.

Inside was a trove of documents, rolled blueprints, and a single metal box. Marcus reached for the box first, carefully opening it to reveal a set of small, intricate tools and a notebook with the *Reichsadler*—the Nazi Imperial Eagle—embossed on its cover.

"This is it," Marcus said, pulling out the notebook. "It's a log. Field notes."

Hana peered over his shoulder as he flipped through the pages. The handwriting was precise, accompanied by diagrams of train cars, weapon systems, and an annotated cross-section of a tunnel.

"'*Sonderlager IV*,'" Marcus read aloud. "That means 'Special Camp Number Four.' Look"—he pointed to the wall map—"number four is the site closest to us." He looked back at the notebook. "And here it says 'Final repository for...'" He paused, his breath catching. "'For materials vital to the Reich's future.'"

Hana raised an eyebrow. "Materials? That's vague."

"Deliberately," Marcus said. "But look at this." He pointed to a sketch of the train's interior. "Compartmentalized. Each car was designed to carry something different—gold, art, documents, and..." He hesitated again, his brow furrowing. "'Experimental technologies.'"

Michael, who had been scanning another corner of the room, pivoted. "Experimental technologies? What does that mean?"

Marcus shook his head. "I don't know. But whatever it is, it's important enough that they buried it with untold treasures and under every layer of defense they could."

Hana gestured to the blueprints in the cabinet. "What about these? Do they match the site?"

Marcus unrolled one of the blueprints, his eyes narrowing as he studied it. "They do. This is the entrance to the train's chamber. It's built into a natural cave system, with reinforced tunnels leading to the main depot. This is our way in."

Suddenly, Karl's voice crackled over the comms, blunt and urgent. "Marcus, you've got company. Lenk's regrouping."

Marcus folded the blueprint and stuffed it into his satchel with the map from the wall. "How many?"

"Too many," Karl replied. "They've brought reinforcements. You've got maybe twenty minutes before they reach you. We'll catch up with you before they do."

Marcus turned to the team, his expression hard. "We've got what we need. Let's move."

Hana slung her pack over her shoulder. "You sure this is everything?"

Marcus nodded. "It's enough to find the train."

As they exited the bunker, the mountain seemed to rumble faintly beneath their feet, a reminder of the fragile system they had left behind. Marcus glanced at the map one last time, his mind locked on the marked coordinates for Special Camp Number Four.

The train was closer than ever. But so was Lenk—and the danger he represented.

THE PATH LEADING AWAY from the bunker was narrow and perilous, carved into the side of the mountain with sheer cliffs dropping into misty abysses below. The team moved in silence, their breaths visible in the crisp, thinning air. Marcus led the way, the artifact in his hand vibrating slightly, its faint glow a guide through the rugged terrain.

"We need to pick up the pace," Karl said, his voice low as he scanned the trail behind them. "Lenk won't stop just because we slowed him down."

Hana adjusted the straps on her pack, her eyes darting to the artifact. "That thing's pulling us forward, but is it leading us into another trap?"

"It's leading us to the train," Marcus replied, his tone confident but his mental acuity racing. "The artifact's resonance is getting stronger. It's designed to react to specific locations, and the closer we get to *Sonderlager IV*, the clearer the signal."

Michael, who had been walking quietly, glanced at the steep cliffs on either side of the trail. "The Nazis hadn't just interred the train. They buried it under layers of defenses. Even if we get there first, we might not have time to breach it."

"We'll make time," Marcus said, his jaw tightening. "We have to."

As they rounded a bend in the trail, the artifact's vibrations grew sharper, its glow intensifying. Marcus slowed, holding it up as he scanned the terrain. The trail widened slightly into a clearing, but something about the scene made him pause.

"Wait," he said, raising a hand. "Something's off." He realized the artifact now vibrated with a sudden and different rhythm.

Karl moved ahead cautiously, his trained eyes sweeping the ground. He crouched, brushing away a layer of dirt and revealing a thin, nearly invisible wire stretched across the path. "Tripwire," he muttered. "Old, but functional."

Hana knelt beside him, inspecting the wire. "It's connected to something over there." She pointed to a cluster of rocks, where the faint outline of a metal canister was visible.

"Anti-personnel mines," Karl said grimly. "Nazis loved these tricks. One step in the wrong place, and this whole trail goes up."

Marcus scanned the area, his mind working quickly, as he held his hand out to stop any of them going forward.

Karl said, glancing over his shoulder. "Lenk's men could be on us any minute."

Marcus ignored him and stepped forward, his eyes on the artifact. Its glow pulsed in a pattern, almost rhythmic, as if responding to the danger. "The artifact," he said suddenly. "It's not just reacting to the train—it must be calibrated for these defenses."

Hana shot him a skeptical look. "You're telling me that thing's a mine detector now?"

"It may even be more than that," Marcus said. "I suspect the Nazis didn't just use it as a key. It was part of their system—designed to interact with every layer of their defenses."

Slowly, he walked to the side, through underbrush beyond the canister, and watched the pulsing vibrations. Once beyond the canister, the vibrations and glow returned to their former levels.

"It does react to the defenses," Marcus said, exhaling sharply. "It serves as a key and also is tuned to the defense mechanisms in its path. Come on." He waved for them to follow around the tripwire's explosive canister, and they hurried on.

The trail narrowed again, this time leading into a steep ravine. The walls of the cliffs on either side were jagged and unstable, with loose rocks threatening to tumble down at the slightest provocation. Marcus held the artifact tightly, its glow dimmer now but still guiding them forward.

"We're exposed here," Lukas said, his voice tense. "If they've got snipers, this is where they'll take us out."

Karl nodded, his expression grim. "And if they don't, the cliffs will. One wrong step, and we're done."

Hana glanced at Marcus. "The artifact—is it still pointing this way?"

Marcus nodded. "It's the only path. *Sonderlager IV* is just ahead. This ravine is the final approach."

Michael looked up at the cliffs, his expression dark. "The Nazis didn't just choose this place for its remoteness. They chose it because it's a natural fortress."

As they moved cautiously through the ravine, a distant sound echoed through the air—the crack of a gunshot. The bullet struck the rock wall just centimeters from Karl, sending shards of stone flying.

"Snipers!" Karl shouted. "Get to cover!"

The team scrambled, ducking behind boulders and outcroppings as more shots rang out. The echoes of the gunfire reverberated through the ravine, masking the shooters' positions.

"We need to keep moving!" Marcus shouted, his

voice barely audible over the gunfire. "The tunnel is just ahead!"

Hana crouched beside him, her weapon drawn. "We won't make it if we stay pinned here. We need a distraction."

Karl nodded grimly, reaching into his pack. "Smoke grenades. It'll give us cover, but we'll have to move fast."

"Do it," Marcus said.

Karl pulled the pin and tossed two grenades into the center of the ravine. Thick plumes of white smoke billowed upward, obscuring their movements. "Go!" he shouted.

The team sprinted through the smoke, their footsteps echoing in the confined space. The sound of gunfire continued, but the smoke provided enough cover to keep them moving, the bullets missing them.

As they reached the end of the ravine, Marcus glanced back, his heart pounding. The snipers had stopped firing, but the smoke was beginning to clear. He knew they were still being hunted—and that their time was running out.

CHAPTER

THIRTEEN

The smoke began to thin as the team cleared the ravine, the air heavy with the acrid scent of burnt chemicals and the echo of gunfire still ringing in their ears. Marcus led the way, the artifact clutched tightly in his hand as it continued to vibrate faintly, its glow a beacon against the darkening sky.

Karl was the last to emerge, his rifle trained on the ridge behind them. He scanned the cliffs for movement, his breath steady despite the adrenaline coursing through his veins. "They'll be coming through the smoke any second," he said. "We've got maybe five minutes to get to cover again."

Marcus nodded, his eyes fixed on the dense forest ahead. "The artifact's pull is stronger now. We're close. The entrance to *Sonderlager IV* has to be just in front of us."

"Let's hope the Nazis didn't leave us another

'welcome' like the last one," Hana said, her tone edged with tension as she checked her weapon.

"Even if they didn't," Michael added, his voice low, "Lenk's team will catch up soon. We need to find cover and figure out our next move."

As they pushed deeper into the forest, the artifact's vibrations intensified, its glow pulsing in a steady rhythm. The terrain became rockier, the trees thinning to reveal jagged outcroppings that jutted from the ground like broken teeth. Marcus stopped suddenly, his gaze locking on a large boulder partially obscured by moss and vines.

"This is it," he said, his voice filled with certainty.

Karl moved to his side, his eyes scanning the area. "A rock? That's what we came for?"

"Not just a rock," Marcus replied, crouching to examine the base of the boulder. He brushed away a layer of moss to reveal faint carvings etched into the stone. The runes matched those on the artifact and the parchment.

"It's a marker," Marcus continued. "The Nazis built their systems to blend into the landscape. This isn't just a boulder—it's a hidden door."

Hana stepped closer, her brow furrowing as she studied the runes. "A hidden door? How do we open it?"

Marcus held up the artifact, aligning its glowing runes with the carvings on the stone. As he adjusted its position the vibrations grew stronger, and a low, mechanical groan echoed from beneath the ground.

"Whatever you're doing, do it fast," Karl said, his tone urgent. "Lenk's men won't wait."

With a final adjustment, the artifact locked into place, and the ground beneath the boulder shifted. They jumped back as the stone slid aside with a deep, grinding sound, revealing a dark passageway that descended into the earth. A faint rush of cool air spilled out, carrying with it the metallic tang of old machinery and the slight scent of oil.

"Bingo," Marcus said, a hint of relief in his voice. "This is the entrance."

Michael peered into the darkness, his expression wary. "If the defenses up here were this well-hidden, I can't imagine what they've built down there."

"Only one way to find out," Marcus said, stepping toward the opening.

THE PASSAGEWAY WAS narrow and steep, the walls carved from rough stone and reinforced with rusted steel beams. Their footsteps echoed faintly as they descended, flashlights cutting through the darkness. The air grew warmer with each step, the silence broken only by the distant hum of machinery.

"This isn't natural," Hana said, her voice hushed. "The Nazis must have hollowed this out."

"They didn't just hollow it out," Marcus replied. "They engineered it. Look at the walls—vents, drainage systems. This place was designed to last."

"And to keep people out," Karl added, his weapon raised as he scanned the shadows. "Keep your eyes open. If they've got defenses down here, we'll walk right into them."

The passage leveled out, opening into a wide chamber that took their breath away. The ceiling arched high above, supported by massive steel girders. Tracks ran along the floor, leading deeper into the mountain, and rows of rusted crates lined the walls. At the far end of the chamber stood a massive steel door, its surface adorned with more runes and the faded insignia of the Third Reich.

"This is it," Marcus said, his voice barely above a whisper. "The entrance to *Sonderlager IV*."

Hana stepped forward, her flashlight illuminating the steel door. "Looks like it hasn't been touched in decades."

"Which means it's probably rigged," Karl said, his tone grim. "They wouldn't leave this unprotected."

Marcus examined the door, the artifact's glow illuminating faint seams and mechanisms hidden within its surface. "The artifact will open it," he said, "but it might take time."

Michael glanced back toward the passage they had come through. "And what about Lenk? If they're behind us, we don't have time. We'll be trapped."

"We don't have a choice," Marcus said, his eyes locked on the door. "If we don't get in now, they'll take everything."

FOURTEEN

The chamber was eerily silent except for the faint hum of the artifact in Marcus's hand. The massive steel door loomed before the team, its surface cold and smooth, etched with faded runes and symbols that told of its purpose: to guard whatever lay beyond. The door's edges were seamlessly fused with the walls, a testament to the precision engineering of the Nazi architects.

Marcus crouched before the door, the artifact glowing brighter as he held it near the carvings. The vibrations were strong now, pulsing in a rhythmic pattern that resonated through his hands. He glanced back at the team, his voice low but steady. "This is it. The artifact should unlock it, but we need to be ready. If it's connected to the defenses, activating it could trigger... anything."

Karl nodded, his rifle raised. "We'll cover you. Just don't take too long."

Hana knelt beside Marcus, her flashlight illuminating the door's intricate mechanisms. "Any idea what we're looking at? It doesn't look like a simple lock."

"It's not," Marcus said, his fingers tracing the runes. "It's a system. The artifact acts as a key, but the runes indicate some kind of sequence. If I activate the wrong one..." He trailed off, the implication clear.

"Then don't," Hana said dryly, her eyes scanning the room. "We've had enough explosions for one day."

Marcus aligned the artifact with a central indentation in the door, the glow of the runes intensifying as it clicked into place. The vibrations stopped, replaced by a low, resonant hum that seemed to emanate from the walls themselves.

A light emanated from behind the runes on the door and began to shift from one to another, in a sequence. Marcus studied them intently, his mind striving to match the sequence with the inscriptions on the parchment. He reached out, pressing one of the illuminated symbols. The hum grew louder, and the door shuddered slightly.

"Is that supposed to happen?" Michael asked, his voice tight with apprehension.

"Hopefully," Marcus replied, pressing another rune. As he activated the sequence, a sharp metallic click echoed through the chamber, followed by the sound of gears grinding deep within the walls.

The door began to move, sliding upward with a slow, deliberate motion. Beyond it lay darkness, the faint outlines of another tunnel barely visible in the dim light.

"It's open," Marcus said, standing and stepping back.

But before anyone could move, a sudden hiss filled the air. From hidden compartments in the walls, narrow steel tubes extended, releasing a fine mist that spread rapidly through the chamber.

"Gas!" Karl shouted, pulling a scarf over his face. "Get out of the mist!"

The team scrambled, retreating toward the edges of the room as the mist thickened. Marcus coughed, his eyes burning. "It's a defense mechanism—meant to flush out intruders."

Hana reached into her pack, pulling out a thick, folded map. "Here!" she said, tossing it toward Marcus. "Clear the air near the artifact!"

Marcus grabbed the map, fanning the airflow away from them. The mist began to dissipate around the door, but the mechanism continued to hum, as if preparing for the next stage of its defenses.

As the mist cleared, Marcus peered into the open passage beyond the door. The tunnel was lined with steel beams, its floor marked with faint tracks that hinted at the train's location deeper within. He glanced at the artifact, which, he now realized, had that same odd vibration it had when they had encountered the tripwire. He hadn't had time to notice it before the mist burst out. But why hadn't it returned to normal now that the danger was—

"Hold up!" Karl said, his tone sharp, his eyes on the

ground, his flashlight cutting through the darkness. "Pressure plates."

Marcus stepped closer, illuminating the floor with his flashlight. The faint outlines of square plates were visible, almost indistinguishable from the surrounding surface.

"Step on one, and it'll trigger a trap," Marcus said. "Probably explosives or—"

A sudden metallic snap interrupted him, followed by the sound of gears grinding. From the walls of the tunnel, long steel rods shot out and flew through the air, their tips gleaming with deadly sharpness. One rod embedded itself in the wall just centimeters from Karl.

"Spears," Karl said grimly, stepping back carefully. "Because why not?"

Marcus examined the floor, his mind a tangle of thoughts. "The plates are arranged in a pattern—same as the runes on the artifact. If we follow the correct path, we can cross safely."

Hana stepped beside him, her voice tense. "And if we don't?"

Marcus glanced at the steel rods. "Then we don't make it to the train."

Using the artifact's runes as a guide, he began to map out the safe path across the pressure plates. He stepped cautiously, the vibrations from the artifact guiding his movements.

"Stay close," Marcus said, motioning for the others to follow. "One wrong step, and…"

He didn't need to finish the sentence. The team moved in single file, their movements deliberate and precise. Each step was a gamble, the tension obvious as the mechanisms beneath the floor groaned with the weight of their footsteps.

As they reached the end of the tunnel, Marcus pressed the final rune on the artifact. The steel rods retracted, and the grinding of gears ceased. The passage ahead was clear.

"We're through," he said, exhaling in relief.

THE ARTIFACT'S VIBRATIONS, though normalized now, also intensified to the point that Marcus doubted he would be able to identify the differences in pulsations even if it did warn about another defense. As the team moved deeper into the winding tunnels, its glow threw shadows on the rough, damp walls. The air was heavy with the scent of rust and mildew, and the faint sound of dripping water echoed around them. Marcus stopped suddenly, holding the artifact aloft, its glow illuminating an archway carved into the rock ahead.

"This has to be it," he said, his voice tight with anticipation. "The readings match, and the artifact is reacting more strongly than ever."

Hana stepped beside him, her flashlight sweeping over the archway. The stone was weathered but engraved with faint Nazi symbols, barely visible under layers of grime. "Looks convincing enough," she said. "But we've been burned before."

Karl moved to the front. "Let's keep this tight. If this is a decoy—or worse—Lenk won't be far behind."

Marcus nodded, stepping cautiously through the

archway. Beyond it lay a cavernous chamber, its walls reinforced with crumbling steel beams and its floor littered with debris. At the far end of the room stood a massive steel door, similar to the one they had encountered earlier but more deteriorated, its surface marred by rust and erosion.

"This looks promising," Michael said, his tone both hopeful and wary.

"Maybe too promising," Hana muttered, scanning the room. "This place feels... wrong."

Marcus approached the door, the artifact's glow growing almost blinding. As he stepped closer, the floor beneath him groaned, and he froze.

"Wait," he said, raising a hand. "Something's off."

Marcus crouched, inspecting the ground near the door. Hidden among the debris were faint lines— seams that didn't match the rest of the floor. His heart sank.

"It's another pressure plate," he said grimly. "Step on it, and it'll trigger... something."

Hana knelt beside him. "Yet another trap? Great. What do you think it's rigged to?"

Marcus gestured to the walls, where faint outlines of recessed panels were visible. "Could be gas, explosives, or..." He trailed off, his attention drawn to a faint glint of metal above the door. "Spears, maybe. Whatever it is, it's certainly lethal."

Karl tightened his grip on his weapon. "So, this site's a fake?"

"Not entirely," Marcus said, rising slowly. "The artifact's reaction suggests this site is part of the system, but maybe it's not the train's depot. It's designed to look like it, to slow us down—or stop us."

"Classic misdirection," Michael said, his tone heavy with frustration. "The Nazis were masters of it."

Marcus turned the artifact in his hands, the glow of the runes shifting in response to his movements. "The artifact's still reacting. There might be something here worth finding—a clue or a key to the real location."

The artifact began to hum softly, its vibrations taking on a new rhythm. Marcus tilted his head, listening intently. The pattern was different, not the steady pulse they had followed before, nor the warning pulse that indicated defenses, but something more intricate.

"It's signaling something," Marcus murmured. "It's... a different sequence."

Hana frowned. "A sequence? Like a code?"

Marcus nodded, stepping away from the pressure plate and toward the side of the room. The artifact's glow shifted, dimming and brightening as he moved. He followed its guidance to a section of the wall, where a faint outline of a compartment was visible.

"Here," he said, pressing the artifact against the wall. The vibrations intensified, and with a soft click, a hidden panel slid open.

Inside was a small, steel box, its surface engraved with the same runes as the artifact. Marcus carefully removed it, his pulse quickening as he lifted the lid. Inside lay a series of intricate metal pieces, each marked with symbols that matched those on the artifact.

"What is that?" Hana asked, peering over his shoulder.

"A calibration kit," Marcus said, his voice filled with wonder. "The artifact isn't just a key—it's modular. These pieces can change its function, probably to interact with different parts of the system."

Karl glanced at the kit, then back at Marcus. "You're saying this thing can do more than just open doors?"

Marcus nodded, already examining the pieces. "It's designed for more than one purpose. The Nazis must have built multiple sites like this, each requiring specific configurations."

Michael crossed his arms, his expression dark. "So this was all just another step in their game. How many more of these places are there?"

Marcus set the box down, his mind sharpened, sifting through facts at lightning speed. "This kit might tell us. If I can decode the sequence, it could reveal the locations of the other sites—or even lead us directly to the train."

Before the team could move, the faint sound of voices echoed through the tunnel. Karl stiffened, raising his weapon. "Lenk. He's here."

Marcus grabbed the box, carefully placing it in his satchel along with the artifact. "We need to move. Now."

Hana pointed toward a side passage they hadn't explored. "This way. It might loop back to the main tunnel."

The team moved quickly, the sound of Lenk's forces growing louder behind them. As they slipped into the side passage, Marcus felt a renewed sense of importance. The artifact's deeper mysteries were beginning to unfold, and he knew the stakes were higher than ever.

"We're not just racing for the train anymore," Marcus said, his voice low but steely. "We're racing to stay ahead of a game the Nazis started—and that Lenk is determined to finish."

THE ATMOSPHERE in the narrow tunnel was stifling, every sound amplified by the cold, unyielding stone surrounding them. The faint glow of Marcus's flashlight flickered over the uneven walls, and the vibrations from the artifact in his satchel seemed to mirror the pounding of his heart.

Behind them, the sounds of Lenk's forces echoed ominously—harsh commands, hurried footsteps, and the faint clatter of equipment. The pursuit was relentless.

"They're gaining on us," Hana said, her voice low but urgent. She glanced over her shoulder, her flashlight sweeping the darkness behind them. "We need to pick up the pace."

"We can't afford a misstep," Marcus replied, his tone tense as he navigated the winding passage. "These tunnels might be unstable. One wrong move, and we could bring the whole place down."

"That might not be the worst idea," Karl muttered. "If we can trap Lenk in here…"

"Not if we trap ourselves too," Michael countered, his voice tight with strain.

The tunnel forked abruptly, splitting into two narrow

paths. Marcus hesitated, his flashlight moving between the options. The left path descended steeply, its floor slick with moisture, while the right veered upward, its incline marked by jagged rocks and crumbling walls.

"The artifact," Hana prompted. "Does it say which way?"

Marcus pulled the artifact from his satchel, its glow brightening as he pointed it toward the descending path. "Left," he said. "But let's exercise caution."

Karl scanned the path to the right with his flashlight. "And this one isn't exactly inviting either. If they're following us, they'll have to split up to cover both."

"Which gives us an advantage," Lukas said, his tone grim. "We can funnel them into a choke point."

Marcus nodded, already moving toward the left path. "We'll take the lower route. It's riskier, but the artifact's guiding us."

"What about the other path?" Michael asked. "If Lenk sends men that way, they'll flank us."

Karl adjusted his pack. "I'll lay some surprises."

From his pack, he pulled a handful of small, crude charges, their timers set manually. He worked quickly, attaching them to the unstable walls of the lower passage.

"Three minutes," Karl said, stepping back. "I'm thinking they'll assume we boobytrapped the path we took—in order to stop them. At the very least, it might buy us time as they try to unblock it or figure it out. Yet this will leave us an exit for later."

The team descended the left path, the air growing

warmer and damper with each step. The sound of dripping water echoed through the tunnel, mingling with the creak of shifting rock. The slope was steep, forcing them to move carefully to avoid slipping on the slick surface.

Marcus held the artifact tightly, its vibrations intensifying. "We're heading deeper into the mountain. This path must connect to another site."

Hana steadied herself against the wall, her flashlight revealing faint carvings etched into the stone. "Look at this," she said, motioning for Marcus to join her. "Symbols—like the ones on the artifact."

Marcus examined the carvings, his fingers tracing the weathered lines. "They're markers. We're on the right track."

A distant rumble shook the tunnel, followed by a distinct crack that echoed through the passage. The charges.

Karl said, his voice clipped, "That'll slow them down, but it won't stop them."

Only the rumbling didn't stop. Loose stones fell from the ceiling, and the ground beneath their feet trembled violently. Marcus's stomach sank as he realized the danger. "The charges destabilized both paths of the tunnel!"

"Move!" Karl shouted, pushing the team forward.

They sprinted down the passage, their footsteps echoing over the roar of collapsing stone. The vibrations grew stronger, the walls groaning under the strain.

"Up ahead!" Hana called out, her flashlight catching

on an opening at the end of the tunnel. "There's a chamber!"

The team burst into the open space just as the tunnel behind them gave way, a deafening crash reverberating through the mountain. Dust and debris filled the air, forcing them to cough and cover their faces.

Karl looked behind them at the totally blocked tunnel. "Well, so much for only collapsing the other tunnel."

When the dust settled, they found themselves in a large, circular chamber. The walls were lined with metal supports, and in the center stood a pedestal with an intricate mechanism atop it. The artifact in Marcus's hand pulsed brightly, as if recognizing its counterpart.

Marcus moved to the pedestal, setting the artifact atop it, the two halves fitting together seamlessly. The vibrations stopped and the mechanism hummed faintly as it activated. The room filled with a soft, golden light as hidden carvings on the walls illuminated, revealing a detailed map of the surrounding tunnels.

"This isn't the depot," Marcus said, his voice filled with awe. "It's a waypoint—a navigation hub."

Hana moved closer, her eyes scanning the map. "Look at this. These paths—they lead to other sites."

"And the train?" Michael asked.

Marcus studied the map, his brow furrowing. "It's here, but the direct path is blocked. The Nazis must have collapsed it intentionally. We'll need to navigate through another site to find an access point."

Karl, still watching the collapsed tunnel behind

them, turned abruptly. "That's great, but we've destroyed our only exit."

"Then we use this," Marcus said, motioning to the map. "Activating the mechanism might lead us to the next site—and give us another way out."

FIFTEEN

The golden glow of the navigation hub faded as Marcus removed the artifact from the pedestal. The intricate map etched into the walls dimmed, leaving only the faint outlines of tunnels burned into their memories. The team stood in silence, the weight of their next move settling over them like the cold, damp climate of the chamber.

"This way," Marcus said, pointing toward one of the passages marked on the map. "It leads to the next site. If the artifact's calibration holds, it should guide us."

"Should?" Hana asked, her eyebrow arching skeptically.

Marcus adjusted the artifact in his hand. "This isn't an exact science. But the Nazis built these systems to work together. The artifact reacts to the locations—if we follow its guidance, we'll get there."

Karl moved to the front. "Let's hope it doesn't lead us into another trap."

The new passage was narrower than the others, its walls rougher and less reinforced. The air grew warmer as they descended, the faint hum of the artifact the only sound breaking the oppressive silence. The team's flashlights illuminated crude carvings along the walls, their shapes twisted and strange.

"These symbols," Michael said, his voice echoing softly in the confined space, "they're different. Not like the others."

Marcus stopped, running his fingers over one of the carvings. "You're right. These aren't Nazi. They're older —much older."

Shining her flashlight farther down the tunnel, Hana asked, "Older? How much older?"

"Centuries, maybe more," Marcus said, his voice shaded with awe. "The Nazis didn't just use this mountain for its isolation. They chose it because of its history. These symbols—they're part of something predating their involvement. Something they must have discovered when they were building these sites."

The passage opened into a cavern that took their breath away. Stalactites hung like jagged teeth from the ceiling, glistening with moisture, while a wide chasm split the floor in two. A narrow stone bridge, barely wider than a person, spanned the gap, its surface worn smooth by time.

But it was what lay beyond the bridge that drew their attention.

A massive stone altar stood at the far end of the cavern, its surface covered in runes similar to those on the artifact. Behind it, carved into the rock wall, was an intricate relief depicting a serpent coiled around a tree, its scales glinting faintly in the dim light.

"The serpent again," Hana said, her voice hushed. "It's everywhere."

Marcus nodded, stepping cautiously onto the bridge as the others watched. The artifact's glow pulsed stronger now, its vibrations almost insistent. "It's not just a symbol. It's a key part of the artifact's origins."

Michael's eyes scanned the carvings. "The serpent—chaos, forbidden knowledge. It's the same across so many cultures. The Nazis must have thought there was power in it."

"They weren't wrong," Marcus said quietly, reaching the altar.

Karl glanced at Marcus, his expression hard, as he held his arm out to hold the others back from the tenuous bridge. "And now we're walking into it."

Marcus set the artifact on the altar, its glow intensifying as it aligned with the runes etched into the stone. A low hum filled the cavern, and the relief behind the altar began to shift, revealing a hidden compartment.

Inside was a metal cylinder, its surface engraved with the same symbols as the artifact. Marcus lifted it carefully, his heart pounding as he realized what it was.

"It's a data cache," he said, his voice trembling with excitement. "The Nazis must have used these to store information. If we can decrypt it, we might find out what they were really doing here."

Hana's eyes narrowed. "And what about the

artifact? Could the cache explain why the artifact reacts the way it does?"

Marcus turned the cylinder in his hands, his mind racing. "Maybe. If this cache contains schematics or records, it might."

Before he could say more, the ground beneath them rumbled violently. Stones fell from the ceiling, and a booming crack split the air as part of the bridge collapsed into the chasm.

"Move!" Karl shouted, rushing forward to grab Marcus's arm, yanking him back across the remaining bridge. The cavern shook as more debris rained down around them. The artifact's glow flickered, its vibrations erratic as if reacting to the instability.

"Whatever you did," Karl said, his voice strained as he hauled Marcus onto solid ground, "you just woke this place up."

At another shake of the floor, Michael snatched Hana away from the remaining stone edge as it crumbled at their feet and pulled her toward the tunnel.

The team sprinted back through the tunnel, the rumbling growing louder with each step. Behind them, the cavern collapsed entirely, the sound of falling rock echoing like thunder.

They emerged into the relative safety of another chamber, the tunnel behind them sealed by the collapse. The artifact's vibrations had steadied, but the air was heavy with tension.

Hana leaned on Michael, her hands on her knees as she caught her breath. Then she turned to Marcus.

"We've found a data cache, collapsed half a mountain, and nearly died—and for what? What did we learn?"

"It's the cache," Marcus said, clutching it tightly. "The system's responding to the artifact's activation of the cache. We triggered something."

"Like what?" Hana demanded.

"I don't know," Marcus admitted, his voice tight. He looked at the cache in his hands, his expression resolute. "This isn't just about the train anymore. The Nazis weren't just hiding treasures. They were hiding knowledge—knowledge they thought could change the course of the war."

Michael leaned against the wall, an arm still around Hana, his tone grim. "Knowledge like what?"

Marcus met his gaze, his voice low. "That's what we need to find out. The artifact—it's not just a tool. It's a map, a key, and a trigger. And whatever's on this cache might tell us how to use it."

Karl, ever pragmatic, glanced toward the sealed tunnel. "And if Lenk finds out what we're carrying?"

"Then we'll be racing him to more than just the train," Marcus said. "We'll be racing to stop him from unlocking something far worse."

THE TEAM MOVED CAUTIOUSLY through the twisting tunnels, taking turns that led to what the map indicated was yet another site. Marcus held the artifact tightly, its glow steady but subdued, as if waiting for the next step. The metal data cache was secured in his satchel, its mysterious contents adding another layer of mystery to their mission.

As they emerged into a wider chamber, the walls around them grew smoother, the rough-hewn stone giving way to precisely cut surfaces. Faded Nazi insignias adorned the walls, interspersed with inscriptions and runes that matched those on the artifact.

"This isn't just another tunnel," Marcus said, his flashlight sweeping across the room. "This was a central point—another operations hub."

Karl scanned the room, his rifle at the ready. "Doesn't look like anyone's been here in a long time. But that doesn't mean it's not dangerous."

Hana moved to a large, rusted control panel embedded in the wall. The buttons and levers were labeled in German, and a faint layer of dust covered the surface. "This looks like it controlled something big. A door, maybe?"

Marcus joined her, his eyes narrowing as he studied the panel. "Not a door. A lift system." He pointed to a schematic etched into the metal beside the controls, showing a series of interconnected shafts and platforms. "This was how they moved materials—and people— through the mountain at different levels."

Michael, standing near a stack of crates marked with more faded Nazi symbols, added, "If this is a hub, there might be records or blueprints here—something to tell us where the train is."

As Marcus examined the control panel, the artifact began to vibrate again, its glow intensifying. He held it near the panel, and a low hum emanated from the machinery.

"It's responding," Marcus said, his excitement tempered by caution. "The artifact's activating something."

Karl scowled at him, not at all pleased that yet another "activation" could be happening.

With a snapping click, a hidden compartment in the wall slid open, revealing yet another cylindrical tube, this one wrapped in metal bands. Marcus carefully removed it, recognizing the engravings as similar to those on the data cache.

"It's another cache," he said, his voice filled with awe. "This one might be linked directly to the lift system."

Hana tilted her head, her flashlight fixed on the panel. "Can it tell us where the train is?"

Marcus studied the runes on the cylinder, aligning them with the artifact's glowing symbols. "Not directly. But if we combine the data from both caches, it might give us coordinates—or another piece of the puzzle."

Working quickly, Marcus placed the new cache beside the artifact on a makeshift table. He opened the first cache and carefully removed a series of small, intricately carved metal plates. The engravings on the plates shimmered faintly, reflecting the glow of the artifact.

"These plates," he said, arranging them into a grid. "They're part of a map—an overlay that interacts with the artifact."

Hana leaned in. "So, where does it point?"

Marcus adjusted the plates, aligning their symbols with the artifact's vibrations. As the grid clicked into place, the artifact pulsed brightly, projecting a faint holographic image onto the wall.

The projection showed a series of interconnected tunnels and chambers, with one location marked prominently at the center. The inscription beside it read *Hauptlager*.

"There's the main depot," Marcus said, pointing to the marked site. "That's the train's true location."

Michael crossed his arms, his expression skeptical. "And how do we get there? It's not on the lift system map."

Marcus nodded, already examining the projection. "It's not connected directly, which means the main route was probably destroyed or blocked. But there's another path." He traced a secondary line on the map. "Here. It's longer, but it's our only way in."

Karl studied the map, his expression grim. "If this path exists, it's probably rigged with more traps—or worse."

"Worse?" Hana asked, raising an eyebrow.

"Collapses, floodgates, maybe even chemical traps," Karl said. "The Nazis didn't just bury the train. They buried everything around it."

Marcus nodded, his determination unwavering. "We don't have a choice. If we can reach the *Hauptlager*, we'll find the train—and everything the Nazis hid with it."

Michael gestured to the lift system. "And what about Lenk? If he takes another route and sees this hub, he'll know exactly where we're going."

"Then we make it harder for him to follow," Lukas suggested, motioning to Karl.

His partner nodded, moving toward the control panel. "We can disable the lift system—or rig it to collapse. We know the alternate way to the train; they'll assume the lift would be the access."

Hana glanced at Marcus. "That'll likely slow them down, but it won't stop them. If the lift is destroyed, they'll look for an alternate route—and find the one we're taking."

"It'll buy us time though," Marcus said, already packing away the caches and the artifact. "And right now, time is the one thing we need."

THE TUNNEL SEEMED to stretch endlessly, the darkness pressing in on all sides as the team pushed forward. The vibrations of the artifact grew erratic in Marcus's hand, its glow flickering like a dying flame. Hana's keen eyes scanned the path ahead while Karl brought up the rear, his rifle ready and his movements precise.

"I don't like this," Karl muttered, his voice low. "It's too quiet."

"Enjoy it while it lasts," Hana said, though her tone betrayed her unease. "Lenk's not far behind. He never is."

As if on cue, the faint echo of voices reached them, bouncing off the stone walls. It was Lenk's men, and they were getting closer. Marcus's stomach tightened as he quickened his pace, the artifact's pull leading them toward a distant glimmer of light at the end of the tunnel.

"We're almost out," Marcus said, his voice taut with urgency. "But if they catch us in the open…"

"They won't," Karl interrupted, his voice hard. "Not if we set the right trap."

The tunnel opened into a wide cavern, its jagged walls and uneven floor providing both cover and danger. Stalactites hung like swords from the ceiling, dripping water into shallow pools.

"Perfect spot for an ambush," Karl said, scanning the space with a practiced eye. "We can funnel them through the tunnel and pick them off one by one."

"We don't have enough ammo for that," Hana countered, her tone acute. "And they've got more men."

"We don't need to outgun them," Marcus interjected, holding up the artifact. "We just need to slow them down. This can do that."

Karl frowned at the idea of yet another destabilizing "activation" from the artifact. But he nodded, already moving to position himself near a cluster of boulders. "Then get to work. We'll cover you."

Marcus's eyes scoured the floor for something, anything that—and there it was. In the center of the floor, he knelt near a patch of exposed rock, where carvings were half obscured by layers of dust. The artifact glowed brighter as he pressed it into the surface. The vibrations intensified, and he moved it about until a faint hum filled the air, growing louder as he aligned the artifact with the carvings.

"What are you doing?" Michael asked, crouching beside him.

"These markings," Marcus explained, his voice steady despite the tension. "They're part of the system. If I can activate them, I might be able to open a path out for us."

THE FIRST SHOTS RANG OUT, penetrating and ear-splitting in the confined space. Lenk's men had arrived, their tactical lights sweeping the cavern as they fanned out in disciplined formation.

"Contact!" Karl shouted, returning fire from behind a boulder. His shots were precise, forcing the advancing mercenaries to scatter for cover.

Hana fired from her position near the cavern wall, her movements quick and deliberate. "There's at least a dozen of them," she called out, her voice echoing. "And they're packing heavier gear."

Marcus worked feverishly, the artifact humming louder as the carvings around it began to glow faintly. "I need more time!" he shouted, sweat beading on his forehead.

"You've got thirty seconds!" Karl barked, his voice tight as he reloaded.

Lenk's voice cut through the chaos, calm and commanding. "Dr. Russo! This is pointless. You can't win. Give me the artifact, and I'll make this painless."

Marcus ignored him, his focus unwavering as he pressed the artifact deeper into the carvings. The vibrations reached a crescendo, but instead of a secret opening appearing for their escape, a deep rumble shook the cavern.

The rumbling intensified, and cracks spread across the ceiling as rocks began to fall. Lenk's men hesitated, their attention divided between the firefight and the impending collapse.

"Fall back!" one of the mercenaries shouted, but Lenk held his ground, his eyes fixed on Marcus.

"Don't let them escape!" Lenk ordered, his voice cold and unyielding. "The artifact is all that matters."

Karl took advantage of the chaos, launching a grenade toward the tunnel entrance. The explosion sent debris flying, forcing Lenk's men to retreat farther into the tunnel.

"Move!" Karl shouted, signaling the team. "The whole place is coming down!"

Marcus grabbed the artifact, its glow dimming as the carvings around it stopped humming. "It's destabilized the tunnel," he said, his voice breathless. "We need to get out now." He looked to the far side of the cavern to see a grinding sheet of rock upon rock creating an opening in the wall. Apparently, the mountain's efforts to open it from the artifact's activation had also triggered the collapse around them.

The team sprinted toward the opening at the far side of the cavern as massive chunks of stone crashed to the floor behind them. Lenk's voice was lost in the chaos, but Marcus didn't look back.

They emerged into another tunnel just as the cavern behind them collapsed completely, the sound of falling rock deafening. Dust filled the air, and the ground trembled beneath them.

Michael struggled to hold Hana up as she doubled over, coughing as she tried to catch her breath. "Tell me that bought us more than thirty seconds."

Karl leaned against the wall, his face streaked with grime. "It would take them hours to dig through that, if they even could."

Marcus held the artifact tightly, its glow faint but steady. "It's good enough for now. We'll find the next location—while they're stuck behind us."

Hana straightened, her sharp eyes fixed on Marcus. "Like you said, 'for now.' Because Lenk will be back— and next time, he won't ask for the artifact. He'll shoot first and then just take it."

CLARA FELT the ground beneath her tremble, then heard the thunderous roar. Her head snapped up, as a crack appeared in the side of the mountain and a few boulders tumbled away. Her heart thudded in her chest. This was the third such disturbance after Lenk had entered the tunnel. Were they from his own explosives, or had he activated the device that he wanted so dearly? Or was this the mountain itself belching at his presence? This time, consequences be damned, Clara wasn't about to wait to find out. She quickly gathered her communications devices—radio, cell phone, satellite system, which had all been useless to communicate anyway—and threw them in her backpack, rushing down the mountain path toward town.

CHAPTER
SIXTEEN

The new tunnel was eerily quiet, the only sounds the distant groans of shifting rock and the team's labored breathing. The air was cooler here, the dampness clinging to their skin as they slowed their pace, finally stopping at a small, widened section of the tunnel. Marcus set his satchel on the ground, pulling out the artifact and the two caches they had recovered.

"Let's figure out where this thing wants to take us next," Marcus said, his voice steady but tinged with doggedness.

Karl slung his rifle off his shoulder, his sharp gaze scanning the boulder-blocked tunnel behind them. Lukas took up watching the tunnel as his partner sat down on the dusty tunnel floor. Michael took hold of Hana's hand, and the two of them, likewise, sat for a moment's reprieve.

Marcus still stood, focusing on the artifact. Its glow was faint but constant, and as he turned it in his hands, the vibrations aligned with a subtle rhythm that seemed to pulse in harmony with the surrounding rock. He opened the first cache, carefully extracting the metal plates they had found earlier.

"These plates form a puzzle," Marcus explained, kneeling to arrange them in a grid. "The runes on the artifact interact with them—like a key fitting into a lock."

Hana crouched beside him, her flashlight illuminating the intricate engravings on the plates. "So, what's the next move? Another hidden chamber? Another dead end booby trap?"

Marcus adjusted the plates, aligning their markings with the artifact. The grid clicked into place, and a faint holographic projection flickered to life, displaying another map of the mountain, this time the images slightly distorted from the angles of the tunnel wall. Yet this one was also more detailed, with additional layers of tunnels and chambers illuminated in faint golden light.

"There," Marcus said, pointing to a new location marked with the inscription *Nebenlager III*. "This site— Auxiliary Site Three—isn't part of the main path. It's a side location, but the artifact is reacting to it."

Michael leaned closer, his expression skeptical. "Why would the Nazis build yet another site? Wasn't the train supposed to be their primary focus?"

"It might be a supply cache," Marcus said. "Or a testing ground for their defenses. Whatever it is, it's tied to the artifact. If we want to reach the *Hauptlager*, it looks like we need to follow through this lead off the main path first."

As Marcus packed up the artifact and caches, Michael stood, his brow furrowed. "There's something we're missing," he said. "The Nazis didn't just hide the train. They created an entire system to guard it, with layers of defenses and false paths. Why go to such extremes?"

"They weren't just hiding the train," Marcus replied, his voice quiet but certain. "They were hiding what's on it. Something they thought was worth more than gold, more than art."

"Secrets," Hana said, her voice laced with suspicion. "But what kind? Military? Scientific?"

Marcus glanced at the artifact, its glow reflecting in his eyes. "Something dangerous enough that they didn't want anyone—even themselves—accessing it easily."

Lukas checked his weapon, his expression grim. "If this next site is anything like the last one, we're going to need a plan. The Nazis didn't leave these places unguarded."

Hana pulled out a map, cross-referencing it with the holographic projection. "The terrain ahead is rough— steep inclines, narrow passages. If Lenk's men have found another way in and are smart, they'll set up ambushes along the way."

"Then we don't give them the chance," Marcus said. "We take the most direct route to *Nebenlager III*, using the artifact to guide us."

Michael gestured toward the tunnel behind them. "And if they catch up?"

"We make sure they regret it," Karl said simply.

Hana glanced at Marcus, her expression serious. "And this next site—whatever we find there—it's not going to give us all the answers, is it?"

Marcus shook his head. "No. But it'll get us closer. Every piece we uncover brings us one step closer to understanding what the Nazis were protecting—and why."

The team moved quickly, their pace steady as they navigated the narrow tunnel. The artifact's glow grew stronger as they progressed, its vibrations guiding them like an invisible compass. The path ahead was uneven and treacherous, forcing them to climb over jagged rocks and squeeze through tight passages.

The deeper they went, the more the air changed— warmer, heavier, and tinged with a faint metallic scent that set Marcus's nerves on edge.

"This place feels different," Hana said, her voice hushed. "Like we're walking into something we're not supposed to find."

"We are," Marcus replied, his tone determined. "And that's exactly why we have to keep going."

THE TUNNEL WIDENED as the team descended, its rough-hewn walls giving way to smoother, reinforced stone. The artifact in Marcus's hand pulsed with rhythmic vibrations, its glow illuminating the path ahead. He found the side path that had been indicated on the map, and the artifact reacted positively as he led them that route.

"We're close," Marcus said, his voice cutting through the silence. "The artifact's reaction is getting stronger."

Hana shone her flashlight ahead, catching the faint glint of metal embedded in the rock. "Look at that," she said, stepping closer.

The metal was part of a door—massive, reinforced, and marked with faded Nazi insignias. It was partially hidden behind layers of rockfall and debris, but its presence was undeniable.

"This is it," Marcus said, examining the door. "*Nebenlager III.*"

Karl approached, his rifle at the ready. "What's the plan? Another key-and-lock situation?"

Marcus held up the artifact. "If this site is like the others, the artifact should trigger the mechanism to open."

Karl lifted an eyebrow. "Without a cave-in this time?"

Marcus grimaced. "Right."

He stepped forward, the artifact glowing brighter as he held it near the door. A faint hum filled the air, and the runes etched into the metal began to glow faintly. He aligned the artifact with an indentation in the center of the door, and the vibrations intensified.

With a deep, resonant groan, the door began to shift, sliding slowly into the rock wall. Dust and debris fell from the ceiling as the hidden mechanisms creaked to life, revealing a dark passage beyond.

Hana stepped back, her flashlight fixed on the opening. "That wasn't ominous at all."

Karl scanned the shadows ahead. "Let's move. Whatever's in here, we need to find it and get back on the main path before Lenk catches up."

The passage led to a large, circular chamber, its walls packed with shelves and cabinets filled with rusted equipment, yellowed documents, and decaying crates.

"This was a storeroom," Marcus said, his flashlight sweeping over the contents. "But for what?"

Michael moved to a nearby table, brushing away a thick layer of dust to reveal blueprints and diagrams. "Look at this," he said, holding up one of the papers. "Schematics for... something. Engines? Machines?"

"Not just machines," Marcus said, studying the drawings. "These are rail systems. They were designing something to move through the mountain—something massive."

Hana crouched beside a crate, prying it open with her multitool. Inside were metal containers, their surfaces engraved with the same symbols as the artifact. She held one up, her expression cautious. "What do you think these are?"

Marcus examined the canister, his brow furrowing. "I'd guess fuel cells. But not for any technology we're familiar with."

Karl gestured toward a far corner of the room, where a rusted locker stood partially ajar. "Over here."

Marcus approached, his flashlight revealing what was inside: tattered uniforms, faded photographs, and a stack of journals. He pulled one of the journals out carefully, the leather binding cracking under his touch.

Flipping through the pages, he frowned. "These are personal logs—written by someone stationed here."

"What do they say?" Hana asked, peering over his shoulder.

Marcus translated aloud, his voice low. "'We've completed the final tests on the containment unit. The energy is volatile—unstable. We've lost three men already. But the Führer insists it's worth the risk.'"

Michael's face darkened. "Containment unit? For what?"

Marcus continued reading. "'Without the containment key, the train cannot be accessed, and the power within cannot be harnessed.'"

"Containment key?" Karl questioned.

Marcus and Michael both nodded, Marcus holding up the artifact.

"Power?" Hana asked, her voice sharp. "What kind of power?"

Marcus set the journal down, his mind processing every detail with relentless precision. "The Nazis weren't just hiding treasures. They were experimenting with something—something they may have thought could turn the tide of the war."

He returned to the table, his focus on the journal and the artifact. "This site was a testing ground," he said. "The Nazis were experimenting with something tied to the artifact. Whatever they were trying to contain, it's connected to the train."

Michael gestured to the schematics. "And the train's location?"

Marcus nodded. "This confirms it. The train is at the Hauptlager. But they didn't just bury it. They locked it behind layers of systems designed to not just protect it —but contain some unstable power."

THE TEAM MOVED CAUTIOUSLY BACK to the main tunnel. Marcus clutched the artifact tightly, its glow pulsing with a new rhythm. He shuddered to think what this new rhythm threatened: yet just another level of danger or the green light to a finale no one wanted?

"This thing's been leading us around like a treasure map," Hana said, her voice low and laced with frustration. "But it's starting to feel more like a ticking time bomb."

"It's both," Marcus replied, his tone grim, his feelings mirroring hers. "The Nazis didn't just design it to guide—it's a part of the system. Whatever they built, it's tied directly to this."

Walking a few steps behind, Michael added, "If it's tied to the train, what happens if Lenk gets his hands on it?"

Marcus hesitated, then shook his head. "He won't."

The tunnel opened into another chamber, this one smaller but intricately carved with runes and symbols that glowed faintly as the artifact's light touched them. The room was dominated by a circular dais in the center, surrounded by faintly luminescent panels embedded into the walls.

As Marcus stepped closer, the artifact in his hand began to vibrate violently, its glow intensifying to a blinding brilliance. He fought the visceral instinct to drop it, to run.

"Marcus," Hana warned, taking a step back. "What's it doing?"

"I don't know," Marcus said, his voice now filled with trepidation. "But it's… connecting to something."

The artifact hummed louder, and the panels on the walls flared to life, projecting not just images on the walls but fully formed holographic images into the air. The images were chaotic—a series of blueprints overlaid with symbols, fragmented diagrams of a train car's interior, and what looked like a glowing containment chamber at its core.

"This is the train," Marcus said, his eyes darting between the projections. Amazement at the technology and clarity of the holograms now replaced his earlier fears. "Or part of it."

Michael pointed to one of the images, his expression grim. "What's that?"

Marcus twisted the artifact a bit and the projection shifted, zooming in on the diagram of a spherical device in front of the train surrounded by intricate mechanisms. Text in German scrolled across the image, and Marcus translated aloud:

"'Primary containment unit. Energy source volatile —requires the conductor's synchronization for activation or stabilization.'"

"Energy source?" Hana asked, her brow furrowing. "What kind of energy?"

Marcus's stomach sank as he read further. "'Classified substance—potential catastrophic release if improperly accessed.'" He looked up, his voice dropping. "The artifact isn't just a key—it apparently also acts as a fail-safe. Without it, the train's contents could be… lethal."

As Marcus studied the projections, the artifact began to emit a low, pulsating tone that resonated through the chamber. The symbols in the air shifted, their light flickering as the tone grew louder.

"What's happening now?" Karl asked, his rifle raised as he scanned the room. Lukas stood with his back to his partner, so the two had full visibility, but all they could see moving were the holograms.

"It's activating another layer of the system," Marcus said, his voice tense. "It's responding to something, likely to the artifact's presence in this chamber, but I don't know what it's triggering.

"The artifact isn't just a key—it's a regulator. Without it, whatever's in that containment unit could…" He hesitated. "Could destroy everything."

Michael crossed himself, his voice grim. "God help us. So now we're carrying a potential bomb."

"Not a bomb," Marcus corrected. "A fail-safe. If we keep it and stop it from being misused, we can control the system. But if Lenk gets his hands on it…"

Karl finished the thought. "Then he has the power to release whatever the Nazis were hiding—and weaponize it."

The team stood in silence. The artifact, once just a mysterious key, had become something far more dangerous. It was both their greatest asset and their greatest liability.

"We need to move," Marcus said finally, packing the artifact and the caches they had found carefully into his satchel. "If this is what they were hiding, the *Hauptlager* isn't just a storage site. It's a containment facility."

"And Lenk wants to open it," Hana said, her voice grim.

"Not if we stop him first," Karl said, his rifle at the ready.

Marcus nodded, his resolve hardening. "Then let's make sure we stay ahead of him—before he unleashes something none of us can control."

THE TUNNELS ahead were darker and narrower, their jagged walls forcing the team into single file as they pressed forward. Marcus led the way, the artifact's glow casting faint light on the uneven floor. Its vibrations had steadied, now guiding them with an unerring precision toward the *Hauptlager*.

"We're getting close," Marcus said, his voice tight. "The artifact's resonance is stronger here—it's leading us straight to the depot."

"Then we've got to pick up the pace," Karl muttered, glancing over his shoulder. "Lenk's men won't be far behind."

The sound of distant echoes pulled them all to a stop: the sharp clatter of boots on stone, the faint hum of equipment. The sound came from somewhere behind the right side of their tunnel wall. Slowly, the sounds faded, as if the tunnel Lenk's troops were apparently using had veered away from their own. Had Lenk taken a false pathway? The team looked at each other, each wondering the same thing. Was it Lenk or themselves on a decoy path? Or... would they all emerge at the depot?

"We've got to pick up the pace," Karl muttered. The others nodded.

The artifact's glow intensified as they entered a wider chamber, its walls lined with strange machinery— long-dead devices whose purpose was long forgotten. Ahead, the path was blocked by a massive steel grate, its edges fused to the rock with a precision that defied its age.

Marcus approached the grate, the artifact humming in his hand. "There's a mechanism here," he said, pointing to a faint outline of runes carved into the wall. "The artifact should unlock it."

Hana frowned, her flashlight scanning the room. "*Should* unlock it? That's not exactly comforting."

"It's the only way forward," Marcus replied, aligning the artifact with the carvings. The vibrations grew stronger and, with a harsh click, the grate began to rise.

The moment it moved, the ground beneath their feet rumbled, and a series of hidden panels in the walls slid open. Mechanical turrets emerged, their long barrels swiveling toward the team.

"Move!" Karl shouted as one of the turrets opened fire. Bullets ricocheted off the walls, the thunderous sound filling the chamber.

Marcus scrambled toward the grate, the artifact still

glowing as he worked to open the grate. "Keep them off me!" he yelled, his voice barely audible over the gunfire.

Hana and Karl flailed their arms, their movements swinging the turrets in their direction as they dodged the turrets' attacks. Michael joined in the distraction, his breathing ragged as he shouted, "How much longer?"

"Almost there!" Marcus called back, the vibrations of the artifact intensifying. With a final adjustment, the grate slammed open and the turrets powered down, their barrels retracting into the walls.

"Go!" Karl barked, ushering the team through the opening.

The path beyond the chamber was steep and treacherous, forcing the team to climb over jagged rocks and navigate narrow ledges. The artifact's glow guided their way, its vibrations quickening as they drew closer to their destination.

The air grew colder as they climbed, the sound of their footsteps swallowed by the oppressive silence.

At last, the tunnel opened into a cavern with a massive door, its top disappearing into darkness. They spied rail tracks beneath them that came out from under a wall of boulders to one side and went under that massive door just as they had seen in the first cave they had encountered. Surely, this was the *Hauptlager*, the depot of the Nazi Gold Train.

"We're here," Marcus said, his voice a mix of relief and dread. "This is it."

. . .

As THE TEAM neared the *Hauptlager's* towering doors, the artifact in Marcus's hands began to vibrate with a deep, resonant hum, its tone so powerful it seemed to echo in their very bones. The air around them grew charged, prickling with static electricity as the artifact pulsed brighter, casting eerie, golden light across the ancient runes etched into the colossal doors. Marcus's breath hitched as the runes, dormant for decades, suddenly flared to life, glowing from an unknown energy that bathed the chamber in a soft light.

"It's the key," Marcus murmured, his voice barely audible over the rising hum. He stepped forward, his movements deliberate despite the weight of awe and tension hanging in the air. "But it's more than that... it's connected to whatever lies inside. It's part of this place."

He carefully aligned the artifact with a central slot on the door, a perfect fit as if it had always been meant for this moment. The instant it locked into place, the humming deepened, reverberating through the stone walls and shaking loose small clouds of dust. The doors groaned in protest, their ancient hinges straining as they began to creak open. Light spilled out through the widening gap, dim and diffused but enough to hint at the enormity beyond.

When the doors fully parted, the team froze. Before them towered a vast, fortified depot carved into the rock. Its walls were lined with reinforced steel, and a catwalk circled high above the floor.

And in the vast, cavernous depot, the legendary Nazi Gold Train dominated the space, its massive, armored cars gleaming faintly under the diffuse glow of recessed lights that flickered to life as if awakened from a long slumber. The air seemed to hum with latent energy, as though the train itself were alive, its menacing iron-and-steel presence a testament to both power and secrecy. Insignias of the Third Reich adorned its sides, half-obscured by grime and the passage of time, yet still potent enough to send a chill through the group.

Marcus took a hesitant step forward, the echo of his boots swallowed by the dismal stillness. The train wasn't just massive—it radiated an almost magnetic pull, a sinister allure that seemed to draw them closer. But even as the view of this mammoth train gripped the team, something else then seized their attention: the object at the heart of the depot—the sphere they had seen in the hologram.

Suspended within a shimmering, golden containment field, a spherical device hovered less than a meter above the floor in defiance of gravity. Its surface was covered in intricate runes and shifting patterns that writhed like living things, morphing too quickly for the eye to follow. The artifact's energy had awakened it, and the low hum emanating from the sphere was now palpable, reverberating in their chests like a heartbeat.

"What is that?" Hana whispered, her voice trembling as her gaze locked onto the sphere.

Marcus's fingers twitched, an almost magnetic need to understand pulling at him. He said, his voice heavy with realization, "This is what they were hiding. The train was incidental—and I'd bet this is the real secret."

The group's sense of discovery was tinged with

foreboding. The hum of the sphere seemed to grow louder, as though it were responding to their presence. Whatever this device was, it wasn't just a relic of the past—it was alive with power, a relic of dangerous knowledge meant to stay buried. Yet, here it was, and they had awoken it.

Marcus stepped closer, his gaze fixed on the device. "It's the containment unit," he said. "The Nazis weren't just hiding the train—they were hiding this."

Michael's voice was tense. "And what exactly is it?"

Marcus hesitated, the weight of realization settling over him. "It's... power. Pure, unstable energy. The artifact was probably designed to control it—to stabilize it. Like its name, 'the conductor or director,' implies."

"Or to release it," Karl said, his rifle raised. "If Lenk gets his hands on this..."

Marcus nodded, his voice grim. "Then he could unleash something catastrophic."

The artifact glowed brighter as Marcus approached the containment unit, its hum intensifying. The device's runes pulsed in response, their patterns shifting as if alive.

"This is why the Nazis built all of this," Marcus said, gesturing to the depot. "The train, the defenses, the artifact—it was all to keep this contained."

Hana stepped closer, her expression serious. "And now it's our responsibility."

Before Marcus could respond, the sound of boots on stone echoed through the chamber. Lenk's voice cut through the air, cold and commanding. "Indeed, Dr. Russo. But that responsibility doesn't belong to you."

The team turned to see Lenk's men entering the depot from a side tunnel that had been unnoticed in the shadows, their weapons trained on them. The tension was electric, the stakes higher than ever.

Marcus tightened his grip on the artifact, his consciousness crackling with restless energy. The choices before him were impossible—but the consequences of failure were unimaginable.

CHAPTER
SEVENTEEN

The *Hauptlager* was bathed in an eerie golden light as the containment unit pulsed faintly, its shifting runes casting strange shadows across the cavern. The team stood frozen, their breathing visible in the chilled air, as Lenk and his mercenaries spread out across the depot. The tension was discernible, the hum of the artifact in Marcus's hand now a loud and steady hum that filled the air.

Lenk emerged from the shadows, flanked by a half dozen more heavily armed mercenaries. His sharp eyes swept the depot, landing on the open train car and its contents. A faint smile tugged at his lips.

"Dr. Russo," Lenk said smoothly, stepping forward, his weapon holstered but his men armed and ready. He spoke up over the constant hum. "You've done remarkably well to get this far. We've succeeded just as we'd planned. But you must understand, this isn't your fight."

"This isn't anyone's fight," Marcus replied, his voice steady despite the weight of the moment. "Whatever's in that containment unit was buried for a reason."

"And now it's time to unearth it," Lenk said, his eyes fixed on the artifact. "The Nazis understood its value, even if their methods were... crude. But with modern resources, its potential is limitless."

Hana snorted, her weapon raised and steady. "Potential for what? Blowing up the planet?"

"Or ruling it," Lenk replied, his smile faint but dangerous. "This artifact, this energy—it's a weapon, a source of power unlike anything the world has ever seen. And it will be mine."

Karl's gaze swept over the mercenaries, noting their positions. "He's got at least ten men," he muttered to Marcus, under the pervasive hum. "Snipers on the catwalks, and the rest spread out. They've got us pinned."

Marcus nodded, his mind processing every detail. "We can't let him have the artifact. If he uses it to access the containment unit—"

"Then the whole world's screwed," Hana finished grimly. "So, what's the plan?"

"We stall," Marcus said quietly. "Buy time to figure out a way to secure the unit—or destroy it."

Lenk, seeing the whispered exchange, inclined his head. "Dr. Russo, you don't seem eager to cooperate. That's disappointing. But no matter—you'll hand over the artifact, one way or another."

Marcus straightened, holding the artifact aloft. Its glow intensified, projecting shadows across the cavern.

"You don't know what you're dealing with, Lenk. This isn't just a key. It's a regulator. Without it, that containment unit will destabilize."

"Then you'll have to stay close, won't you? Lucky you, I need you alive. But not them," Lenk replied, his tone icy. "Now, hand it over or your friends die."

Marcus saw the numerous gunsights aimed at his team.

"No, none of this belongs to you," he replied. "This treasure was stolen. It belongs to the families and nations the Nazis plundered, not to you. And this containment unit needs securing, not detonation."

Lenk's smile faded, replaced by cold determination. "You're naïve, Dr. Russo. The world isn't kind to idealists. Hand it over, or my men will take it by force."

Before Lenk could give the order, Karl fired the first shot, the sound deafening in the enclosed space. Chaos erupted as Lenk's mercenaries scattered, diving behind steel supports and crates.

Lukas and Karl took the advantage, opening fire and forcing the mercenaries to scatter in the depot. Gunfire echoed off the steel walls, and the acrid scent of gunpowder filled the air.

Lenk, undeterred, moved toward Marcus, his weapon drawn. "You can't win, Dr. Russo!" he shouted. "This is bigger than you!"

Marcus ignored him, his focus on the artifact and the unit. Lenk raised his weapon, aiming directly at Marcus. Before he could fire, Lukas turned, his rifle trained on Lenk.

"Drop it," Lukas commanded, his voice cold.

Lenk hesitated for a moment, then smirked. "You think killing me changes anything? My men—"

A sharp crack echoed through the depot as Lukas fired. Lenk staggered, his weapon falling to the ground as he collapsed. His mercenaries, disoriented and leaderless, ran off or fell quickly under Hana and Michael's precise fire.

A final shot rang out, and the depot fell silent.

As the smoke cleared and the ringing in their ears lessened, the team slowly stood, assessing the damage. Lenk and a couple of his men lay still on the cavern floor. None of their team appeared injured, and they nodded to each other in recognition of the battle being over. Then a movement caught their eye.

Lenk had moved.

Karl looked to Marcus for orders, but Marcus shook his head as he approached and knelt beside the dying man. "It's over, Lenk."

Blood dribbled from the man's lips as a sneer reached his eyes. "Oh, but you are mistaken, Russo. Do you think this was my task alone? The New Order has its tentacles everywhere, and my superior, Klaus Jäger, won't stop until he has what he wants. We will rise once more and..." He gasped as blood filled his mouth and his eyes lost all life.

Michael came up to Marcus and touched his shoulder. Marcus nodded and rose to stand by the others as Michael crossed himself and gave a silent prayer over the body of their adversary. The priest then approached each of the other fallen and did likewise.

The team regrouped around the train, their collective breaths heavy and their faces etched with exhaustion.

Hana, her voice tinged with relief, said, "Lenk's gone."

Marcus nodded. "But there are others, it seems, this Klaus Jäger and his people. But for now, we have work ahead of us." His gaze fixed on the containment unit.

Lukas glanced at it as well. "What do we do with that?"

Marcus's expression hardened. "We secure it. Find a way to hide it where no one can find it again."

Michael placed a hand on Marcus's shoulder. "You think that'll be enough?"

Marcus looked at the team, his voice resolute. "It has to be."

THE *HAUPTLAGER* WAS EERILY silent in the aftermath of the confrontation, the faint hum of the containment unit the only sound in the cavern. The team gathered around the artifact and the unit, their faces a mix of exhaustion and unease.

Marcus knelt beside the containment unit, his hands moving over its surface as he studied the intricate runes. The artifact, still embedded in its slot, pulsed faintly, its glow steady but subdued.

"This unit," Marcus began, his voice low but steady, "it wasn't just designed to hold energy. It's... alive, in a way."

"Alive?" Hana asked, her tone brusque with skepticism. "What does that mean?"

"The energy inside—it's not just power. It's a fragment of something greater. Something ancient."

Michael stepped closer, his expression dark. "Ancient like what? A weapon? A machine?"

Marcus shook his head. "Not exactly. The Nazis must have believed it was a manifestation of something that defied the laws of nature. They didn't understand it fully, but they were terrified of it. That's why they built all of this—to contain it."

Karl crossed his arms, his face grim. "And now we're the ones stuck with it."

Marcus removed the artifact from the unit, its glow intensifying as he held it aloft. The runes on the containment unit shifted, forming new patterns that pulsed in rhythm with the artifact.

"The artifact isn't just a key or a regulator," Marcus said, his voice filled with awe. "It's a conduit. It interacts with the unit, but it also connects to something beyond it."

"Beyond it?" Hana repeated. "Like what? Another unit? Another... thing?"

"Maybe," Marcus replied. "Or maybe it's part of a larger system—something the Nazis never fully uncovered. But they knew enough to be afraid."

Michael's voice was quiet but firm. "And now, like Karl said, we're the ones stuck with it. So what do we do?"

The team sat in a rough circle around the containment unit, the artifact hovering between them. The cavern's golden light gave the moment an almost sacred quality, but the weight of their discovery felt anything but holy.

"If we destroy it," Hana began, "we could eliminate the promise for its good uses. But we could also trigger whatever fail-safes the Nazis built into this thing."

"And if we don't destroy it?" Michael asked, his tone heavy. "What then? Do we bury it and hope no one ever finds it again? Because that worked so well for the Nazis..."

Karl leaned forward, his voice measured but firm. "We can't just leave it. This New Order isn't going to stop, and if Jäger gets his hands on this..."

"He'll weaponize it," Marcus finished. "Or worse, unleash it."

Hana tilted her head, her gaze fixed on Marcus. "But what if he's right? What if this thing really is a source of power? Something that could change the world?"

Marcus hesitated, the weight of her question pressing on him. "It could. But that's exactly why it's too dangerous. The Nazis thought they could control it, and look where that led them. Some things simply aren't meant to be used."

As the others continued their debate, Marcus stood and walked to the edge of the cavern, the artifact clutched tightly in his hand. He stared into the darkness, his thoughts racing.

Hana joined him, her voice soft. "You're thinking about keeping it, aren't you?"

Marcus shook his head, though his expression betrayed his conflict. "No. But... I can't stop thinking about what it could mean. For science, for history. For us."

Hana placed a hand on his shoulder. "For us, it's a nightmare waiting to happen. You've seen what it can do—shake an entire mountain, and that is before it's actually released. You've seen what people like Lenk are willing to do for it."

Marcus turned to her, his eyes filled with uncertainty. "What if we're wrong? What if there's a way to use it safely—to understand it without unleashing it?"

Hana's gaze hardened. "And who decides that? Us? Some government? The man Lenk called Jäger? There's no version of this where it doesn't get abused."

Marcus returned to the group, his resolve clear. "We need to take the artifact and the unit out of here. If there's a way to secure them permanently, we'll find it. But we can't leave them for anyone else."

Michael looked at the containment unit, his expression tense. "And if we can't secure it? If there's no way to contain this thing for good?"

Marcus's jaw tightened. "Then we destroy it. No matter the cost."

The team exchanged heavy glances, the enormity of their task sinking in. The artifact's glow seemed to pulse in agreement, as if acknowledging the weight of their decision.

CHAPTER

EIGHTEEN

The containment unit hummed faintly, its golden glow displaying long shadows in the cavern. The team stood silently, each of them lost in their own thoughts. The artifact rested in Marcus's hand, its vibrations steady but its purpose now a question that gnawed at them all.

Michael broke the silence, his voice cutting through the tension. "We've been chasing this artifact, these defenses, and this containment unit—but what about the train? That's what started all of this."

Marcus nodded, his brow furrowed. "You're right. The train is at least part of the reason the Nazis built all of this. Whatever's in it—treasure, artifacts, documents, weapons—could be connected to the containment unit."

Hana crossed her arms, her expression skeptical. "So, we open the train and hope we don't find another ticking time bomb?"

Karl's gaze swept the cavern, his tone calm but firm.

"We don't have a choice. If we leave the train untouched, someone else will find it. We have to know what we're dealing with."

With a new imperative, the team approached the train. Its massive cars loomed in the dim light, their reinforced, ironclad surfaces marked with faded swastikas and runes that mirrored those on the artifact. The sense of history—and danger—was palpable.

"This isn't just a train," Marcus said, running his hand along the cold metal. "It's a vault on wheels. Whatever's inside, the Nazis didn't want anyone getting to it."

Hana crouched beside one of the dozen or so cars, inspecting a heavy locking mechanism. "This is military-grade. It would've taken them hours to secure just one car. More hours for us to open one."

Lukas glanced at his partner. "So that's the connection."

"Huh?" Karl and the others looked at Lukas.

Then Marcus grinned. "Of course. That's one way the train is likely connected to the unit and the artifact," he replied, holding the artifact up. Its glow intensified as he approached the lock, the runes on the surface beginning to shift and align.

As the lock clicked open and the heavy metal door groaned on its ancient hinges, the team stood transfixed. A warm, golden light spilled from the depths of the car, refracting in delicate patterns through the dust-choked air. It was as though the train itself was exhaling a long-held secret, the glow intensifying with each second as the team's flashlights danced across the interior.

Marcus moved forward, his breath catching as the light revealed what lay within. Crates and chests of varying sizes, meticulously arranged, radiated an aura of untouchable opulence. Gold bars stacked in one corner gleamed with an almost ethereal brilliance, each marked with the Reichsbank eagle and swastika. Their polished surfaces seemed to hold the weight of stolen futures, glinting in accusation and awe.

Hana knelt beside an open crate, her hands trembling as she lifted a delicate goblet, its surface encrusted with rubies and emeralds that glimmered like fire in the glow. "These aren't just treasures," she whispered. "They're relics of unimaginable value. Pieces of history stolen and buried in the dark."

Michael's flashlight swept to the back of the car, catching the edge of a large, open wooden container revealing a fresco—an intricate depiction of a saintly figure haloed in gold. The painting, impossibly intact despite its journey, bore the unmistakable strokes of a Renaissance master.

Marcus approached the artwork, reverently brushing away a layer of dust. "This is a Caravaggio," he murmured. "One of the lost ones. They must have taken it from an Italian church."

Moving on to the next car, Karl and Lukas pried open another crate, revealing a collection of shimmering jewelry—tiaras encrusted with diamonds, ceremonial crowns, and necklaces that looked as though they had been forged from liquid sunlight. The craftsmanship spoke of dynasties and empires long past, treasures that belonged to nations, not men.

But it wasn't only the gold and jewels that captivated them. Deeper into the car, they uncovered stacks of manuscripts bound in ancient leather, their spines bearing Latin inscriptions. Hana delicately opened one, revealing illuminated pages depicting biblical scenes, the colors as vivid as the day they were painted. "These... these are priceless," she said, her voice almost breaking. "They belong in a museum, not in this tomb."

Michael's light caught on another container, slightly ajar, and he stepped closer. Inside, a golden reliquary lay cradled in velvet, its intricate carvings glinting as though lit from within. He recognized the style immediately—a sacred artifact, likely stolen from a cathedral or abbey during the war. "These aren't just museum pieces," he said, his voice heavy with realization. "These are pieces of faith, stolen and desecrated."

Hana walked up to Michael and placed her hand on his arm, recognizing the anguish of a priest seeing sacred relics so violated. "This train—it's not just a treasure trove. It's a monument to everything they destroyed."

Marcus nodded, his eyes lingering on the gold bars and priceless artifacts. He shivered as the reality hit him that this wealth had been amassed not through triumph but through atrocity. "And now it's our responsibility to ensure it's never hidden again."

As they stood among the train's luminous contents, the weight of their discovery bore down on them. The glow of the treasure seemed to pulse like a living thing, illuminating not just the car but the enormity of what had been stolen—lives, history, and faith—all waiting to be reclaimed.

"Look further," Michael urged, his flashlight catching on a set of larger containers at the back of the car. "What's in those?"

The team pried open the larger containers, revealing objects that defied easy explanation: strange devices, meticulously preserved documents, and diagrams that hinted at experimental technology.

Marcus sat on the edge of a metal crate, his fingers carefully turning the pages of a fragile document he had retrieved from one of the train's sealed containers. Hana and Michael stood nearby while Lukas and Karl kept a watchful eye on the cavernous space around them.

Hana crossed her arms. "So, what is it? Another inventory list? More schematics?"

Marcus shook his head, his voice subdued but intense. "No. This is… different. It's a report—detailed, almost obsessively so. They called it *Projekt Vulkan*."

"*Vulkan*? As in volcano?" Hana stepped closer, peering over his shoulder.

Marcus nodded. "Yes, it was more than just a code name. They performed an operation to tap into the volcanic heat for geothermal energy. They weren't just planning to use it. They were—or *are*—using it." He began to translate aloud:

"'PROJEKT VULKAN: Established 1944 in the Mývatn volcanic fields of Iceland. Objective: Harness geothermal energy to power self-sustaining military and industrial operations. Phase One: Successful installation of steam turbines and magnetic generators at subterranean facilities.'"

HANA'S EYES WIDENED, her nerves buzzing with a hundred urgent possibilities. She gestured toward the cavern walls beyond the train car. "Wait a minute. That explains it. I've been wondering this whole time how this entire mountain complex is still energized. The lighting in the tunnels, the elevators we passed, the ventilation systems—they're all powered by something. Geothermal. It's still operational."

Marcus flipped to another page, his voice steady as he read:

"'Through controlled drilling and the deployment of advanced steam turbines, *Projekt Vulkan* has successfully converted subterranean steam into electricity. The integration of heat exchangers allows for efficient energy recycling, ensuring the system remains operational indefinitely.'"

Michael frowned, stepping closer. "They created a closed-loop system. They weren't just generating electricity—they were creating a sustainable power source. In the 1940s."

Marcus continued, the weight of the words settling over them:

"'Phase Two: Construction of interconnected geothermal plants in volcanic zones across Europe. These facilities will ensure the continued power of the Reich in the event of territorial loss or prolonged conflict. By mastering the earth's energy, the Führer's vision of an eternal Reich will be achieved.'"

Hana let out a breath, shaking her head. "They weren't just thinking about the war. They were thinking decades—centuries—beyond it. This was part of *Operation Eisenkreuz*, wasn't it? Preparing for a shadow Reich to outlast their collapse."

Marcus nodded grimly. "It gets worse. They weren't just using this for power. They were experimenting with weaponized applications of electricity—early versions of directed energy weapons, according to this." He held up a page covered in faded schematics. "This is their blueprint for a high-energy discharge system. Crude by today's standards, but for 1944? Revolutionary."

Father Michael rubbed his temples, his voice low and grim. "They were turning the earth itself into a weapon. The mountains, the steam, the energy—they weren't just infrastructure. They were potential tools of destruction."

Hana paced the length of the train car, her boots clanging against the metal floor. "And it's still here. Not just the power source but the potential for all of it to be used again. That's why this Klaus Jäger and the New Order wanted this train so badly. They don't just want the blueprints. Or treasure. They want to reactivate this network."

Marcus closed the report, his hands resting on the cover as though trying to contain its dark power. "If even part of this system is still operational—and from what we've seen, it is—it means the neo-Nazis behind Operation Iron Cross could have access to unlimited power. They could restart Vulkan or use it as a blueprint to expand the operation."

The group stood silently for a moment, the hum of the mountain's hidden machinery vibrating faintly underfoot. Hana broke the quiet. "This isn't just about history anymore. This is active. Live. And if Jäger gets his hands on it, he'll use it."

Marcus exhaled slowly, nodding. "Then we can't let that happen. We'll secure this site and figure out how much of *Vulkan* is still operational. And we'll start mapping out the other locations mentioned in the report."

Michael's expression was somber but resolute. "This isn't just about stopping Jäger. This is about ensuring this technology doesn't fall into the wrong hands. Ever."

Marcus tapped the cover of the document. "The Nazis believed this would be their future."

Karl glanced toward the tunnel that Lenk's group had used. "And now Jäger wants it to be his future. The New Order may now know where it is and the path to get here."

"He'll take the artifact, the containment unit, documents like these, and the train," Michael finished grimly. "And he won't care about the consequences."

Hana stepped forward as she fingered her computer, then punched at her cell phone. "Michael, I don't think so. Inside this mountain, I've had no signals, no readings of any kind to indicate any communications can get out of here. Between the solid rock and the geothermal energies and"—she glanced at the containment unit—"possibly the energy this thing emits, nothing gets through."

She looked up at the others. "I think Lenk's boss may know where he came inside, but no more than that. Between the charge Karl set off where the tunnels forked and the collapse of that one cavern, I doubt anyone could make their way into here."

Lukas stepped forward. "And we make our way out of here how?"

The team looked at each other.

Marcus replied, "We'll figure that out. But first, we finish this."

CHAPTER

NINETEEN

T he air in the *Hauptlager* was thick with dust and tension as the team worked in silence. A heavily secured crate sat near the back of the train car. Unlike the others, this one was lined with thick steel, its edges marked with the faded insignia of the SS. The rusted but formidable lock gave way with a satisfying snap under Karl's multitool. Then Marcus carefully pried it open.

The team stood in stunned silence, their flashlight beams sweeping over the treasure trove of meticulously preserved documents. The air was thick with the smell of aged paper and leather, and the eerie quiet of the room seemed to amplify the weight of their discovery. They spread across a long, polished wooden table the blueprints, maps, and dossiers, all sealed in protective casings as if their creators had anticipated the need for their survival. The precision of the documents was chilling, the stark black ink outlining a vision that made the team's blood run cold.

"These aren't just logistical records," Marcus said, his voice low and steady as he carefully lifted a detailed map of post-war Europe from its casing. His eyes scanned the bold, clean lines and annotations. "These are plans—plans for the Reich's survival."

Hana leaned in, her brow deeply furrowed as she studied the map under the dim light. Her finger traced a series of marks scattered across Europe, South America, and the United States. "Look at these locations," she murmured, her voice laced with a mix of awe and dread. "They're not random. Safe houses, escape routes… they were preparing to vanish and start over."

Standing across the table, Michael flipped through a stack of dossiers with grim determination. His fingers paused mid-turn as his eyes locked onto a page. "And these aren't just coordinates or facilities," he said, his tone crisper now. "These are people. Names. Affiliations. Sympathizers."

Marcus moved to stand beside him, his stomach tightening as he read over Michael's shoulder. The names leapt off the pages like ghosts from a sinister past: influential figures from history—industrialists, scientists, bankers—all meticulously cataloged. Alongside the names were cryptic notes, scrawled in a shorthand Marcus could only partially decipher but that he recognized as the ominous fingerprint of a far-reaching conspiracy.

"'Loyal until *Phase Zwei*,'" Marcus read aloud, his voice barely a whisper. He looked up, meeting

Michael's eyes. "Phase Two. They weren't just planning to escape and hide. They were planning to rebuild."

Hana's eyes flicked to another dossier, her journalist instincts kicking in. She opened it with care, revealing pages of photographs, detailed biographies, and timelines. "It's more than rebuilding," she said, her voice hardening. "This is a blueprint for infiltration. These names—look at their roles. Bankers, media moguls, researchers—they weren't just hiding in the shadows. They were embedding themselves into the fabric of society."

Marcus exhaled slowly, the implications settling heavily over him. "They planned for a future where the Reich wouldn't just survive—it would thrive in plain sight, waiting for the moment to rise again."

Michael's hand hovered over another stack of files, his gaze hardening as he read. "And they didn't act alone," he said grimly. "These notes—'negotiated terms,' 'alliances secured.' They were working with external entities, forming partnerships. This was no longer solely a Nazi operation. It's a group of interconnected entities."

The room seemed to close in around them as the enormity of their discovery sank in. Maps marked with escape routes, dossiers on individuals with unchecked power, and the ominous phrase *Phase Zwei* all painted a picture of an operation that had transcended time and borders. What they held in their hands was more than history—it was a warning.

"This changes everything," Hana said, her voice

barely above a whisper. "If even a fraction of this is true..."

"It means they're still out there," Marcus finished for her, his jaw tightening. "And they've been preparing for decades."

The documents, aged but meticulously preserved, seemed almost alive under the dim light, the black ink as bold as the intent it represented. The team worked with silent urgency, and once the table had filled, they spread more files across a makeshift table improvised from crates and boards. Each page added to the dark, insidious puzzle that, once assembled, painted a picture too vast and horrifying to comprehend all at once.

Marcus murmured, his voice heavy with realization. "This was a blueprint for domination—quiet, patient, and methodical."

Now the team, each sorting through a separate section of documents, sifted and searched, only speaking when another clue came to light.

Hana's eyes focused on a detailed schematic of a rail system. She pointed to a series of notations scattered along the intricate web of lines. "These blueprints," she said, "show how they moved the treasures. But look here." She tapped a cluster of marks surrounded by cryptic symbols. "These aren't just transfer points. They're installations. Factories, research facilities. They were building something."

At the far end of the table, Michael sifted through another pile of documents with deliberate care. His eyes locked on a diagram that seemed ordinary at first glance —a simple office building, unassuming in every detail.

But as he read the notes scrawled in the margins, his face hardened. "This," he said, holding the page up for the others to see, "is marked as a bank. But these annotations..." He paused, scanning the coded phrases, then continued, his voice taut. "It was a front. They used it to launder stolen wealth into legitimate channels. They weren't just hiding assets. They were embedding them into the global economy."

Across the table, Karl had been rifling through a bundle of dossiers. He stopped suddenly, pulling out a thick file and tossing it onto the table. "Here's your smoking gun," he said, his tone grim, his military instincts fully engaged. With his background as a Swiss Guard, he didn't read the ancient languages as others in the room did, but he knew German, plus the format of—and relevance of—a detailed inventory list. The file's cover bore an unassuming stamp, but its contents were far from any ordinary inventory.

The team leaned in, their breathing shallow as they examined the pages. It was a list—a damning list of individuals who had benefited from the covert network.

"These are post-war assets," Karl said, his voice growing harder with every word. "People who used this treasure to buy power, influence. And they're not just Nazi leftovers. Look at these names." He jabbed a finger at a few entries, his expression dark. "Some of these people, at least their generational descendants, are still in power."

Marcus hesitated before pulling the file closer. His heart pounded as he read the list. It was a roll call of influence, a who's who of the modern world: politicians whose decisions shaped nations, CEOs who controlled the flow of resources and information, and even celebrated public intellectuals who had guided the course of post-war philosophy and policy. Each name came with a set of cryptic notations—transactions, meetings, and coded phrases that suggested allegiance, if not complicity.

"These are powerful people, yes, " Marcus said, his voice hollow, "but in reality, they're architects. Architects of a world built on the back of this network."

Hana's fingers tightened on the edge of the table. "This explains so much," she whispered, her thoughts scattering like startled birds, impossible to corral. "How certain regimes rose, how industries consolidated power so quickly. They were shaping the post-war world. Yet some of these names are ones that just disappeared."

Michael's gaze shifted to another file he had noticed, this one filled with photographs and timelines. Each image told a story of transition: Nazi officers shedding their uniforms for suits, scientists quietly absorbed into industrial and academic roles, and financiers stepping seamlessly into the global banking system. "They didn't just disappear," he said, his voice dark. "They rebranded. They became part of the system."

Karl grunted, picking up another sheet. "And the system didn't just let them in. It welcomed them. Look at this," he said, holding up a memo stamped with the insignia of an allied intelligence agency. "Some of them were protected—used as assets in exchange for their knowledge or resources. The West turned a blind eye because it suited them."

The air grew heavy as the implications sank in. This wasn't just history—it was a living legacy, an insidious undercurrent that had persisted for decades, reshaping the world in its image.

Hana exhaled abruptly, breaking the silence. "But why keep these records?" she asked, her eyes darting over the piles of evidence. "Why not destroy them?"

Marcus's expression hardened. "Because they believed in it," he said. "They believed they were building something that would survive and that this would document their legacy."

Michael's fingers traced the edge of a dossier, his thoughts racing. "And now we're holding their playbook," he said, his voice low. "The question is, what do we do with it?"

As they all pondered the question, Marcus swept his flashlight over the train car's shadowed interior, and something caught his eye—a leather-bound volume tucked into the corner of a crate, its cover adorned with an intricate insignia that gleamed faintly in the dim light. His breath caught as he stepped closer, carefully lifting the codex from its resting place. The symbol on the cover was unmistakable: the red cross of the Knights Templar, embossed in worn gold leaf.

"This can't be..." he murmured, running his gloved fingers over the aged leather. The codex was thick, its edges frayed, and the faint scent of old parchment rose as he unbuckled the strap holding it shut. Inside, the pages were covered in Latin script, the text dense and precise, interspersed with diagrams and maps that hinted at something far more significant than a simple historical record.

Hana, drawn by his tone, stepped up beside him. "What is it?"

"A Templar codex," Marcus replied, his voice hushed. "It's a record—or a guide. These symbols..." He traced one with his finger. "They match some of the notations from *Operation Eisenkreuz*. The Nazis must have used this as part of their plan to locate and secure relics. I wonder if this is what Cardinal Severino was hoping to find."

He tucked the codex under his arm. "We need to make sure this codex doesn't end up in the wrong hands."

The team exchanged glances, the weight of their discovery settling on their shoulders. They had unearthed a conspiracy that spanned continents and generations, one that had quietly rewritten the rules of power. And they had to wonder: to what degree did that conspiracy now run the world?

THE OPPRESSIVE SILENCE in the room was broken only by the rustle of paper as the team pored over the documents, their unease deepening with every page. What they held in their hands wasn't just evidence of a hidden trove of treasure but the blueprints of a shadowy network that had wormed its way into the fabric of modern society.

Each gold bar, each piece of priceless art, and each rare manuscript listed in the records came with an annotation—details of payments made to specific individuals and institutions. The notes were chilling in their precision, marking not just the transfer of wealth but its weaponization.

Hana's voice, tight with tension, broke the heavy silence. "'Nineteen forty-four—Transfer to neutral accounts via Zurich,'" she read aloud, her finger tracing the line. "'Funds allocated to key sympathizers in Allied nations.'" She handed the journal to Marcus.

Michael's face was pale, his jaw clenched. "The Nazis bought their way into the New Order. These people they paid off aren't just remnants of a defeated regime—they and their descendants are now part of the foundations of our modern system."

Karl, who had been studying another stack of dossiers with the methodical precision of a soldier analyzing an enemy's strategy, looked up. His expression was as hard as his voice when he spoke. "And if this gets out? If people learn how deep this goes in today's society?"

Standing over the table with a grim expression, Marcus let out a slow breath. He flipped through a document that listed names and corresponding payouts, his finger stopping on a familiar name—one that carried significant weight even in the present day. "It would tear governments apart," he said heavily. "The fallout could destabilize entire countries. Alliances would crumble. Economies could collapse."

Hana, her reporter's instincts firing on all cylinders, picked up another dossier, her sharp eyes scanning the pages. "Which," she said, her tone laced with dread, "is why they hid all this under so many layers of security."

Michael nodded slowly, his mind working through the implications. "If even half of this is true, it explains so much. The rise of certain political movements, the inexplicable consolidation of wealth in specific industries... They weren't just infiltrating—they were manipulating."

Karl's gaze darkened. "And what about the rest of the treasure?"

"The rest?" Lukas asked.

"Yes. If this much was used to buy influence, and we've found so much here as well, who is to say how much is still out there, waiting to be found?"

Marcus picked up a blueprint of the rail system they had found earlier. It detailed not just transportation routes but also hidden depots and supply caches. He tapped the map with his pen, a sinking feeling growing in his gut. He said, "I don't know if this is the main cache or only one of many. But this network—these depots, factories, safe houses—they're still out there. And they could hold more of what we see here. This wasn't just a contingency plan or storage plan. It's a system, and it's still operational."

Hana's eyes narrowed. "Which means someone's still pulling the strings."

Michael leaned heavily on the table as he tried to steady himself. "So someone—or some group—is playing a very long game. They're not interested in rebuilding the Reich as it was. They've evolved. This is about power on a global scale without a shot being fired."

"We can't let this stay buried," Hana said firmly, her reporter's confidence overriding her fear. "The world deserves to know."

"But at what cost?" Karl countered, his tone acute. "If this goes public, it won't just be the guilty who suffer. Innocent people will pay the price— economically, politically, socially. You can't tear down a foundation this deep without collapsing the whole structure."

"That's what they're counting on," Marcus said, his voice heavy with resignation. "That no one would dare risk the fallout. It's their ultimate insurance policy."

Michael straightened, his resolve hardening. "Then we have to find another way," he said. "This isn't just a fight for the truth of the past. It's a fight for the future. If we don't handle this carefully, we'll be playing right into their hands."

The enormity of their task loomed over them, but one thing was clear: they were no longer just uncovering the past. They were battling a present-day threat that had been decades in the making, and the stakes had never been higher.

The room seemed to close in around them as the implications sank in. Every creak of the train car, every distant rumble from the mountain felt amplified in the oppressive silence.

Marcus opened to the last page of the journal Hana had handed to him. Its pages were filled with dense handwriting, the ink still vivid after decades. As he translated the German, his voice grew quieter, more somber.

"'Our defeat is not the end,'" he read. "'The Reich's spirit will live on, not in flags or uniforms, but in the hearts of those who understand its purpose. We will not fight with guns but with ideas, wealth, and patience. The world will come to us, even as they believe they are free.'"

A shiver ran through the group as Marcus closed the journal. "This served as more than just a backup plan. This was their real plan."

Hana crossed her arms. "So what do we do with this? Expose it? Destroy it?"

Marcus hesitated, the weight of the question settling over him. "We decide carefully. Because whatever we do, the world won't be the same after this."

He stepped away from the glowing treasures within the train, his flashlight beam lingering for a moment on the gilded reliquary before he turned to face the group. His expression, usually marked by the excitement of discovery, had grown somber. The magnitude of what they had uncovered was undeniable—but so too was the danger of staying any longer.

"Let's gather up as many of these official Nazi documents as we can carry, especially those revealing connections to the Vatican," Marcus said. "There's got to be much more in here that merits closer inspection.

"This changes everything, my friends," he continued as he gathered up a passel of documents, his voice steady but laced with persistence. "But we can't do anything for this train or its contents down here. We need to get back to Rome, regroup, and figure out how to handle this without blowing it wide open. We don't even tell Cardinal Severino we found the train. Not yet anyway."

Hana, still kneeling beside a stack of manuscripts, glanced up. "You're right. If we stay, we risk drawing more attention—or worse, getting trapped. Whoever orchestrated this hoard won't want us to walk away with the knowledge we've gained."

Karl and Lukas, always alert, exchanged a quick nod. "The way we came in is blocked from our defenses against Lenk," Lukas said. "But they found a side tunnel, and there may be others branching off before the main cavern. We need to find another way out."

"Let's move, then," Marcus said, his tone firm as he gestured for the team to follow. "We can't risk being discovered."

The group extinguished their flashlights, plunging the cavern back into the eerie glow of the treasures under the geothermal-powered security lights as they turned away from the train. Glancing back one last time, Michael muttered under his breath, "This is going to be a nightmare to explain."

The team retraced their steps, Karl and Lukas taking the lead with their weapons at the ready. The tunnels twisted and turned, the cold air thick with the damp scent of earth and stone. The echoes of their footsteps were their only company until Karl raised a hand, signaling for the group to halt.

Before them, a wall of rubble stood in their way.

Whether from the cave-in earlier or the charge that Karl had set at the fork in the tunnel, they couldn't tell. But this was the end of their path.

"Okay," Marcus said, "let's backtrack but keep an eye for other offshoots, too."

They turned and spent untold minutes searching the way they had come and other side tunnels, often encountering more rubble. Some of it was old, dust-covered rock speaking to decades of time. Other blockages showed the fresh signs of their recent interference with this formidable mountain.

"Here," Karl said at last, breaking the silence. Near yet another of the recently tumbled boulders, he pointed to a narrow passage marked by faint scratches on the wall. "This could lead to the surface. It's tight, but it looks clear."

One by one, they slipped through the passage, its rough walls brushing against their shoulders as they navigated the incline. After several tense minutes, the tunnel opened into a larger chamber, where a faint shaft of moonlight filtered down through a crack in the rock above.

"A camouflaged exit," Hana breathed, relief evident in her tone.

The team climbed carefully, Karl and Lukas ensuring the path was stable. Finally, they emerged onto the mountainside, the crisp night air filling their lungs. Below them, the Owl Mountains stretched out in shadowy waves, the distant lights of civilization blinking like stars.

"We'll make for Wrocław," Marcus said, scanning the terrain. "From there, we'll secure transport back to Rome. We need to review all this information back in the Vatican immediately."

CHAPTER
TWENTY

The first light of dawn spilled through the arched windows of St. Peter's Basilica, casting a golden glow across the cobbled courtyards outside, but the team's thoughts were far from the serene beauty of the Vatican. Deep within the Vatican Secret Archives, in a chamber fortified with centuries-old security, they convened around a large oak table. The room was dimly lit, the shadows of its vaulted ceiling adding to the solemnity of the moment.

Marcus unfolded a map and spread out a series of photographs, aged documents, and hastily scribbled notes across the table's polished surface. Each piece was a fragment of the puzzle they had uncovered—photographs of the train's treasure, faded manifests of stolen art, and dossiers of individuals whose lives had been touched—or tainted—by the hoard's legacy.

Michael leaned over, his fingers tracing the edge of an image depicting a gilded reliquary, its surface encrusted with jewels and its design unmistakably medieval. His brows furrowed as he studied the intricate carvings. "This piece alone is priceless," he murmured, his voice reverent. "But it's not just about its value. It's what it represents. And its connections to the Church and Vatican is undeniable."

Across the table, Hana sat with her laptop open, typing furiously as she cross-referenced notes on what they had found. Her face was illuminated by the screen's pale glow, her expression a mixture of awe and determination.

Michael explained further. "The Vatican's involvement in this discovery places us at the heart of a moral and spiritual dilemma. We need to approach this with absolute caution. This isn't just a historical artifact —it's a revelation. And if it falls into the wrong hands, even within these walls..." He paused, his voice tinged with unease. "The consequences could be catastrophic."

Hana looked up from her laptop, her gaze meeting Michael's with unwavering resolve. "Then we make sure it doesn't," she said firmly. "This isn't just about exposing the truth—it's about protecting it. If we don't control how this information is handled, someone else will. Someone with an agenda."

Karl, standing by the door, crossed his arms and leaned against the stone wall. Secured now back within the walls of the Vatican, Marcus had suggested both guards could resume their normal duties, but Karl and the others felt safer having him still accompany them. Lukas had resumed his Swiss Guard duties for the time being. "You're talking about keeping this under wraps," he said, his tone skeptical. "But how long can you suppress something like this? Sooner or later, someone will dig too deep."

Michael's gaze shifted to Karl. "I'm not talking about suppression. I'm suggesting stewardship. This is more than a discovery—it's a responsibility. One we didn't ask for, but one we can't ignore."

Marcus, still studying the map before him, pointed to a cluster of locations marked in faint ink. "These depots and safe houses—they're more than hiding places. They're strategic points, part of a larger network. And from what we've found, this network didn't end with the war. It adapted and evolved. I believe there are likely people out there who know about it and are still using it."

Hana's eyes narrowed as she clicked through another set of documents on her screen. "If that's true, then we're not just dealing with the past. We're up against a living, functioning system. And if this network is still operational, it's not just about protecting the truth. It's about stopping them."

The weight of her words settled heavily on the team. For a moment, no one spoke. The silence was broken only by the distant pealing of church bells marking the hour.

"So, what's the plan?" Karl asked, his voice breaking the stillness. "We can't just sit here theorizing. What's our next move?"

Marcus straightened, his expression unhesitating. "We follow the threads," he said. "These documents, these clues—they lead somewhere. If this network still exists, we need to find it. And if there are people protecting it, we need to know who they are."

Michael nodded. "Agreed. But we need to tread carefully. If we make a wrong move, we risk exposing ourselves—and everything we've found. The Vatican can provide us with resources and security, but that also means keeping this operation within a very tight circle."

Hana leaned back in her chair, her legs crossed, tapping her pen rhythmically against the side of her notebook. The tension in the room was stark, a mix of exhaustion and the nagging realization that their mission in Poland had raised more questions than it answered.

"I keep coming back to it," Marcus said finally, his voice breaking the silence. He gestured at the document spread before him. "*Operation Eisenkreuz.* It served a purpose beyond simply moving the train from Allied control. There was something more."

Michael looked up, rubbing his temple. "Something bigger, you mean."

"Exactly." Marcus leaned forward, his eyes intense. "Think about it. The Gold Train was laden with treasure —gold, art, even sacred relics. But if *Eisenkreuz* was just about safeguarding assets, why leave the Templar manuscript? Why the mention of the Covenant of the Iron Cross in every fragment we've found?"

Hana uncrossed her legs and leaned forward, flipping open her notebook to a page densely covered in notes. "We didn't have time to dig deeper into that manuscript Severino kept bringing up. But it was there, mentioned alongside *Eisenkreuz* in that priest's account we found in Poland." She pointed to a specific line. "'Blood will seal this Covenant.' It's repeated over and over. A connection to the Knights Templar, no doubt, but… what kind of Covenant were they referring to?"

Michael set down the ledger with a heavy thud and laced his fingers together. "It wasn't just about protecting the treasures," he said. "It was about control. The Templars—and later the Nazis—knew the relics weren't just symbols. To some, they represented power. Influence. The ability to shape history."

Hana raised an eyebrow. "And that's why *Operation Eisenkreuz* becomes relevant again. The Nazis used the Gold Train as a diversion. What if *Eisenkreuz* was their fail-safe? A way to ensure the most important pieces were hidden, even if the Allies—or anyone else—found the train?"

Marcus exhaled sharply, his mind reeling, grasping desperately for a solid conclusion. "And the manuscript. If it held instructions or even a map to other caches, then… then it wasn't just about relocation. It was about obscuring the truth. About ensuring that whatever was buried stayed buried—until their kind rose to power again."

Michael's gaze turned sharp. "And now Severino wants us to find it—the manuscript. The one we very nearly had no time to recover because we were busy blowing up tunnels and saving our own lives."

"And you think it's connected to what we uncovered in Poland?" Hana asked, her tone skeptical but tinged with curiosity.

"I don't think," Marcus replied, his voice low and

deliberate. "I know. The relics allegedly on the train—the fragment of the True Cross, the reliquary—they're valuable, of course, but meant to distract. *Operation Eisenkreuz* wasn't a smuggling operation. It was a blueprint for something much larger. And that manuscript holds the answers."

Hana nodded, closing her notebook with a decisive snap. "Then we're not finished. Not by a long shot."

Michael smiled faintly, though there was no humor in it. "We never are."

CHAPTER
TWENTY-ONE

The following evening, Marcus, Hana, Michael, and Karl reconvened, and the tension in the room was tangible. What had started as a unified mission was beginning to splinter under the weight of their discoveries. Michael sat at the head of the table, his fingers steepled as he considered the growing mountain of facts. His expression was grave, and his voice was steady but firm when he finally spoke.

"I think we need to consider the consequences of what we're doing here," he said, his gaze shifting from Marcus to Hana. "Some of these secrets… they've been buried for a reason. Unearthing them now could cause more harm than good."

Standing near the table, arms crossed, Marcus turned to Michael. "Buried for a reason? Michael, you're a historian. Isn't it our job to uncover the truth, no matter where it leads?"

Michael leaned back, his jaw tightening. "There's a difference between uncovering the truth for understanding and wielding it recklessly. This isn't just about artifacts or wealth—it's about power. Power that could destabilize everything if handled poorly."

Hana, who had been scrolling through her notes on her laptop, looked up quickly. "And who decides what's 'handled poorly'?" she asked, her voice edged with frustration. "Michael, if we start picking and choosing what truths to reveal, we're no better than the people who kept these secrets in the first place."

She rose and walked over to Michael, sitting beside him and holding his hands in hers on the table. They looked into each other's eyes, and both understood more than they had spoken.

Michael had publicly chosen Hana as his life partner only recently, but he still functioned for the time being as a priest and chief archivist of the Vatican archives. The Church hierarchy knew of his plans to concentrate on a married life but had yet to authorize his leave. The resultant limbo that he and Hana lived in had been awkward. Yet their time together, now open and fulfilling, had been worth the sacrifice he knew he would make in choosing this new life with her. But now his religious background, his priestly duties, and his guardianship of Vatican history, warred with his new partner's journalistic desire to expose the Church in what would be negative, even disastrous terms.

They both understood his dilemma: He wanted to safeguard the Church that had been his home and was his spiritual anchor. Yet the logical analytical side of him believed the truth should supersede ignorance. How this all might end was the big unknown.

Michael's gaze met hers, his voice calm but unwavering. "I'm not saying we suppress everything, Hana. I'm saying we need to think about the consequences. A revelation like this could destroy lives, institutions, faith itself."

Marcus stepped closer to the table, his frustration mounting. "And what about the lives that have already been destroyed because this network was allowed to persist? What about the people who deserve to know how their histories, their nations, were manipulated? You can't just bury that."

Michael's voice rose slightly, his frustration beginning to show. "This isn't about what I want to bury. It's about understanding the bigger picture. If we release this without caution, it's a Pandora's box. Do you think the Vatican—or any institution, for that matter —is equipped to handle the fallout?"

Hana stood, her chair scraping back loudly. "And what's the alternative, Michael? Pretend we never found it? Let this network keep operating in the shadows, influencing the world? You're asking us to perpetuate the very thing we're trying to expose."

Marcus gestured toward the documents. "We've seen the evidence, Michael. These people infiltrated governments, industries, and, yes, the Church. If we don't do something about it, we're complicit."

Michael's voice was pointed now. "Doing something doesn't mean throwing everything into the public eye without a plan. You're thinking like an archaeologist,

Marcus. And you like a journalist, Hana. I'm thinking about what happens next."

"And you're thinking like a priest, protecting the Church at all costs," Marcus countered.

No one spoke for a moment. Michael felt his checks heat as there was some truth to his long-time friend's words. But there was more as well. "Think, Marcus. The riots. The loss of trust in *every* institution touched by this —entire governments. Do you understand the scale of the chaos this could cause?"

The room fell silent for a moment, the weight of his words hanging in the air. Hana folded her arms, her eyes narrowing. "So we just sit on it? Keep it locked away in some archive? Let the people who built this system off the backs of stolen lives and treasures continue to profit while the world remains in the dark?"

Michael rubbed his temples, trying to find the words to explain the delicate balance he felt compelled to maintain. "It's not that simple. We need to proceed cautiously. Strategically. If we act rashly, we could lose control of this entirely—and the wrong people could seize it."

Marcus shook his head, his voice tinged with disbelief. "Caution is one thing, Michael. Paralysis is another. You're so focused on what might happen, you're ignoring what already is."

The tension was thick enough to cut with a halberd.

Karl cleared his throat, drawing their attention. "You're all making good points," he said gruffly. "But while you're arguing about what to do, you're forgetting one thing: Lenk was working under the rule of Jäger and the New Order. They *are* watching. And if we don't move fast, they will."

Hana exhaled sharply and sat back down. "Fine," she said. "But I'm not stopping. We find a way to reveal this responsibly—but we do reveal it."

Michael's lips pressed into a tight grimace, but he gave a reluctant nod. "Then we need to do it the right way. No rash decisions. Every step has to be deliberate."

Marcus nodded, his frustration giving way to determination. "Agreed. There's too much at stake to let fear dictate our choices."

The uneasy truce left them still a team, but the cracks in their unity were beginning to show. And as they turned back to the mountain of evidence before them, each knew the path forward would not only challenge their enemies—it would test their bonds.

MARCUS REACHED for the leather-bound codex he had recovered from the Gold Train. Its brittle parchment pages were filled with meticulous script in a blend of Latin and old Sütterlin German, along with symbols and diagrams that defied immediate interpretation. Hana and Michael followed his movements closely, their expressions equally grim, while Karl lingered near the door, his watchful eyes scanning their surroundings.

Marcus carefully opened the book, revealing a page marked with the title *Operation Eisenkreuz* written in ornate script. Beneath it was an intricate sigil, an overlapping design of a Templar cross and a Nazi swastika, surrounded by unfamiliar glyphs.

"*Eisenkreuz*," Marcus began, his voice low but steady. "We've seen references to it in other documents— always tied to the treasure and those safe houses. But this..." He tapped the page, his finger skimming a line of text. "This is different. It wasn't just about protecting treasures. It was about protecting something else— something they considered too dangerous to leave unguarded."

Hana leaned forward, her pen poised over her notebook. "The sphere energy unit we found?"

Marcus shrugged, his expression conflicted. "I don't think it's that simple. Look here." He flipped a few pages to reveal a diagram, a circular chamber etched into stone, surrounded by layers of defenses. Arrows indicated concealed entrances, underground passages, and traps. At the center of the chamber was a pedestal bearing a symbol Hana recognized immediately: an ouroboros, the serpent devouring its own tail.

"That's not Nazi," she said, her voice sharp. "That's much older, from the Egyptian culture."

"Exactly," Marcus said, meeting her gaze. "This design predates them by nearly three millennia. The Nazis didn't create *Eisenkreuz*—they inherited it. It was built by someone else, long before the war. And from what I can gather here..." He flipped another page, revealing more writing in faded Latin. "The Templars were involved."

Michael, who had been quietly listening, straightened at the mention of the Templars. "The Knights Templar?" he asked, his brow furrowing.

Marcus nodded. "This says *Eisenkreuz* was originally

designed as a containment system—'*custodia ultima,*' the final guardian. Whatever it was meant to hold, the Templars believed it was dangerous enough to seal away forever."

Karl spoke up. "Then why were the Nazis so interested in it? They didn't seem like the 'seal it forever' type."

Marcus hesitated before responding. "There are references here to attempts to 'harness' it." He flipped to another section, showing a rough sketch of strange machinery surrounding the chamber. "The Nazis thought they could control it. Use it. But something must have gone wrong."

Michael's face darkened. "Or they realized they couldn't control it and decided to bury it again."

"Right," Marcus agreed. "Hence their use of the artifact to connect to it as a fail-safe, the diagrams we found, the levels of security we had to negotiate until we found it in the depot." They all fell silent, recalling the gravity-defying sphere they left behind as they escaped for their lives, before he finished with, "And we've left it behind, unguarded and deactivated... at least for now."

"What's our next step?" Karl asked, breaking the resulting silence.

Marcus glanced at Michael, then Hana, before replying. "We follow the clues in the documents. There are coordinates here—locations that might lead us to *Eisenkreuz.* But we proceed carefully. If the Nazis couldn't control this, we need to understand why before we even consider going further."

Michael nodded reluctantly, his voice low but resolute. "Agreed. But let me be clear—this isn't just about discovery anymore. It's about ensuring that whatever lies at the heart of *Eisenkreuz* stays out of the wrong hands."

Hana's gaze flicked between the two men, her resolve hardening. "Then we'd better make sure we're not the wrong hands," she said.

TWENTY-TWO

Michael had made the arrangements quietly, understanding the gravity of granting such unprecedented access. Hana's credentials as a journalist and her unwavering commitment to uncovering the truth had convinced him, but it wasn't a decision he had made lightly. She now had temporary clearance to access the Vatican's vast digital repository of ancient texts, correspondence, and codices. Though the Archives' physical vaults held treasures that remained off-limits, the digital records were extensive, and Michael had ensured she could sift through them with minimal interference. It was a gesture of trust— and one he knew could raise eyebrows among the more traditionalist factions in the Vatican.

The conference room was quiet except for the rhythmic tapping of Hana's fingers on her laptop and the soft rustle of pages as Michael and Marcus pored over ancient texts. The emotional strain in the room was palpable as they sifted through fragments of forgotten history, piecing together a mystery buried deep in the annals of time.

Hana's urgent voice broke the silence. "Got something," she said, her eyes fixed on the screen. "The phrase *'Blood will seal this Covenant'*—it isn't just a metaphor. It's literal."

Michael looked up from a yellowed manuscript. "What do you mean, literal?"

Hana turned the laptop around to show a digitized scan of an old Templar codex. The text, written in Latin, was accompanied by a vivid illustration of a ceremonial altar. The imagery was stark: a circle of knights surrounding a robed figure, blood pooling in intricate grooves carved into the stone. In the background, a Vatican seal loomed large over the scene.

"This," she said, pointing to the illustration, "is the Covenant of the Iron Cross. It was a pact—a secret agreement between the Templars and early Vatican officials. It involved a ritual that, according to these texts, required a blood offering. The phrase 'Blood will seal this Covenant' refers to the creation of an unbreakable bond."

Marcus leaned closer, studying the screen. "A bond over what, though? What was so important that it required this kind of pact?"

Hana scrolled down, her voice tightening as she read aloud. "'To guard against the apocalypse, to preserve the sanctity of the faithful, and to ensure the destruction of that which would unmake the world.'" She glanced up, her eyes wide. "This went beyond a simple political alliance. This was about something existential."

Michael stood, pacing the length of the room as he processed the revelation. "If this is true, it suggests the Templars and the Vatican were aware of something—something they believed could end the world as they knew it."

"And they didn't just want to guard it," Marcus said, tapping the screen. "They created instructions for its destruction. That means they thought it was powerful enough to be used, but dangerous enough that it had to be destroyed."

"This sounds more like a weapon than a relic," said Karl.

Hana shook her head. "Not necessarily. The wording here is ambiguous—'relics of apocalyptic power.' That could mean anything: physical objects, knowledge, or even something spiritual."

Michael stopped pacing, turning back to the table. "And the blood ritual? What role did it play?"

Hana pursed her lips, scrolling further through the text. "It's tied to the concept of sacrifice. The Covenant required a binding act—a blood offering—as a means of sealing their oath. This had a deeper meaning than symbolism. It's described as an activation ritual, one that binds the participants and their descendants to the pact."

Marcus flipped through the manuscript he had been studying, his finger stopping on a page. "Look at this," he said, holding it up for the others. The text described a chamber beneath a cathedral, its walls inscribed with

Latin prayers and warnings. At its center was a reliquary surrounded by symbols of both the Templars and the Vatican. "'The Covenant's heart lies where light cannot reach, sealed until the day of reckoning.'"

Michael's face clouded over. "That sounds like a hiding place."

"Or another fail-safe," Marcus countered, "if these relics—or whatever they are—might have been hidden away as part of the Covenant."

Hana typed quickly, cross-referencing the locations mentioned in the text. "There's a connection here. The phrase 'where light cannot reach' comes up repeatedly in different contexts. It could refer to physical locations —crypts, caves, underground chambers—but also to knowledge. Something deliberately kept in darkness."

Karl frowned. "And if we're following this thread, where does it lead?"

Hana's fingers stopped, her eyes narrowing as she read a passage aloud. "'In the shadow of the four keys, the Covenant lies.'" She looked up. "Four keys. That's got to mean something."

Marcus nodded. "Templar symbolism often used keys to represent access—both literal and metaphorical. They could be locations, artifacts, or even people tied to the Covenant."

Michael folded his arms, his mind racing. "If the Covenant is tied to relics of apocalyptic power, and there are instructions for their destruction, we need to understand what we're dealing with. We're not just chasing history anymore. This could have real, immediate consequences."

Hana's gaze was purposeful. "Then we start with the keys. If we can figure out what they are, they'll lead us to the Covenant's heart—and to understanding whatever it's protecting."

Karl nodded grimly. "And let's hope we're not the only ones looking for these keys."

The room fell silent, considering Hana's reading of the cryptic phrase, "'In the shadow of the four keys, the Covenant lies.'" The weight of the words hung in the air like a challenge issued across centuries.

Michael, leaning heavily on the table, ran a hand through his hair, his expression thoughtful.

"What do we know about Templar symbolism?" he asked. "If they referred to keys, they might not be just talking about literal objects. They could be sites, concepts, or even people."

Marcus nodded, flipping through the Templar codex they had uncovered. "Templars often used the key motif to signify guardianship or access. It's rarely literal. Look here—this illustration shows a knight holding a key, but it's overlaid with the image of a tower. The 'key' could easily be a location tied to the Templar network."

Hana was already typing on her laptop, cross-referencing the codex with other records Michael had given her access to. "If we're dealing with four keys, we're looking for something that connects them—a unifying factor. They might be physical locations tied to the Covenant."

Karl crossed his arms, watching them work. "If that's true, they could be anywhere. How do we narrow it down?"

Hana paused, her eyes narrowing as she scrolled through a digitized archive of Vatican maps and correspondence. "Wait," she said, pointing to a fragment of text on her screen. "This is from a Templar correspondence dated 1291. It references 'the four corners of sanctity, where our Covenant endures.' That sounds a lot like the four keys."

Michael straightened, his interest piqued. "Four corners of sanctity. That could align with Templar sites of major importance."

Marcus tapped his chin, his voice thoughtful. "The Templars operated across Europe and the Holy Land, and they had strongholds in key locations. If the 'four keys' are connected to significant sites, they might be places where the Templars had the most influence."

Hana nodded, excitement growing in her voice. "Jerusalem, obviously—their center of operations. Paris —their administrative stronghold before the purge. Maybe London? And…"

Marcus interrupted, his tone sure. "Tomar, Portugal. It became a refuge for the Templars after their official disbandment. The Order of Christ carried on their legacy there."

Karl asked, "What was the Order of Christ?"

Michael explained, "In reality, it was just a new name for the Knights Templar. When the Church tightened up on them, King Denis of Portugal granted them exclusive use of the Tomar Castle to protect the assets of the Templars from the Catholic Church." He smirked. "With, of course, considerable compensation to the king for his protection. And a new name as the Order of Christ."

Karl nodded. "So it was greed on all counts, from the Templars themselves to the Church it served."

Michael sighed. "Yes, I'm afraid so. The Templars, established by Pope Honorius II, had become a military and financial powerhouse. They appeared as warriors, protecting Christian travelers, but they were also bankers. The order created one of the first international banking systems, allowing nobles and monarchs to store and transfer wealth across continents. This wealth brought fear to the Church for the power their wealth wielded."

He then frowned. "So, back to our current situation. I'm afraid we're looking at a possible network of locations. But what connects them? And how do we know which sites are tied to the Covenant?"

Hana glanced back at the codex, her fingers brushing the edge of the illustration of the four keys. "The phrase 'in the shadow' stands out to me. It implies proximity— either something hidden at these sites or something they're symbolically tied to."

Marcus leaned over the map they had been compiling of Templar locations. "We're missing something. The 'shadow' could mean a connection that's less obvious. A shared architectural element, a specific symbol, or a set of rituals tied to these places."

Michael folded his arms, his voice growing more contemplative. "Or something they were all guarding. The Templars were meticulous. If this Covenant was that important, they would have left clues—not obvious ones, but something discoverable to those who understood their methods."

Hana tapped her pen on the table. "We need to focus on records tied to these locations—correspondence, relic inventories, anything that mentions four guardians or a shared purpose. Michael, is there anything in the archives that could help?"

Michael hesitated, considering. "There's a restricted section—records tied to sites that were under Vatican protection after the Templar dissolution. It's a long shot, but if any documents survived connecting those locations, they'd be there."

Karl glanced at him. "How restricted are we talking?"

Michael sighed. "Highly. It's not something I can just walk into. I'll need clearance from Cardinal Severino, and even then, we'll have to tread carefully."

"Who is responsible for them if not you as Prefect of the Archives?" Marcus asked.

Michael smiled. "I oversee the main archives, yes, but the Vatican has layer upon layer of sections, both in the hierarchy and physical locations. There are a couple of priests responsible for those other small areas."

Hana looked between them, her determination evident. "We don't have a choice. We have to follow the trail if these locations hold the keys to the Covenant—or whatever they were guarding. This isn't just about history anymore. It's about ensuring this stays out of the wrong hands."

Karl sat back, arms folded. "So, really, we have two issues. One is unlocking whatever this Covenant of the

Iron Cross represents that the Templars and Vatican agreed to hide in their pact in the 1300s. Then, fast-forward, the Nazis in the 1940s stumbled on some of those hidden things in their travels. And they effectively made an agreement with the Vatican to hide those things plus more from the Vatican as well as their looted items. This was their Operation Iron Cross."

Michael said, "Right. Likely the Nazis came across that original Covenant pact and realized the Vatican was holding more pieces of the puzzle to unlock even more power for their regime's plans. Now we have a neo-Nazi group resurrecting all this for their goals."

Marcus nodded. "Agreed. So, let's start at the beginning of that scenario. We start with those Templar sites—Jerusalem, Paris, London, and Tomar. If the Vatican records hold anything that can guide us further, we'll need to cross-reference them with what we already have."

Michael groaned, his responsibility as both a custodian of the Vatican Archives and a member of the team weighing heavily. "I'll speak to Cardinal Severino. But once we open this door, there's no turning back. We'll be dealing with secrets some people would kill to keep buried."

The team exchanged a solemn glance, the magnitude of their task crystal clear. They were chasing shadows cast by history's most secretive order, unraveling a Covenant that could either safeguard the world—or destroy it.

. . .

THE RESTRICTED SECTION of the Vatican Secret Archives was unlike anything Hana had experienced, even with her expanded access. Dimly lit by carefully placed lamps, the room seemed to pulse with the weight of its contents. Michael had already laid out the necessary texts on a long oak table, their bindings cracked and pages yellowed with age. These were records that hadn't been touched in centuries, reserved for only the highest echelons of the Church's scholars.

"This is everything tied to Templar activities related to Jerusalem, Paris, London, and Tomar," Michael said, gesturing to the collection. "If the four keys exist, the clues will be in here."

Hana opened her laptop, ready to document anything significant, while Marcus carefully thumbed through an illuminated manuscript. Karl, as usual, kept a watchful eye on the room's entrance, ensuring their work remained undisturbed.

Michael pulled a thick volume closer, flipping to a bookmarked page. "This is a record from the Council of Vienne in 1312," he said, his voice heavy with the gravity of their task. "It references four strongholds that were to remain under surveillance after the Templar dissolution. The descriptions align with Jerusalem, Paris, London, and Tomar, but the text is cryptic." He ran his finger along a line of faded Latin script. "'Let the keys be kept in shadow, their sanctity guarded by the faithful until the end of days.'"

Hana leaned forward. "What does that mean? Are these keys literal objects, or something else?"

Marcus studied an illustration in one of the

manuscripts—a knight holding a key overlaid with a tower. "Templar symbolism often used keys to represent access or guardianship. It doesn't have to be literal. It could signify locations, ideals, or even relics tied to their mission."

Hana typed quickly, her brain whirring like a machine pushed to its limits. "If these keys are symbolic, they might correspond to something tangible. Something tied to the Templars' principles."

Michael nodded. "The Templars were guardians of relics and knowledge. If these keys were tied to the Covenant, they'd represent something central to their identity."

Marcus flipped to another page, revealing a diagram of an ancient chamber. "Here's something. This mentions Jerusalem—a 'Pillar of Fortitude.' It's described as both a relic and a test, meant to challenge those who seek it. That aligns with the Templar ideals."

Hana scrolled through her notes. "Paris was their intellectual center. I found a reference to a 'Crown of Wisdom'—kept in their headquarters before the purge. It's described as illuminating, something that would guide the worthy."

Michael opened another book, scanning quickly. "London. A hidden chapel kept the 'Chalice of Faith' safe, supposedly one of the relics brought from the Holy Land. It's described as enduring unyielding devotion."

Hana glanced up. "And Tomar?"

Marcus flipped through the codex. "The 'Scales of Justice.' They were part of the Convent of Christ, a religious house where the Knights lived. The text says they weren't just physical scales—they balanced truth and judgment, challenging those who sought to misuse them."

Michael leaned back, his expression thoughtful. "Fortitude, wisdom, faith, and justice. These aren't just relics or symbols—they're virtues. The Templars tied them to their core values, but they also represent thresholds. Each is a test."

Hana's fingers flew over the keyboard as she typed. "This makes sense. The Covenant wasn't just a pact between the Vatican and the Templars. It served as a safeguard within the Templar Order itself—a way to ensure that only those who embodied these virtues could access its secrets."

Karl frowned from his post near the door. "And what happens if someone unworthy tries?"

Michael's expression became somber. "The Templars wouldn't have left that to chance. They would have built fail-safes—traps, destruction mechanisms. Their entire purpose was to guard whatever they were hiding against misuse."

Hana scanned another document, her eyes narrowing. "Here's something else. The phrase 'in the shadow of the four keys'—it doesn't mean the locations themselves. It's symbolic. The 'shadow' is their combined meaning. Together, they unlock understanding of the Covenant."

Marcus nodded, his archaeologist instincts kicking in. "So the keys aren't objects we need to retrieve— they're concepts we need to understand. By combining the virtues, the Covenant's purpose becomes clear."

Michael leaned over the table, pulling a final document into the light. It was a weathered letter from a Templar knight. "'To unlock the Covenant, one must embody the keys in thought and deed,'" he read aloud. "'Fortitude to face the challenge, wisdom to uncover the truth, faith to endure the trial, and justice to act righteously.'"

Hana exhaled deeply. "That's it, then! We've found the four keys, and what you just read confirms it. It's a moral code. The Covenant was hiding something not just guarded by the Templars—it was designed to make that hiding place inaccessible to anyone who didn't uphold their principles."

Michael closed the book in front of him, his expression resolute. "Which means this isn't just about understanding history. If this hiding place still exists, in order to access it, we'll be tested by the Covenant that protects it."

The room fell into silence as the enormity of their realization sank in. The four keys weren't objects to be found—they were ideals to be proven. The Templars had created a system that ensured only the virtuous could access the Covenant's secrets, leaving the team to confront not just the mysteries of the past, but the strength of their own characters.

TWENTY-THREE

arcus's study in his Trastevere apartment was a space that balanced academic order with the chaos of an ongoing investigation. The room was lined with tall, dark wood bookshelves crammed with texts ranging from ancient theology to modern archaeology, their spines faded from years of use. A wide oak desk dominated the center, its surface scattered with open journals, maps, and folders filled with hastily translated Nazi documents recovered from the *Hauptlager*. The faint scent of aged paper mingled with the aroma of strong espresso that lingered from the kitchen nearby. A large window overlooked the cobblestoned streets below, its curtains partially drawn, letting in shafts of golden sunlight that contrasted sharply with the somber weight of the work inside. Despite its clutter, the study felt insulated, almost sacred —a refuge where history's ghosts could be confronted without distraction.

The quiet hum of the study's air conditioning barely masked the tension in the room. Marcus sat at the desk, the recovered documents spread out before him—blueprints, names, and notes that hinted at a far larger Nazi network than he had ever imagined. Hana stood near the window, her arms crossed, gazing out at the narrow Roman street. Michael lingered nearby, scanning a stack of dossiers.

A harsh knock at the front door startled them all. Marcus and Michael exchanged a glance.

"Expecting someone?" Michael asked.

"No," Marcus replied, his voice tense. "Stay quiet."

Reaching for the phone, he pressed the intercom button. "Who's there?" he called out.

The voice replied, smooth and faintly accented. "Klaus Jäger, Dr. Russo. I represent an interested party. Trust me, you will want to hear what I have to say."

Marcus stiffened, glancing at the team. Neither Karl nor Lukas had joined them at his apartment; the team had felt secure in this private residence. But now…

Michael and Hana both nodded to Marcus, and he then pressed a button to open the electronic lock on the door. He got up and went to meet the man as he entered the apartment.

Klaus Jäger was a tall man in a perfectly tailored suit, his movements deliberate. He had strong features, pale blond hair, and icy blue eyes that seemed to take in the entire apartment with a single glance.

"Dr. Russo," Jäger said, his faint smile almost polite. "It's a pleasure to finally meet you." The two men shook hands as Marcus silently sized up the man. Then he gestured toward the hallway. "Please, join us in the study."

Marcus made introductions, then said, "So, you've got our names. Who are you?"

Jäger inclined his head slightly, introducing himself to the group. "Klaus Jäger, a representative of an organization you've recently encountered—though indirectly. We call ourselves *Die Neue Ordnung*—the New Order."

Michael inclined his head. "Let me guess. Anton Lenk worked for you."

"Lenk was a tool," Jäger said with a faint hint of disdain. "A blunt instrument, a man too focused on immediate power to see the broader vision. My colleagues and I operate on a far more sophisticated level."

Marcus's jaw tightened. "Your 'work' being what? Reviving the Reich?"

Jäger's smile grew, but his eyes remained cold. "Revival suggests resurrection. The Reich never died, Dr. Russo. It adapted. We learned from history's mistakes—brute force, overt control. The New Order is built on influence, on embedding our collective ideals within the structures of power. Governments, corporations, research institutions… you name it, we are there."

Jäger stepped closer to the desk, his eager gaze scanning the documents. "What you've uncovered is just the surface. A fragment of the network we've spent decades perfecting. The names you see in those files—

they are only a few of the countless allies who serve our vision. Many don't even know they do."

Marcus's heart pounded as Jäger continued. "Your discoveries at the *Hauptlager* weren't just remnants of the past. They were the foundation of a global infrastructure. Wealth transferred, influence secured, alliances built—all to ensure the ideals of the Reich persist in every corner of the modern world."

Michael crossed his arms. "That's a bold claim."

Jäger turned his icy gaze to him. "Bold, yes, but undeniable. We've shaped elections, steered research, and controlled industries. Do you think the chaos of the modern world is a coincidence? The chaos we control creates opportunity, and the New Order thrives in it."

Marcus's voice was low but firm. "If your network is so powerful, why come here? Why not just take what you want?"

Jäger's faint smile returned. "The exact location and access to the train, the containment unit—these are critical to our work. We needed you to translate what we'd failed to in order to locate them. And you did. But you've complicated things, Dr. Russo, by keeping that to yourself."

"You mean by not letting your henchman Lenk take it from us."

Jäger shrugged. "In a manner of speaking. And now, thanks to your interference, what we seek is at risk of falling into the wrong hands."

Marcus leaned forward slightly. "And by 'wrong hands,' you mean anyone but yours."

"Precisely," Jäger replied. "You see, Dr. Russo, the

New Order doesn't rely on loyalty alone. It relies on necessity. The artifacts and documents you've recovered are more than just relics—they are tools. With them, we can maintain stability, ensure control, and prevent unplanned chaos from destroying what we've built."

Michael's voice was harsh. "You mean enslave the world."

Jäger waved a hand dismissively. "We mean to save it. The world is already controlled—by greed, by indecision, by weakness. We simply offer a more efficient system."

Marcus's stomach churned as he stared at the man across the table. "And you think we're just going to hand over the location of the train and the containment unit?"

Jäger's expression didn't falter. "I think you'll consider the alternatives carefully. Resistance is admirable, but futile. You've made yourself a target, Dr. Russo. Others are watching—some less diplomatic than I. Aligning with us ensures your survival."

Marcus narrowed his eyes. "And if we don't?"

Jäger's smile faded, replaced by a steely intensity. "Then you will face the full weight of an organization embedded in every aspect of your world. We don't employ just mercenaries like Lenk did—we use systems. Bureaucracies. Scandals. We dismantle lives, reputations, careers. You will lose everything, and when you do, we will still take what is ours."

Hana, silent until now, stepped forward. "That sounds like a threat."

"It's a promise," Jäger said coldly. "But one I'd prefer

not to fulfill. You have something we need, Dr. Russo, and I have the resources to ensure its safe use. The train's exact location and access. The containment unit. Give them to us, and this ends cleanly."

Marcus's jaw clenched. "You're not getting anything from me."

Jäger studied him for a long moment, then nodded slowly. "I expected as much. Very well. You've chosen your path. Let's see where it leads."

Without another word, Jäger turned and exited the room, his footsteps echoing in the corridor. The front door clicked shut behind him, leaving the team in heavy silence.

Michael exhaled slowly, breaking the tension. "We just made a very dangerous enemy."

"We already had one," Marcus said, his voice firm. "Now we know how big they are."

Hana turned back to the window, her gaze watching Jäger get into a waiting Mercedes limousine. "And how far they'll go."

Marcus looked down at the documents, the weight of Jäger's words pressing on him. "This isn't just history anymore. It's war."

CHAPTER
TWENTY-FOUR

Cardinal Severino sat at his ornate mahogany desk in his private quarters in the Vatican, the soft glow of a brass desk lamp leaving faint shadows across the gilded walls. A thin layer of papers—recent reports, event schedules, and confidential Vatican correspondence—lay scattered across the surface. Despite the late hour, he showed no signs of fatigue, his restive eyes fixed on a folder marked with a discreet, faintly embossed symbol along with the title for the New Order in German: *Die Neue Ordnung*.

The quiet hum of his secure phone interrupted his concentration. The cardinal reached for it without hesitation. The call was expected, and the name on the encrypted display confirmed it: Klaus Jäger.

Severino answered, his voice calm but laced with authority. "Jäger. I trust you have news."

On the other end of the line, Klaus Jäger's voice was smooth, precise, and unhurried. "Good evening, Cardinal Severino. It seems our mutual friend, Dr. Russo, has been rather… industrious."

Severino's grip on the receiver tightened slightly. "What do you mean? Did he uncover the location, as we'd hoped he would?"

"Oh, yes. Your confidence in his abilities held true. He found the entrance and route we'd searched for in vain using his apparent knowledge of the runes and the artifact we knew he'd find. But did he reveal that to you? Report to you as instructed?"

The cardinal sat back, his jaw tight. "No. I've heard nothing from him."

"Exactly. And now he has his own agenda—not yours, or I should say, ours—that he follows."

"How serious is it?"

"Serious enough," Jäger replied. "He has uncovered not only the location of the train but also documents that tie our organization to post-war activities. His possession of these materials presents a risk that cannot be ignored."

The cardinal leaned back in his chair, his gaze drifting to the frescoes on the ceiling above. "Russo is intelligent, but he doesn't fully understand what he's dealing with."

"That may be true," Jäger said, his tone hardening. "But intelligence and idealism make for a dangerous combination. He's already sharing his findings with his team, and his next steps could bring unwanted attention to our work. If he exposes even a fraction of what he's uncovered, it will be catastrophic for all of us."

Severino closed his eyes briefly, considering the weight of Jäger's words. "What are you asking of me?"

"Pressure him," Jäger said, his voice cold but deliberate. "You have the influence to sway his decisions. Appeal to his sense of loyalty to the Church, if you must. Convince him that continuing on this path is not only dangerous but unnecessary. And if he refuses…"

Jäger let the silence hang for a moment, his meaning clear.

Severino sighed softly, his voice lowering. "I will handle it. But Russo is not a fool. If I push too hard, he will suspect my motives, perhaps maybe even my affiliation."

"Then tread carefully," Jäger replied. "But ensure he understands the consequences of defiance. The New Order cannot afford interference—especially not from an archaeologist with a penchant for uncovering inconvenient truths."

After the call ended, Severino placed the phone down gently and rested his hands on the desk. For a moment, he sat in silence, his mind a whirlwind of questions and half-formed conclusions. Marcus Russo had often been a thorn in his side, though his discoveries frequently proved useful to the Church. But this… this was different.

The cardinal opened a drawer and retrieved a rosary, running the beads through his fingers absently as he stared at the folder before him. The New Order's interests aligned with his own ambitions—order, control, and the preservation of certain truths. But Marcus's idealism threatened to upend decades of carefully constructed influence.

He leaned forward and pressed a button on his intercom. "Sister Beatrice, arrange a meeting with Dr. Russo. I want him in my office tomorrow morning."

"Yes, Eminence," came the crisp reply.

Severino released the button and stood, his silhouette framed by the dim light. He would use all his authority, all his cunning, to steer Marcus away from this path. And if the archaeologist refused?

Well, even the Church had its limits.

THE VATICAN OFFICE of Cardinal Severino in the Apostolic Palace exuded authority and opulence. High vaulted ceilings were adorned with frescoes depicting scenes from the lives of saints, and a massive, ornately carved desk dominated the room. Shelves lined with centuries-old books framed the cardinal as he sat in a high-backed chair, his hands folded calmly in front of him.

Marcus entered with measured steps, his satchel slung over one shoulder. Despite the grandeur of the setting, he had always felt at ease here—until now. Severino's summons had been uncharacteristically urgent, and he felt a tension in the air as he approached.

"Dr. Russo," Severino greeted him warmly, rising

from his chair and extending a hand. "Thank you for coming on such short notice."

Marcus shook the offered hand, noting the cardinal's firm grip. "Of course, Your Eminence. How can I help?"

"Please, sit," Severino said, gesturing to a chair across from his desk. As Marcus settled in, the cardinal's gaze lingered on the satchel. "I had hoped for a report, and then I heard you were already back in Rome and, well..." He lifted an eyebrow as if curious at the lack of any word of their journey.

Marcus understood that Severino had given him the document that set him on this journey under the condition that Marcus report back only to him. Yet every fiber in Marcus wrestled with whether to believe the cardinal's interests were sincere. "Yes, I returned only recently, and my team and I are still sorting out our discoveries." Russo offered a pleasant smile, watching the eyes of the cardinal carefully.

Severino nodded as if accepting the excuse. "So, I trust your recent endeavors in the Owl Mountains were... enlightening?

"They were challenging," Marcus replied carefully. "Rewarding in small ways. But we have more to understand, more to learn."

"Rewarding," Severino repeated, leaning back slightly. "That is what I hoped to speak with you about." He steepled his fingers, his tone calm and measured. "You are an exceptionally gifted archaeologist, Dr. Russo, with a deep respect for the Church and history. It is precisely because of your talents that I requested this task of you. But I must caution you. There are some discoveries—some truths—should you come across them, that are better left undisturbed."

Marcus raised an eyebrow, his curiosity piqued. "Are you referring to the Gold Train, Your Eminence?"

"Among other things," Severino replied, his gaze steady. "You know as well as I do that these endeavors are not just about history. They attract interest from dangerous individuals and organizations, many of whom would stop at nothing to exploit what you uncover."

"That's true," Marcus said. "But isn't it the Church's role to protect the truth? To ensure that treasures and knowledge are preserved and used wisely?"

"Preservation," Severino said softly, "is not the same as exposure. The Gold Train and the myths surrounding it carry a weight that could destabilize far more than you realize. Entire nations could be drawn into chaos. Since requesting your assistance, I have pondered these factors and now believe this is best not exposed to the public."

Marcus straightened in his chair. "With all due respect, Your Eminence, the train isn't just a collection of stolen artifacts. It's a part of history, and history demands accountability. If I stop now at unraveling the secrets behind the document you entrusted me with, someone else—someone far less scrupulous—will take up the search."

While Severino's expression grew somber, his voice held its composure. "And if you succeed? What then? Do you believe you can control what happens next?

That those treasures and truths won't be used for destruction instead of good?"

"I can't control everything," Marcus admitted. "But I can ensure that what I do uncover is handled responsibly."

Severino's chair creaked faintly as he leaned forward. "Responsibly. An admirable sentiment, but naïve. You see only the surface, Dr. Russo. The Gold Train is not just a repository of stolen artifacts. It is a symbol—a beacon to those who would use its discovery to reignite old ambitions."

When Marcus didn't reply immediately, Severino's tone sharpened. "Do you think the Nazis' influence vanished with the end of the war? That their wealth and plans evaporated with their defeat? That train represents more than gold—it is a legacy of power and ideology that persists even now."

A chill ran down Marcus's back at the cardinal's words, but he kept his voice steady. "I'm aware of those dangers, Your Eminence. That's why it's so important to uncover the truth. We can't fight shadows." Russo knew now that the cardinal himself had concealed himself in one of those shadows.

Severino's eyes hardened. "No, but we can ensure that those shadows remain buried. Dr. Russo, I am asking you—no, I am advising you strongly—to abandon whatever additional pursuits you may have in mind. Give me whatever information you have gathered, which had been my request from the outset. I will handle it with the utmost responsibility. Focus your considerable talents elsewhere."

"And if I don't?" Marcus asked, his tone still respectful but firm.

For the first time, a flicker of frustration crossed Severino's face. He rose from his chair, the full weight of his authority emanating from his stance. "Then you risk far more than your career, Dr. Russo. You risk opening doors that should remain closed. I urge you to consider the consequences of your defiance."

Marcus rose as well, meeting the cardinal's gaze evenly. "With all due respect, Your Eminence, I believe it's my responsibility to bring those consequences into the light. Secrets like these fester in the dark."

Severino's lips pressed into a thin line, and for a moment, the room was silent. Then, with a nod, he gestured toward the door. "Very well, Dr. Russo. You've made your position clear. But I pray you reconsider. The Church has always valued your contributions, and it would be... unfortunate to see you stray into dangerous waters."

Marcus inclined his head politely. "Thank you for your concern, Your Eminence."

Without another word, he turned and exited the room, the weight of Cardinal Severino's warning lingering heavily in his mind.

As the door closed behind Marcus, Severino returned to his chair, his expression dark and contemplative. He reached for the secure phone on his desk and dialed a familiar number.

The voice on the other end was calm and precise. "Yes, Cardinal?"

"He refuses to back down," Severino said grimly.

"Prepare the next steps. Dr. Russo needs to be... redirected."

"Understood," came the reply.

Severino hung up and leaned back in his chair, his fingers steepled once more. "May God forgive you, Marcus," he murmured, "for what your defiance will cost."

CHAPTER
TWENTY-FIVE

The late afternoon light filtered through the large window of Marcus's study in Trastevere, casting mottled sunbeams over the cluttered desk. Maps, documents, and translation notes were scattered in organized chaos, remnants of their work on the discoveries from the *Hauptlager*. Hana leaned against the bookshelves, arms crossed, her expression tense. Michael sat in one of the leather chairs, flipping through a dossier distractedly, but clearly waiting for Marcus to return from Cardinal Severino's office.

Marcus entered the room, closing the door behind him with a decisive click. He dropped his satchel onto the desk and looked at his two closest allies, his expression grim.

"That bad?" Hana asked, breaking the silence.

"Worse," Marcus replied, rubbing the back of his neck. "Cardinal Severino is part of this."

Michael's head snapped up. "Part of what? The New Order?"

Marcus nodded. "I'm almost certain. He didn't ask outright if we found the Gold Train, but everything about his questions, his warnings, and his tone—it all pointed to the fact that he already knew what we'd discovered."

Hana frowned, shifting her weight. "How could he know? You didn't tell anyone."

"I didn't," Marcus said firmly. "But someone did. Severino must've gotten his information from another source. And I think that source is Klaus Jäger."

Michael leaned forward, his fingers interlaced as he spoke. "So Severino and Jäger are collaborating. That explains a lot. It's not just about the train or the treasure —it's about control. Severino's been pushing for years to centralize more of the Church's power."

"Exactly," Marcus said, pacing behind his desk. "He tried to steer me away from pursuing this any further. Said it was too dangerous, that it could destabilize entire nations. But what he didn't say was even more telling."

Hana raised an eyebrow. "Such as?"

"I told him we'd made discoveries and found 'small rewards,' yet he never asked for specifics," Marcus replied. "That means he already knew. He didn't need to ask—he just wanted to warn me off."

Michael nodded, his expression dark. "Because if you push too hard, you risk exposing him and the New Order. If Jäger and Severino are working together, they've been watching us for a while."

Hana uncrossed her arms and moved to the desk,

tapping one of the open documents. "If Severino's involved, we've got a bigger problem than we thought. He's not just any cardinal—he's got access to resources, people, influence. He can make life very difficult for us."

"More than that," Marcus added, his voice low. "He's positioned to keep the Church aligned with the New Order's goals. Think about it—if the Vatican Secretary of State is part of their neo-Nazi network, it gives them a foothold in one of the most powerful institutions on earth."

Michael sighed, leaning back in his chair. "So what do we do? Confront him? Expose him?"

"No," Marcus said quickly. "Not yet. He doesn't know I suspect him. If we act now, we'll tip our hand, and he'll bury us under his authority."

Hana crossed her arms again, her gaze intense. "Then we need to stay ahead of him—and figure out how far this goes. If Jäger's pulling Severino's strings, what's the endgame?"

Marcus sat down, his hands resting on the edge of the desk. "We start by looking at the documents from the *Hauptlager*. There has to be something in there—something that ties Severino and Jäger to the larger network. Names of forbears, Vatican relationships, transactions, anything."

Michael nodded. "And the train?"

Marcus exhaled deeply. "We still need to keep its location a secret. As long as they don't know where it is, we have the upper hand. But we can't sit on this forever. We have to decide what to do with the train and its contents—and sooner rather than later."

Hana glanced out the window, her voice quiet but determined. "And if Severino and Jäger push harder?"

Marcus's eyes hardened. "Then we push back. But for now, we work quietly. The more they underestimate us, the better chance we have of surviving this state of affairs."

The room fell silent, the weight of their next steps pressing on them. For the first time, the scope of the conspiracy they were up against felt suffocating—but none of them was willing to back down.

THE ATMOSPHERE in Marcus's apartment study the next day was tense but focused. The entire team had gathered—Hana and Michael, Karl and Lukas—seated or standing around the room, their attention riveted on Marcus as he prepared to address them. The scattered documents, maps, and notes from the *Hauptlager* covered every available surface, a visible testament to the magnitude of their discoveries.

Marcus sat on the edge of his desk, arms crossed, the weight of what he was about to say etched into his expression. "All right," he began, his tone calm but resolute. "It's time we lay everything out. We're dealing with something far larger than just the Gold Train. What we've uncovered goes beyond treasure or stolen artifacts—it's part of a system, a network. And unless we understand the full scope, we'll never be able to stop it."

Marcus unfolded a large, weathered map of Europe,

marked with red dots at various locations, and pinned it to the corkboard behind him.

"Let's start with *Operation Eisenkreuz,*" he said, gesturing to the map. "This was more than a treasure hoarding operation—it was a carefully constructed plan for the survival and resurgence of the Nazi regime after the war. The documents we recovered in the *Hauptlager* outline its three main goals."

He raised a finger. "First, to hide vast amounts of stolen wealth—gold, art, cultural artifacts—in secure, secret locations across Europe. The Gold Train was one such location, but it wasn't the only one. *Eisenkreuz* involved a network of bunkers, tunnels, and hidden caches."

"Like *Nebenlager III,*" Lukas interjected, his arms resting on the back of a chair.

Marcus nodded. "Exactly. These locations weren't just about safeguarding wealth—they were leverage. Resources that could be used to forge alliances, fund covert operations, or control key players in the post-war world."

He raised a second finger. "Second, *Eisenkreuz* supported the development of advanced technology and weapons. The containment unit and artifact are prime examples. These weren't just relics—they were experiments. The Nazis believed they could use these items to manipulate energy, create weapons, or maintain control."

"And the third?" Michael prompted, leaning forward.

Marcus tapped the map again. "The third goal was

the most ambitious: building a shadow network to infiltrate global institutions. The goal of *Eisenkreuz* wasn't simply to safeguard treasures and technology, but to spread its ideology throughout the post-war era.

He picked up a folder marked with a faint black cross and opened it, revealing a dossier of names, photos, and cryptic symbols.

"That brings us to *Operation Eisenkreuz*," he continued. "This wasn't just a faction—it was a clandestine group within the Nazi regime tasked with ensuring the survival of their vision, no matter what happened to Germany."

"They were the puppet masters," Hana said, her tone sharp.

"Exactly," Marcus agreed. "That third function was fulfilled by Operation Iron Cross, which was composed of SS officers, scientists, industrialists, and financiers—people who understood that brute force alone wouldn't be enough. They swore an oath of loyalty—'Blood will seal this Covenant'—to protect and execute the Reich's most sensitive plans."

Karl, who had been standing silently near the window, spoke up. "And they didn't just disappear after the war, did they?"

"No," Marcus said grimly. "The members scattered but remained active. They funneled resources through the Franciscan Ratlines, escaped to South America and other safe havens, and used the treasures hidden by *Eisenkreuz* to secure alliances with powerful figures in politics, finance, and science—not to mention the Vatican itself."

Michael lowered his head at the mention of the Vatican's involvement. Hana reached a hand over to squeeze his folded hands, and he lifted his head, glancing at her with a sad smile.

Lukas frowned. "So they're still out there. Operating in secret."

Marcus nodded. "More than that—they evolved. They adapted to the modern world, embedding themselves into governments, corporations, research institutions. They became what we now know as the New Order."

Hana gestured toward the documents spread across the desk. "So Severino and Jäger are part of this New Order... with plans to... what? Build another Reich?"

"Not through war," Marcus said, "but through influence. Jäger himself said it: the New Order isn't trying to revive the past—they're shaping the future. They're using the Gold Train and other *Eisenkreuz* assets as tools to consolidate power."

Michael exhaled sharply. "And we're the ones standing in their way."

"Which is why they're coming after us," Karl said grimly. "Severino's already tipped his hand. He knows about the train, and he knows we're a threat."

Marcus stepped forward, his voice steady. "Here's what we're up against: If the New Order gets its hands on the Gold Train and the containment unit, they'll have the resources, wealth, and power to expand their influence even further. They've spent decades embedding themselves into the world's systems, and this could push them over the edge."

"And if we expose them?" Hana asked.

"It could destabilize everything," Marcus admitted. "The names we've uncovered—the connections—would implicate people and institutions at the highest levels. Entire governments could fall. Economies could collapse."

"So what do we do?" Lukas asked, his tone serious.

Marcus looked around the room, meeting each of their gazes. "We keep moving. We stay ahead of them. The Gold Train, the documents, the containment unit—they're all pieces of a larger puzzle. If we can uncover enough, we can stop them before they consolidate their power. How we share that truth without causing chaos, I'm not sure. Not yet, anyway. But our first step is to stop the New Order from gaining more power and burying the facts forever."

Silence fell over the room as the team absorbed Marcus's words. Finally, Hana broke it, her voice firm. "Then we'd better get started. If the New Order wants to bury this, we must ensure the truth sees daylight."

Michael nodded. "Whatever it takes."

Karl and Lukas exchanged a glance, then nodded in unison. "We're with you," Karl said simply.

Marcus felt a swell of determination as he looked at his team. The road ahead was dangerous, but they were all in this together. And for the first time in days, he felt a glimmer of hope.

"All right," he said. "We better get to work."

CHAPTER
TWENTY-SIX

The small, unmarked envelope sat on Marcus Russo's desk when he returned to his working quarters in the Vatican. Its plain appearance might have gone unnoticed if not for the absence of any identifying marks. No sender, no official seal, not even a name scrawled on its front. Marcus's first instinct was to leave it untouched, but curiosity tugged at him. Who would leave something so nondescript in such a secure place?

The weight of the day—long hours spent poring over manuscripts in the Vatican Archives with Michael and Hana—pressed heavily on him. But this... this was new. He glanced around the room, ensuring he was alone, before cautiously opening it. Inside was a folded sheet of thick paper and a small thumb drive.

Marcus unfolded the paper first, his pulse quickening. The handwriting was elegant but unfamiliar, the Latin precise yet unsettling in its message:

"The past is not what you believe it to be. Your work endangers everything—faith, truth, and the lives of those closest to you. If you truly seek to understand the Covenant, consider what it may bring: salvation... or ruin."

His breath hitched as he read the final line: *"See for yourself."*

He stared at the note for a long moment before reaching for his laptop, his fingers brushing the small thumb drive. Could this help explain more about the containment unit they had discovered? Sliding it into the port, he waited, the hum of the machine filling the silence of the room.

A folder opened automatically on the screen, its title stark: *Sanctum Records.*

Marcus's heart raced. The folder contained several scanned documents, some appearing to be Templar manuscripts, others modern reports. Among them was a grainy photograph of what looked like an excavation site—a chamber partially unearthed, its walls carved with intricate symbols he didn't immediately recognize. In the center of the chamber stood a pedestal, and on it rested a gleaming, black object that defied clear definition.

He cocked his head. A black cube-like object. Not the shining sphere containment unit they had found in the Owl Mountains at all. What was this?

He clicked on the accompanying text file, its contents detailed yet ominous. The artifact was described as an "engine of corruption," a relic capable of twisting the minds of those who sought to wield it. The Templars hadn't sealed it merely to protect humanity from its misuse—they had sealed it to stop its destructive influence from spreading. The file claimed that even indirect exposure had driven men to madness, their actions sparking chaos and violence in their wake.

Another document caught his eye, dated 1942. It was a report, purportedly written by a Nazi officer, detailing an attempt to harness the artifact's power. The language was clinical, yet laced with fear: *"It defies our understanding. Those exposed to its presence have succumbed to uncontrollable impulses. We have lost three men already. The Führer's directive is clear, but I fear this will destroy us before we can control it."*

The final item was a video file. Marcus hesitated, his cursor hovering over it. Something in the pit of his stomach told him not to open it, but his curiosity overruled his caution. He clicked the Play button.

The footage was old, grainy, and silent. It showed the same chamber from the photograph, the camera's perspective jerky as if held by an unsteady hand. Figures in military uniforms—German officers—moved through the space, their faces grim. The camera focused on the pedestal, zooming in on the black object. Even through the poor resolution, Marcus felt an almost magnetic pull emanating from the screen.

Suddenly, chaos erupted. The figures began gesturing wildly, one clutching his head as he fell to the ground, convulsing. Another grabbed a weapon, turning it on his comrades before collapsing himself.

The video ended abruptly, leaving Marcus staring at the blank screen, his chest tight.

He leaned back in his chair, his mind like a room full of shouting voices, each one growing louder. The materials were compelling, but something about them felt... off. If this new artifact was as dangerous as the files suggested, why hadn't they found any record of such incidents in the Nazi archives on board the train? Why would these documents show up now, and why anonymously?

The warning in the note echoed in his mind: *"Your work endangers everything."* For the first time since they began unraveling the mystery of the Covenant, doubt crept into Marcus's thoughts. What if they weren't meant to uncover this any more than they had been meant to discover the containment unit? What if their pursuit of truth was leading them toward a disaster even greater than they already realized?

He closed the laptop and stared at the envelope, its plainness now menacing in its simplicity. Someone wanted him to see this. But the real question loomed larger: why?

Who had sent this? And why now? The materials felt both meticulously curated and strangely incomplete, as though designed to provoke a reaction rather than provide a full picture. He reached for the grainy photograph again, his eyes scanning the chamber's walls. The carvings seemed familiar, but he couldn't place them. Were they Templar symbols? Something older?

A loud knock on the door shattered his thoughts.

Marcus jumped, adrenaline coursing through him. He shoved the laptop shut and slid the envelope and thumb drive into his desk drawer before crossing the room.

"Who is it?" he asked, his voice more tense than he intended.

"It's me, Hana," came the reply, her tone clipped. "We need to talk."

Marcus opened the door, his face carefully neutral. Hana stepped inside, her laptop tucked under one arm, her expression a mix of irritation and insistence. She set her laptop on the desk and turned to him.

"I just got an alert from the Vatican's digital archives," she said, crossing her arms. "Someone accessed restricted files connected to the research areas we'd scoured and didn't log their credentials. It's like they knew how to bypass the system entirely."

Marcus stiffened, his pulse quickening. "And you think it's related to what we're working on?"

"I do, yes," she shot back. "The timing's too perfect. We're closing in on the Covenant, and suddenly someone's pulling data on *Sanctum*? Whoever it is, they're ahead of us."

He hesitated, the weight of the thumb drive in his drawer almost tangible. Should he tell her? Show her what he had found—or rather, been shown? Or would that play directly into whoever sent the materials' plans?

Hana tilted her head, her eyes narrowing. "You're quiet. Something wrong?"

Marcus shook his head, trying to mask his internal

conflict. "Just tired. We've been running ourselves ragged with all this."

She frowned but didn't press. Instead, she flipped open her laptop and gestured to the screen. "Look at this. These files are sanitized. Whoever accessed them left almost nothing behind, but I found fragments in the metadata." She pulled up an image of partially reconstructed text. "'Core of the Iron Cross.' That's all I could recover."

Marcus frowned. "Core of the Iron Cross? What does that mean?"

Hana shrugged, frustration flashing across her face. "I don't know, but it's got to mean something important. The core of the Templars' covenant with the Vatican? Whatever it is, if they went to these lengths to hide it, it's worth following."

The phrase "Core of the Iron Cross" echoed in Marcus's mind, intertwining with the ominous warnings from the thumb drive. He felt the gnawing tug of doubt again. What if this was all connected? What if their search wasn't illuminating history but disturbing something best left untouched?

"Maybe we need to slow down," Marcus said cautiously, watching her reaction.

Hana's eyes narrowed. "Slow down? Marcus, this isn't just a history project. There are people out there— powerful people—who don't want us to find what the Covenant hid. We can't let them win."

"And what if they're right?" The words were out before Marcus could stop them.

Hana froze, her expression shifting from

determination to incredulity. "Right about what?" she asked, her voice low.

"What if the Covenant's purpose isn't what we think it is? What if it's dangerous—not just to the people chasing it, but to the world? Maybe the Templars sealed it away for a reason."

Hana took a step back, studying him carefully. "Where's this coming from? You've never been the one to back off, Marcus. What changed?"

He hesitated, debating whether to show her the materials. If he did, she would push forward without hesitation, convinced it was another clue. But if he didn't, he would carry the burden of what he had seen alone—and the doubt that came with it.

"It's just a feeling," he said finally, his voice subdued. "We need to be sure we're not opening something we can't control."

Hana crossed her arms, her frustration evident. "You sound like Michael. I didn't expect that from you."

Marcus's jaw tightened. "Maybe Michael has a point."

Her smart retort died on her lips as her phone buzzed. She pulled it out and glanced at the screen, her frown deepening. "It's Michael. He says he's found something about the four keys. He wants us back in the archives."

Marcus nodded, grateful for the reprieve, but as Hana turned to leave, her parting glance lingered.

"You're holding something back," she said quietly. "I can feel it. Whatever it is, you'd better figure out which side you're on, Marcus. Because the people we're up against won't wait for you to make up your mind."

As the door closed behind her, Marcus exhaled, the weight of the thumb drive in his drawer heavier than ever. He had a choice to make—trust his instincts and the warning he had received, or stay the course and risk stepping into a trap. Either way, the stakes were growing higher with every passing moment.

CHAPTER
TWENTY-SEVEN

The Vatican Archives were eerily quiet, the soft hum of ancient air circulation systems blending with the faint rustle of parchment as Michael waited in the secluded study room. The atmosphere was heavy with centuries of concealed truths, but tonight it felt even more oppressive. He had uncovered something that would force the team to reconsider everything.

When Marcus and Hana arrived, Michael motioned for them to sit. A worn manuscript bound in faded red leather lay open on the table before him, its edges frayed from centuries of handling. Beside it sat a modern binder, filled with neatly typed pages and annotated diagrams.

"Thanks for coming," Michael began, his tone low but urgent. "I've been piecing together additional context around *Operation Eisenkreuz* and also the Covenant's four keys. What I've found is significant."

Hana pulled out her laptop and immediately began setting up. "Let's hear it."

Michael leaned forward, his hands resting on the manuscript. "We know the Templars had a pact with the Vatican to protect something—some form of dangerous knowledge or artifact. Which we've already discovered is that geothermal energy containment unit in the Owl Mountains. For now, we know it's secure. But for how long? And what I didn't fully understand until now is how deliberately they tied the four keys to more than just virtues or trials in order to protect it."

Marcus frowned. Although his friend's summary seemed correct on the surface—the Templars wanted that unit secured to avoid its dangers—he didn't know about the dangers of yet another object: that black cube. He tried to refocus on Michael's point, asking, "You're saying the keys have a deeper purpose?"

Michael nodded. "Yes, but not in the way we assumed. The keys are metaphysical as much as they are symbolic. They represent humanity's potential to either preserve or destroy what that Covenant guards."

He tapped the manuscript. "This is a rare Templar document—one of their reflections on why they chose to seal the Covenant. It describes the keys as 'threads in a loom,' a metaphor for how fortitude, wisdom, faith, and justice weave together. Without balance, the tapestry unravels. That unraveling, they believed, could doom humanity."

Hana narrowed her eyes, her fingers pausing over her keyboard. "And what does that mean for us? We're not just solving a puzzle; we're untangling something designed to resist being understood."

Michael hesitated, his expression troubled. "There's more. The Covenant wasn't just establishing a vault or hiding place—it was a test of moral readiness. The four keys weren't created to open it; they were created to stop it from being opened."

Marcus's brow furrowed. "But if that's true, why leave the clues behind at all?"

Michael pushed the binder toward him. "This is where things become murky. The Templars believed that while the Covenant was necessary to guard humanity from the power we found in the containment unit, there might come a time when humanity would need its knowledge. They left the keys not as a map, but as a challenge—proof that whoever sought it was worthy of wielding it."

Hana leaned back, her arms crossed. "So, the Templars, even though they created a covenant with the Vatican, didn't trust them, and therefore left clues for those they deemed 'worthy' to reveal these objects, if need be? And what if someone who isn't worthy, like the New Order, finds it first?"

"That's what they feared most," Michael admitted. "The tests aren't foolproof. They can be bypassed—or misunderstood. And from what I've found, there are already groups trying to find these hidden Templar sites, groups who don't care about proving their worth."

Marcus stiffened. "Like the New Order."

Michael nodded grimly. "And whoever sent us chasing this now, if it wasn't them."

Hana sighed, the weight of the revelation settling on her shoulders. "So, what's next? How do we approach this without playing into their hands?"

Michael stood, retrieving a folded map from a nearby shelf. He spread it across the table, pointing to markings that corresponded to Jerusalem, Paris, London, and Tomar. "The Templars scattered their knowledge across these locations. But here's the twist—they didn't hide the Covenant itself in any of them."

Marcus tilted his head. "Then where is it?"

Michael tapped the center of the map. "Somewhere that connects them all. The original Covenant's true location is hidden at a point of convergence—a place tied to the Templars' greatest fear and hope."

Hana leaned over the map, scrutinizing the lines and symbols. "A convergence of what? Geography? Influence?"

Michael shook his head. "Virtues. The Templars believed that only in the unity of the four keys—fortitude, wisdom, faith, and justice—could the Covenant's purpose be understood. But they were clear: this isn't just about finding a physical location so we can read the actual Covenant. It's about embodying the keys in order to find it."

Marcus exhaled sharply. "So even if we find the convergence, if we're not ready—if we're not balanced—it could destroy us."

Michael's face darkened. "That's exactly why we need to proceed with absolute caution. We need to be equipped in whatever way the Templars would find necessary when we find the right location."

Hana closed her laptop with a sharp snap. "Caution is one thing, Michael. But whoever is out there pulling strings—they're not stopping. And they certainly aren't looking to be tested for their wisdom, faith, or justice. All they might have on their side is fortitude."

Marcus looked down at the map, the symbols blurring as doubt crept into his thoughts. The cryptic warnings from the envelope and the thumb drive weighed heavily on his mind. Was their pursuit of the Covenant a step toward salvation—or ruin?

Michael's voice broke through his reverie. "We'll work through this together. Step by step. If we don't, everything the Templars feared could become reality."

THE TENSION in the study room had thickened, an unspoken undercurrent of urgency lingering as Michael rolled up the map and Hana stared at her closed laptop, her fingers drumming against the table. Marcus, sitting across from them, could feel the weight of his hesitation pressing down on him. The envelope and its contents burned in his mind like a secret he wasn't meant to keep.

But he couldn't keep it any longer.

Marcus cleared his throat, drawing their attention. "Before we go any further," he began, his voice steady but low, "there's something I need to share."

Hana tilted her head. Michael leaned back slightly, folding his arms as he studied Marcus.

"What is it?" Michael asked, his voice measured.

Marcus reached into his satchel, pulling out the plain

envelope. He set it on the table with deliberate care, his movements slow, almost hesitant. "This showed up in my quarters earlier today," he said. "It was waiting for me when I got back. No sender, no explanation—just this."

Hana reached out, her fingers brushing the edge of the envelope. "What's in it?"

Marcus opened it, withdrawing the folded note and thumb drive. He passed the note to Michael and set the thumb drive in the center of the table.

Michael unfolded the paper, his brow furrowing as he read the Latin text aloud. "'The past is not what you believe it to be. Your work endangers everything—faith, truth, and the lives of those closest to you. If you truly seek the Covenant, consider what it may bring: salvation… or ruin.'" He glanced up, his expression dark. "Where did this come from?"

"I don't know," Marcus admitted. "But it wasn't random. Whoever sent it knew exactly what they were doing. Plus they had access to my Vatican office."

Hana picked up the thumb drive, turning it over in her hand. "You opened it already?"

Marcus nodded. "It contains documents and a video —things that connect to *Operation Eisenkreuz* and what we're chasing. But the message was clear: whoever sent it wants me to question our mission."

Michael frowned. "What's on the drive?"

"Scans of Templar texts, Nazi reports, and a video of an excavation," Marcus said. "The texts describe the Covenant—or its core—as an 'engine of corruption,' something inherently destructive. The Nazi report

describes failed attempts to control it, and the video..."
He paused, exhaling sharply.

Hana looked at him. "What aren't you telling us?"

"It wasn't the sphere we found that they were trying to control. It was something else. Another object altogether. The video shows chaos. Soldiers turning on each other, losing their minds."

Hana's eyes widened, her expression a mix of fascination and unease. "You think it's real?"

"I don't know," Marcus admitted. "It feels real enough, but the timing is too perfect. This was meant to scare me—or manipulate me."

Michael leaned forward, his hands resting on the table. "And it's working, isn't it?"

Marcus didn't deny it. "It made me question everything. What if we're not uncovering a mystery to preserve history, but a danger—now a second one—that the Templars wanted sealed away forever? Worse yet, what if we're being used to open something that should stay buried?"

Hana placed the thumb drive on the table and crossed her arms. "Or what if this is exactly what the people seeking the Covenant or its core actually want? To scare us off, to make us hesitate while they get ahead."

Michael tapped the note thoughtfully. "It's a calculated move. The language, the delivery—it's designed to destabilize us, to make us question our purpose. But that doesn't mean the information is false."

"That's the problem," Marcus said. "If it's true, we're

risking everything by continuing. If it's a lie, we're being manipulated into doing exactly what they want."

Silence fell over the room as they weighed the implications. Hana broke it first, her voice firm. "We can't let fear dictate our decisions. Whoever sent this—whether they're warning us or manipulating us—they're trying to control the narrative. We need to stay focused on the truth."

Michael nodded slowly. "Agreed. But we need to tread carefully. This thumb drive could be a trap in itself. The information might be bait, or worse, it could contain something meant to mislead us."

Marcus looked at them both, his uncertainty evident. "So, what's the next step? Do we ignore it? Follow the lead? What if we're walking into something we can't handle?"

Michael's expression softened. "We don't ignore it, but we don't let it dictate our path either. We take what we've learned and cross-reference it with what we know. If this information fits, we proceed cautiously. If it doesn't, we treat it as a distraction."

Hana picked up the thumb drive again, her resolve hardening. "Let me take a closer look at this. If there's something in the metadata, maybe I can trace its origin. We need to know who sent it and why."

Michael gestured to the note. "I'll dig through the archives and see if there are any records that align with the descriptions Marcus found. If the Templars documented this 'engine of corruption,' there might be more to it than what's on the drive."

Marcus exhaled, the weight of the secret lifting

slightly. "And what about the video? Should I show you?"

Hana and Michael exchanged a glance. Michael nodded. "Yes. If it's real, it's important. If it's fabricated, we need to understand why someone would go to such lengths."

Hana placed a reassuring hand on Marcus's arm. "We're in this together. Whatever this is, we'll figure it out."

Marcus nodded, a flicker of relief breaking through his unease. As Hana connected the thumb drive to her laptop and Michael turned back to his texts, he felt a small but vital reassurance: he wasn't alone in this.

The glow of Hana's laptop cast dim shadows over the study room as she worked on the thumb drive, her brows furrowed in concentration. Marcus and Michael watched as lines of code scrolled across her screen.

"There's definitely metadata embedded here," Hana muttered, her voice low but focused. "Looks like someone tried to scrub it clean, but they did a less than perfect job."

Michael leaned in slightly. "Anything we can use?"

Hana paused, tilting her head as she decrypted another layer of data. "There. I've got a timestamp and an IP address. It's rerouted through a chain of proxies, but the origin point..." She trailed off, her expression shifting to one of disbelief.

"What is it?" Marcus asked, tension tightening his chest.

Hana turned the screen toward them, pointing to a

line of text. "The origin traces back to Rome. Specifically, a secure Vatican server."

Michael's face darkened. "Someone inside the Vatican sent this?!"

Hana nodded. "And they went to a lot of trouble to make it look like it came from outside."

Marcus sat back, his mind sifting through possibilities, eliminating the impossible with each breath. "So we're not just dealing with external forces. There's someone here, in the Vatican, trying to control what we find."

Michael folded his hands, his voice measured but firm. "This changes things. If someone within the Vatican is involved, they could be monitoring us—or worse, working against us."

Hana narrowed her eyes. "Then we need to move quickly. Whoever sent this knows more than they're letting on, and they're not going to wait for us to catch up."

Michael nodded, his gaze hardening. "We'll dig deeper. But we have to be careful—if they're watching, we need to stay one step ahead. This isn't just about uncovering the Covenant anymore. It's about figuring out who's pulling the strings."

Marcus looked between them, his resolve firming. "Then let's find out who's behind this. And what they're so desperate to keep hidden."

CHAPTER
TWENTY-EIGHT

The revelation of the Vatican server's involvement had sent a chill through the air. Marcus, Michael, and Hana remained seated around the table, the gravity of the situation sinking in. The thumb drive now seemed less like a clue and more like a trap—one designed to manipulate them.

Michael broke the silence. "We can't proceed as we have been. Whoever sent this knows where we're looking and what we've found. They're watching us."

Hana tapped her pen against the edge of her laptop, her face set with determination. "And they're doing more than watching. They're steering us—trying to control what we see and how we react. That kind of manipulation takes planning."

Marcus leaned forward, resting his elbows on the table. "Which means they've been involved for a while. This didn't start with the thumb drive. Someone's been monitoring us since we started digging into any of this."

Michael looked grim. "And if they're embedded within the Vatican, they could have access to every step we've taken. Archives, field notes, our communications... everything."

Hana raised an eyebrow. "Then it's time we started playing them instead of letting them play us."

Michael shot her a wary look. "What are you suggesting?"

"Simple," Hana said, leaning back in her chair. "We set a trap. Whoever sent this thumb drive wanted us to find something specific—or they wanted us to react a certain way. If we don't follow their lead exactly, we might force their hand."

Marcus frowned, skepticism etched across his face. "And what does that look like? How do we outmaneuver someone who's clearly been planning this for years?"

Hana smiled faintly, the glint of a seasoned journalist in her eyes. "We mislead them. We act like we're following their breadcrumbs, but we pivot—dig deeper into what they're not showing us."

Michael considered this for a moment. "It's a risk. If they realize we're onto them, they could retaliate."

"That's a chance we'll have to take," Hana countered. "Right now, we're being reactive. If we don't shift the balance, they'll stay ahead of us."

Marcus sighed, rubbing the back of his neck. "Fine. But we can't ignore the information on that drive. If it's real, it could tell us what *Eisenkreuz* is—and why they're so desperate to keep it buried."

Michael nodded. "We'll split our efforts. Hana, you

follow the digital trail. See if you can pinpoint who accessed the server and planted the data. Marcus, focus on the video and the documents. Cross-reference them with the archives. Look for inconsistencies, anything that could suggest fabrication."

"And you?" Marcus asked.

Michael's gaze was steady. "I'll go higher up. There are cardinals I trust—ones who've been involved with the archives for decades. If there's a faction operating within the Vatican, someone will know."

Hana looked doubtful. "And if they don't? Or worse, if they're part of it?"

Michael hesitated, his voice softening. "Then we'll know exactly how far this conspiracy reaches."

LATER THAT NIGHT, in Marcus's apartment, the study was silent save for the faint hum of his laptop. He sat at his desk, the screen glowing faintly as he replayed the video from the thumb drive. Each time, the same sequence unfolded: the excavation site, the pedestal, the gleaming black object. The soldiers pacing nervously, the sudden eruption of chaos.

He paused the video on the pedestal, leaning closer to examine the carvings. Something about the symbols nagged at his memory. He had seen them before—but where? He opened a separate window, accessing a digitized collection of Templar codices. After an hour of searching, he found it: a nearly identical symbol etched into the margins of a Templar map. The accompanying text read: *"Locus Aeternitatis"*—the Place of Eternity.

Marcus's stomach tightened. The Place of Eternity. Was that a description of the Core of Iron Cross? Or was it only a metaphor?

A knock at the door pulled him from his thoughts. He closed his laptop and stood, his pulse quickening. He wasn't expecting anyone. "Who is it?"

"It's me," came Hana's voice. "Let me in."

Marcus exhaled in relief and opened the door.

Hana stepped inside, her laptop under one arm and a faintly triumphant look on her face.

"I've got something," she said, setting her laptop on the desk. She brought up a series of logs, each one showing timestamps and server activity. "I traced the IP further. Whoever sent that thumb drive didn't just access the Vatican servers—they used them to pull old files from the Vatican Archives."

"What files?" Marcus asked, leaning over her shoulder.

"Documents tied to the Council of Vienne that met in 1311," Hana replied. "Specifically, correspondence between the cardinals and the Templar Grand Master about sealing the Covenant of the Iron Cross. There's also a request—an order, really—for a permanent containment team. They called it *'Custodes Umbrae.'* The Shadows' Keepers."

Marcus frowned. "And what does that mean?"

"It means," Hana said, her voice growing sharper, "that someone within the Vatican hasn't been just aware of the Covenant of the Iron Cross—they've been guarding it. For centuries. Clearly, this represents the 'guardians who cannot be moved' that

I translated from that original document Marcus was given."

Marcus leaned back, the revelation settling heavily in his chest. "So whoever sent this... they're not just trying to stop us. They're part of the system that's been protecting whatever the Covenant is hiding all along."

"Exactly," Hana said. "The question is: why break silence now? Why expose themselves?"

Marcus didn't answer. Instead, his mind drifted to the video and the warning embedded in the note. *Eisenkreuz.*

THE FOLLOWING MORNING, the weight of the previous night's revelations hung heavily over the team. Marcus and Hana joined Michael in the same secluded study room deep within the Vatican Archives. The air was colder, the silence more oppressive. They had all slept fitfully, their thoughts consumed by the shadows *Eisenkreuz* now cast over their mission.

Michael was already at the table when they arrived, an array of manuscripts, maps, and codices spread before him. He looked up as they entered, his expression grim but focused. "I spoke to one of the cardinals last night," he began, skipping any preamble. "Someone I trust."

Hana raised an eyebrow as she dropped her bag onto a chair. "And?"

Michael exhaled briskly. "He confirmed what we suspected. *Custodes Umbrae*—the Shadows' Keepers—is real. It's not just a historical note. It's an active group within the Vatican, tasked with guarding the Covenant."

Marcus stiffened. "Guarding it? Or hiding it?"

Michael's eyes darkened. "Both. They see it as their sacred duty. The cardinal didn't say much—he was cautious—but he mentioned that what the Covenant safeguards represents a threat unlike any other. They've been watching anyone who comes close to uncovering it, and they've been silencing those they consider a risk."

Hana leaned forward, her voice acute. "Silencing? You mean... permanently?"

Michael nodded reluctantly. "It's possible. The cardinal didn't confirm it outright, but he implied that their methods are... absolute."

The words hung in the air like a storm cloud. Hana broke the silence first, her voice tight with anger. "So, we're being stalked by a secret faction within the Vatican that thinks they're the last line of defense against the apocalypse. Great. What else?"

Michael tapped the manuscript before him. "This. It's one of the oldest Templar texts we've found. It outlines the creation of the Covenant seals—what they called the *Clavis Exilis*." He gestured to the text. "The Exiled Keys. The Templars believed that no one could control this object they'd found, not even themselves. They scattered the seals to prevent anyone from activating it. Each key was meant to act as both a safeguard and a warning."

Marcus leaned over the manuscript, his eyes scanning the faded Latin script. "The keys were symbolic, tied to those virtues we already knew were connected somehow—fortitude, wisdom, faith, and justice. But this suggests they were also physical artifacts, doesn't it?"

Michael nodded. "Yes. The text describes them as tangible objects, each one containing a piece of the covenant's purpose. But here's the catch: they weren't just symbols of virtues. The Templars believed each key carried part of the danger they were trying to contain."

Hana frowned. "So they scattered the danger instead of locking it all in one place?"

"Essentially, yes," Michael said. "They thought it was safer that way. Each key was entrusted to a different location and guarded by their own tests and traps. But if someone were to reunite them…"

"…they'd have the power to unlock this powerful object," Marcus finished grimly.

Hana tapped her fingers against the table, her journalist's instincts kicking in. "This *Custodes Umbrae* group—they're protecting the seals, aren't they? Making sure they stay separate? So, they could be the ones warning us with the video to keep back."

"Possibly," Michael said. "But the faction isn't unified. There are those who believe whatever this object is should be destroyed entirely, and others who think it's too important—too powerful—to lose forever."

Marcus clenched his jaw. "And we're caught in the middle, again."

"Exactly," Michael said. He paused, his expression hardening. "There's something else. The cardinal mentioned a recent fracture within *Custodes Umbrae*. A splinter group has broken away, believing the seals must be reunited to reveal the Covenant's true purpose."

Hana's eyes widened. "A splinter group? So maybe they sent the thumb drive. They're trying to entice us to now search out and find those four keys."

Michael nodded. "And if they're using us, it's because they think we'll lead them to the keys. They no doubt know we've already been successful finding the Owl Mountains cache. Either way, we're playing right into their hands."

Marcus stood, pacing the length of the room. "We need to find those keys before anyone else does. Whether they're symbols, artifacts, or something else entirely, they're the only way to figure out what the Templars were really hiding—and how to stop it from getting in the wrong hands."

Hana leaned forward, her voice resolute. "Agreed. But we can't go charging in blindly. If *Custodes Umbrae* is already watching us, we need to stay ahead of them. That means misdirection, careful planning, and, most importantly, figuring out where the keys are."

Michael gestured to the map spread across the table. "We've narrowed it down to those four locations based on the Templar texts. They align with the four virtues. They're tied to specific places in those cities where the Templars faced their greatest challenges."

He pointed to the map, his finger stopping at each location in turn. "Montségur in France, where the Cathars made their last stand. Acre in the Holy Land, the site of their final battle before they lost Jerusalem.

Rosslyn Chapel in Scotland, a place steeped in Knights Templar lore. And finally, the Convent of Christ in Tomar, Portugal, their refuge after the order fell."

Hana's eyes scanned the map, her voice thoughtful. "So these locations hold the keys—or at least the answers to where they might be."

Michael nodded. "Exactly. But we can't visit them directly. It's too risky. *Custodes Umbrae*—or their splinter group—will be watching."

Marcus rubbed his chin thoughtfully. "Then we research them remotely. The archives must have records, accounts, something that ties these places to the keys."

Hana nodded, her determination clear. "Let's get started. The longer we wait, the more we risk someone else beating us to the truth."

Michael nodded. "Agreed. But we move carefully. This object or knowledge was hidden for a reason, and if the Templars thought it was too dangerous to control, we need to understand why before we even think about unlocking it."

The three of them settled into their tasks, the room filling with the sound of flipping pages and the soft clicking of keys. Outside, the Vatican's centuries-old walls stood silent, their secrets protected by layers of stone and shadow. But inside, the team was unraveling the threads of a mystery that could shake those walls to their foundations—and possibly beyond.

CHAPTER

TWENTY-NINE

The late afternoon sun filtered dimly through the small window of the study room, casting elongated shadows over the table cluttered with manuscripts, maps, and digital tablets. Marcus, Michael, and Hana had been working tirelessly, combing through Vatican records, Templar correspondences, and the notes from the mysterious thumb drive. Hours had passed and threads began to converge.

Michael was the first to break the silence. He pushed a thick manuscript across the table toward Marcus, his expression pointed. "Here," he said, his finger tapping a faded Latin phrase. "'*Clavis Exilis*'—the Exiled Keys. This confirms what we suspected about the locations."

Marcus scanned the text, nodding slowly. "It matches the Templar philosophy. The keys were never meant to be reunited, but each one carries a fragment of knowledge about what they have hidden away.

Together, they form a map of its purpose—and its danger."

Hana glanced up from her laptop, her tone urgent. "I've cross-referenced the locations you mentioned—Montségur, Acre, Rosslyn Chapel, and Tomar—with the Vatican's classified excavation reports. The good news? We don't need to visit them. Detailed records were sent back to the Vatican after each site was explored by various factions over the centuries."

"And the bad news?" Michael asked.

Hana leaned back, gesturing toward the screen. "The records aren't complete. Montségur and Acre are missing critical pieces—likely destroyed or deliberately hidden. But Rosslyn and Tomar? Those reports appear intact. And they mention objects retrieved from each site that match descriptions of the keys we found in that 1312 document from the Council of Vienne."

Marcus leaned forward, his pulse quickening. "What do they say?"

Hana began reading aloud. "From Rosslyn Chapel: 'An ornate chalice engraved with the seal of faith, inscribed with a warning of balance to be kept.' From Tomar: 'A blade of blackened steel, unyielding and worn, bearing the sigil of justice.' Both artifacts were removed and placed under Vatican protection."

Michael rubbed his temples, the pieces of the puzzle falling into place. "Justice and faith. That leaves wisdom and fortitude unaccounted for."

Hana nodded. "But if Montségur and Acre were also explored, the keys—or their fragments—might have been moved as well. The problem is, we don't know where those went."

Marcus tilted his head, a storm of thoughts battering his consciousness. "What about *Custodes Umbrae*? If they've been guarding the secrets of the Covenant all this time, wouldn't they have tracked the keys?"

Michael considered this, his expression darkening. "It's possible. If they see the keys as essential to keeping this sealed, they would have kept them close. And how much closer than in the Vatican Archives, the very institution that funds the Shadows' Keepers? But if the splinter faction broke away, they might have taken some of the keys—or their knowledge of them—with them."

Hana tapped her laptop, her voice tight with determination. "Then let's focus on Rosslyn and Tomar. If the artifacts were moved to the Vatican, there must be records. And if *Custodes Umbrae* has them, we'll need to find a way to access their archives."

Michael stood abruptly, pacing the length of the room. "This changes things. If the splinter group has part of the keys and the loyalists have the rest, then the Covenant's seals are already compromised. The factions are playing a game of cat and mouse, and again, we're caught in the middle. One or both sides are using us to pull these pieces together."

Marcus frowned, his thoughts returning to the video on the thumb drive. "And the thumb drive—what if it was a warning from one of the loyalists? A way to scare us off before we inadvertently help the splinter group?"

Michael paused, considering this. "Then why wouldn't they eliminate us outright? But they didn't...

or maybe they want us to reveal the splinter group's next move."

Hana's eyes narrowed. "Then we need to decide which side we're really on. The loyalists want to keep the Covenant sealed, but the splinter group thinks it should be understood—maybe even controlled. Which one is right?"

Marcus exhaled slowly. "Until we know what it is, how can we say which is right?"

Hana leaned forward, her voice firm. "Then we need to find those key artifacts. Hopefully, they're still in Vatican custody."

Michael nodded, his resolve hardening. "I know where to start. There's a restricted section of the Vatican Treasury—artifacts too sensitive even for the main archives. If the chalice and the blade are here, that's where they'll be."

"And you have access?"

Michael hesitated. "Not directly. But I know someone who does."

Marcus stood, his voice steady. "Then let's move. Every moment we wait, the splinter group gets closer to reuniting the keys."

THE VATICAN TREASURY was a fortress within a fortress. Hidden beneath layers of security, it was said to house relics so powerful or controversial that even their existence was denied by the Church. Later that night, Michael's contact, an aging priest named Father Bernard Corvi, slowly escorted them through a maze of corridors, each turn taking them deeper into the heart of the Vatican's secrets.

Finally, they reached a heavy iron door, its surface etched with ancient prayers. Father Corvi stopped, catching his breath. Then he placed his hand on a scanner, muttering a prayer as the door groaned open.

Inside, the air was cold and still. Shelves lined with relics stretched into the shadows, each item carefully cataloged and preserved. Michael led the way, his steps deliberate as he scanned the labels on each shelf.

"There," he said, pointing to a case near the back. Inside rested an ornate chalice, its surface gleaming even in the dim light. The sigil of faith was unmistakable, etched deep into the silver.

"And there," Hana added, gesturing to a second case. Within lay a blackened blade, its edges jagged and worn, the sigil of justice etched into the hilt.

Marcus stepped forward, his breath catching as he stared at the artifacts. "These are the keys."

Michael nodded. "Two of them, at least."

Before anyone could say another word, the lights flickered, and a low hum echoed through the chamber. Father Corvi turned abruptly, his face pale. "My friends, it seems we are not alone."

Hana's hand instinctively went to her bag, where she kept a small but sturdy recorder.

Marcus clenched his fists, his instincts screaming danger.

From the shadows, a voice echoed, calm and precise. "You've come far, but your journey ends here."

The splinter group had arrived.

CHAPTER
THIRTY

The voice was calm yet cold, echoing ominously throughout the chamber. Marcus, Hana, and Michael froze, their eyes darting into the shadows. Father Corvi muttered a prayer under his breath and crossed himself, retreating toward the entrance. But the heavy iron door had already closed behind them.

"Who's there?" Michael called, his voice steady but tense.

A figure emerged from the darkness, draped in black robes edged with crimson embroidery. The sigil of *Custodes Umbrae* gleamed on the front of the robe, unmistakable in the faint light. Behind him, two more figures appeared, their faces partially obscured by the hoods of their robes. They moved deliberately, their presence radiating authority and menace.

"You shouldn't have come here," the first figure said, stepping closer. His tone was authoritative, but there was no anger—only resolve. "You've stumbled into matters far beyond your comprehension."

Hana took a step forward. "If that's true, why not stop us earlier? Why leave breadcrumbs and send cryptic warnings? You wanted us here."

The man tilted his head slightly, a faint smirk curling at the edge of his lips. "Observant, Miss Sinclair. Yes, you were brought here. But not by us." He glanced toward Michael. "You've been led astray, Father Dominic, manipulated by forces that seek to end what we have guarded for centuries."

Michael's jaw tightened. "Led astray? It is the *Custodes Umbrae* who have gone astray. Your sacred vow is to protect the Covenant's charge, to ensure the keys remain separate. But instead you—"

"You misunderstand." The man's expression darkened. "We have not failed. The splinter group you speak of is a corruption within our own ranks that has distorted our purpose. You have been manipulated by forces that seek to end what we have guarded for centuries. Your meddling has accelerated their plans. And now you have given them the opportunity they have been waiting for."

The team glanced at one another. This was not the splinter group?

Marcus stepped forward, his frustration boiling over. "Then help us stop them. That has been our aim all along. You claim to be protectors, yet you've done nothing but obstruct us."

The man's gaze shifted to Marcus, his tone cool and calculating. "And you, Dr. Russo, have been reckless in your pursuit of truth. You have no idea what the Covenant is meant to protect, no comprehension of the destruction it could unleash. Yet here you stand, ready to pry open the seals, believing you are immune to the consequences."

Marcus bristled but said nothing. The memory of the video on the thumb drive—soldiers succumbing to madness—flashed in his mind, an unwelcomed specter.

Hana cut in, her voice sharp. "We're not here to unlock anything. We're here to ensure the powers held by the Covenant remain out of the wrong hands. Already some of those secrets slipped out of your hands into those of the Nazis generations ago in *Operation Eisenkreuz*. Now the New Order wants to relocate a unit of immeasurable danger plus gain access to even more of the secrets you say you protect. But you seem more interested in gatekeeping than solving the problem."

The man's smile returned, but it carried no warmth. "And what solution do you offer, Miss Sinclair? Exposure? Transparency? That would only hasten the world's descent into chaos. This is not a problem to be solved. It is a burden to be carried."

Michael's voice was calm but firm. "Then carry it with us. If you truly believe in your mission, you'll see that we're not your enemies. We want to protect the world as much as you do."

The man studied Michael for a long moment, his expression unreadable. Finally, he gestured to the two artifacts encased before them—the chalice and the blade.

"Those relics are not trophies," he said. "They are warnings. Each represents a fragment of the burden the

Templars sought to bear alone. Reuniting the keys does not reveal the covenant's purpose. It reveals its curse."

Marcus frowned. "What curse?"

The man stepped closer, his voice lowering. "What we are tasked to protect is not simply a relic, nor is it knowledge. It is the culmination of human arrogance—an entity that defies understanding, born of the darkest moments in history. To touch it, to unleash it, is to invite corruption. Even the Templars could not comprehend what they sought to contain."

Michael exhaled slowly. "If that's true, then the splinter group's plans are even more dangerous than we thought."

"They are fools," the man said sharply, his tone tinged with disdain. "They believe this power can be controlled, that it can be harnessed. But the Templars learned the truth too late. The seals are the only thing preventing its influence from spreading. Even fragments of its presence could destabilize nations, destroy faith."

Hana met his gaze. "Then help us. If the splinter group is as close as you say, standing in our way only gives them more time."

The man hesitated, his resolve wavering. Finally, he turned to one of the robed figures behind him and nodded. The figure stepped forward to unlock the cases holding the chalice and blade. The air seemed to grow colder as the artifacts were revealed, their ancient power palpable even at a distance.

Father Bernard Corvi, now slumped against the wall, crossed himself, his face pale.

"These are two of the seals," the man said. "The

others—what you call wisdom and fortitude—have already been taken by the splinter group. They plan to use all four to unlock this dangerous secret. If they succeed, there will be no stopping its devastation."

Marcus's voice was steady. "Then we need to stop them before they can."

The man's gaze hardened. "You have no idea what you're asking for. But I see that you will not be swayed. Take these seals. Use them to draw out the splinter group. But understand this—if you fail, if the seals are reunited in the wrong hands, you will have doomed us all."

Michael nodded solemnly. "We won't fail."

The man stepped back into the shadows, the other robed figures following. His final words echoed through the chamber as they disappeared.

"What you seek is more than you can imagine. Pray you never discover its true nature."

The silence that followed was ominous.

Michael rushed over to Father Corvi and helped steady the old priest to his feet.

The elderly man muttered, "What have I done?"

"We'll handle this, Father. You have done nothing wrong bringing us here." But Michael saw both guilt and fear in the old man's eyes.

Hana turned to Marcus, her expression grim. "So, now we have two seals. And we know who has the others."

Marcus stared at the chalice and the blade, the weight of their task pressing down on him. "Now we set the trap. We make them come to us."

Michael stepped forward, carefully wrapping the artifacts in the cloth on which both cases rested. "And when they do, we end this—once and for all." He returned to take the old priest's arm to escort him out.

The three exchanged a glance of unspoken resolve. The splinter group had the other keys, and the race to stop them was about to reach its breaking point. Whatever this mysterious object truly was, the fate of the world now depended on keeping it sealed—and out of the wrong hands.

The dim light of Marcus's study cast a shadow over the table, where the chalice and the blade now lay, wrapped carefully in protective cloth, the weight of the artifacts pressing on the team like an unrelenting tide. Marcus, Michael, and Hana stood around the table, their faces drawn with exhaustion but keen with purpose.

"We can't wait for them to make the first move," Marcus said, breaking the silence. His voice was steady but tinged with exigency. "If we want to stop the splinter group, we need to force their hand."

Hana nodded, her eyes fixed on the chalice. "We've got two of the seals. That alone makes us a target. If we make it known that we're close to the others, they'll come to us."

Michael frowned. "You're suggesting we bait them? Let them think we have more knowledge of the other two keys than we do?"

Hana crossed her arms, her expression unfaltering. "Exactly. It's the only way to draw them out. If they believe we're about to reunite the keys, they won't be able to resist."

Michael's gaze darkened. "And if they decide to attack? These people aren't just scholars or idealists. They're zealots. They won't hesitate to kill if it means achieving their goal."

"That's why we plan carefully," Marcus interjected. "We control the location and the conditions. If they come after us, we make sure we're ready for them."

Hana pulled out her laptop, setting it on the table. "I can plant the bait digitally. A few encrypted files, maybe a fake communication leak suggesting we've located the other two seals. If they're monitoring us—and I'd bet anything they are—it'll be enough to get their attention."

Michael paced the room, his thoughts clearly racing. "It's risky. If we miscalculate, they could ambush us. Or worse, they might move the remaining seals somewhere we can't reach them."

Marcus folded his arms, meeting Michael's gaze. "Do we have a better option? Right now, they're ahead of us. If we wait, we lose what little advantage we have."

Michael hesitated, then nodded reluctantly. "Fine. But we need a secure location, somewhere we can control the environment and ensure they don't have the upper hand."

Hana smiled confidently. "I think I know just the place."

. . .

THE ATMOSPHERE WAS musty and cool as they descended into the labyrinthine catacombs beneath a secluded chapel on the outskirts of Rome. Michael had secured access through an old Vatican contact, ensuring that no one would disturb them. The narrow corridors, lined with ancient tombs and faintly flickering lanterns, provided the perfect setting for their plan.

Marcus carried the wrapped artifacts carefully, his every step deliberate. Hana walked ahead, her phone lighting the way as she documented their path. Michael brought up the rear, his movements tense and watchful.

"This place is a maze," Hana muttered, glancing back at Michael. "Are you sure they won't be able to sneak in without us knowing?"

Michael gestured to the thick stone walls. "There's only one entrance, and it's locked from the inside. If they want to get to us, they'll have to come straight through."

Marcus set the chalice and blade on a small stone altar at the center of the chamber they had chosen. The room was spacious but enclosed, with high vaulted ceilings that echoed faintly with every sound. Candles flickered along the walls, their light casting eerie shadows over the artifacts.

"This will do," Marcus said, stepping back to survey the setup. "It's defensible, and it keeps the artifacts protected."

Hana knelt beside her laptop, typing rapidly. "I'm setting the bait now. A fabricated email chain, some encrypted files, and a few false breadcrumbs pointing to

Montségur and Acre. If they're monitoring us, they'll think we've tracked down the remaining seals."

Michael watched her work, his expression grim. "And if they don't take the bait?"

"They will," Hana said confidently. "This group has spent years chasing these keys. If they think we're about to reunite them, they won't be able to resist coming after us to do it themselves."

Marcus glanced at Michael. "Do we have everything we need? If this turns into a fight, we need to be ready."

Michael nodded. "I've arranged for discreet backup. Karl and Lukas are stationed outside the chapel. If things go south, they'll intervene."

Hana closed her laptop and stood, brushing the dust from her jeans. "It's done. Now we wait."

HOURS LATER, the first sign of their success came as a faint sound—footsteps echoing through the catacombs. Michael held up a hand, signaling for silence. Marcus and Hana froze, their breaths shallow as they strained to listen.

The footsteps grew louder, accompanied by the faint shuffle of fabric. Shadows flickered at the far end of the corridor, moving closer with each passing moment.

"They're here," Marcus whispered, his voice tight.

Michael nodded, his expression steely. "Stay close. Follow the plan."

Hana's hand drifted toward her bag, where she kept a concealed taser. Her heart pounded in her chest, but her resolve didn't waver. She exchanged a glance with

Marcus, who nodded, his grip tightening on a heavy flashlight that doubled as a blunt weapon.

The figures emerged into the chamber, their faces partially obscured by hoods. There were five of them, dressed in dark robes edged with crimson, the sigil of *Custodes Umbrae* gleaming on their chests.

The leader stepped forward, his voice calm but commanding. "You've gone too far. Surrender the seals, or face the consequences."

Michael stepped forward, his posture unwavering. "We're not your enemies. But if you think we'll hand over the seals without understanding their purpose, you're mistaken."

The man tilted his head, his tone almost mocking. "Understanding their purpose? As if you could understand. The powers inherent in what is under our charge needs to be studied, not secreted for centuries waiting for the likes of you to 'understand' it. Its power could be of supreme benefit to mankind."

Hana took a step forward, her voice curt. "Or destroy it. Your splinter group's actions endanger everything you have vowed to protect. You're the ones breaking the seals, not us."

The man stiffened at her words, his tone hardening. "You have no idea what you're dealing with. That is why you must give us the seals. Only we can know what to do with them."

The tension in the room reached a breaking point. The man raised a hand, and the figures behind him stepped forward, their movements deliberate and threatening.

"Enough talk," the man said coldly. "Surrender the seals. Now."

Marcus glanced at Michael and Hana, his voice low but firm. "Looks like they've made their choice."

Michael nodded, his expression grim. "Then we make ours."

As the chamber erupted into chaos, the true battle began.

CHAPTER

THIRTY-ONE

T he room exploded into action. The flickering candlelight cast chaotic shadows as Marcus, Michael, and Hana braced themselves against the splinter group of the *Custodes Umbrae*'s sudden charge. The five robed figures moved with precision, their steps deliberate and unhesitating as they closed in on the altar where the chalice and blade lay.

Marcus acted first, grabbing the cloth-covered blade and stepping back from the altar, behind the other two. "Not a chance!" he shouted, his voice echoing through the chamber.

The leader of the group barked an order in Latin, his tone sharp and commanding. Two of the robed figures veered toward Marcus while the others moved to intercept Michael and Hana.

Michael stood firm, blocking their path to the artifacts. "You're not taking them," he said, his voice low and inflexible. The nearest assailant lunged at him, but Michael sidestepped, grabbing the man's arm and twisting it with surprising force. The attacker stumbled, but Michael didn't relent, shoving him backward into one of the stone walls.

Hana, meanwhile, ducked as one of the figures swung a baton-like weapon in her direction. She reached into her bag, pulling out the taser she had brought, and jabbed it into the attacker's side. The crackle of electricity filled the air, and the man crumpled to the ground with a groan.

Marcus, clutching the blade tightly, dodged between tombs and columns as his two pursuers closed in. His heart pounded as he darted left, then right, his flashlight swinging wildly in his free hand. One of the robed figures grabbed at him, but he turned brusquely and swung the flashlight with all his strength. It connected with a satisfying thud, and the man staggered backward, clutching his shoulder.

"You're not as untouchable as you think," Marcus muttered, catching his breath.

The leader of the *Custodes Umbrae* faction stepped into the fray, his movements measured but deadly. He advanced toward the altar, where the chalice still rested, his eyes fixed on Michael.

Michael intercepted him, raising his hands in a defensive stance. "If you want it, you'll have to go through me."

The leader smirked, his expression cold. "So be it."

The two clashed, their movements a blur of calculated strikes and counters. The leader was fast, his attacks precise, but Michael held his ground, using the limited space of the chamber to his advantage. He ducked under a wide swing and countered with a pointed elbow to the man's ribs, eliciting a grunt of pain.

Across the chamber, Hana had retrieved the chalice from the altar, its blackened surface gleaming faintly in the dim light. She held it tightly, her eyes darting between the remaining attackers. She shouted, "Let's move!"

Marcus ducked another swing and made his way toward Hana, the blade still clutched to his chest. "We can't leave without Michael!"

Michael delivered a final blow to the leader, sending him staggering backward. "Go!" he barked, his voice ringing with urgency. "I'll cover you!"

Hana hesitated, concerned for Michael's safety, but Marcus grabbed her arm. "He can handle himself. Let's go!"

The two turned and sprinted toward the chamber's exit, the artifacts secured. Behind them, Michael held his ground, blocking the remaining attackers from following. His daily runs, his gym workouts after hours, all came into play as he fought off their attackers. His movements were calculated and controlled, each step a deliberate effort to buy them more time.

As Marcus and Hana reached the heavy iron door, Hana quickly typed a code into the electronic lock. The mechanism groaned in protest but finally gave way, allowing the door to swing open. Marcus looked back, his chest tightening as he saw Michael locked in combat with the remaining figures.

"Michael, now!" Marcus shouted.

Michael delivered a final kick to one of the attackers, sending him sprawling into the remaining man. Without a moment's hesitation, he sprinted toward the door. The leader of the *Custodes Umbrae* group, recovering quickly, called after him. "You can run, but you won't escape! *Operation Eisenkreuz* will consume you all!"

Michael ignored the taunt, sliding through the doorway just as Hana slammed the door shut. She locked it with trembling hands, her breath coming in ragged gasps.

For a moment, the three of them stood in silence, the distant shouts and pounding on the door muffled by the thick stone walls. The cold air of the catacombs pressed against them, but it felt almost refreshing after the suffocating heat of battle.

Marcus finally broke the silence, his voice hoarse but steady. "We've still got the two seals. But this group didn't bring the other seals we need. Now what?"

Michael leaned against the wall, catching his breath. "Now we regroup. The *Custodes Umbrae* won't stop trying to get the two seals we have back into their hands. And neither will the splinter group, to reunite them with the other seals. And this last guy mentioned '*Operation Eisenkreuz* will consume' us. So, either they're conspiring with the New Order or just are aware of them. Either way, we now have three groups after us. We need to figure out where they're going next—and beat them there."

Hana nodded, her grip tightening on the chalice. "We've got two of the keys. If the splinter group already has the others, it's only a matter of time before they make their move."

Michael straightened, his expression persevering. "Then we need to make ours first. Let's get out of here. We've bought ourselves some time, but not much."

Together, they ascended the narrow staircase leading back to the surface, their steps hurried. The battle in the chamber had been a victory, but it was far from the end. The splinter group still had two of the keys, and the seals were dangerously close to being broken.

As they emerged into the night air, the distant church bells of Rome ringing faintly in the distance, Marcus glanced at the blade in his hands. "We can't let our guard down—not for a second."

Hana looked toward the horizon, her eyes narrowing. "They'll come for us again. Next time, we'll be ready."

Together, they moved into the shadows, their determination unshaken.

THE VATICAN ARCHIVES were shrouded in an unnatural stillness as Marcus, Michael, and Hana returned to their secluded study room. The chalice and the blade were carefully placed on the table, their surfaces glinting faintly under the soft glow of the desk lamp. Despite their recent victory in the catacombs, tension hung thick in the air.

"We're on borrowed time," Michael said, pacing the length of the room. "The *Custodes Umbrae* won't stop hunting us, and neither will the splinter group. Not to mention Jäger and his New Order could still be tailing us. If any of them figure out where we're hiding the keys—"

"They won't," Hana interjected sharply. "I've encrypted every digital trace of our movements. But we can't stay on the defensive forever."

Marcus leaned over the blade, his fingers brushing its intricate surface. "We need to figure out what these artifacts actually do. They're more than symbols—they're pieces of a larger mechanism. If the splinter group already has the other two, they must be trying to reunite them for a reason."

Michael stopped pacing, his gaze sharp. "The Templars understood that reuniting the seals could unleash its uncontrollable power. The splinter group and the New Order might think they can control it, but history proves otherwise."

Hana, seated at the table, was already typing vigorously on her laptop. "The *Custodes Umbrae* leader said the seals were warnings, not tools. But if the Templars went to the trouble of designing these keys, they must have a purpose beyond containment."

Marcus frowned, his mind racing. "It is like the artifact we used to find the containment unit in the Owl Mountains. The unit was the power source, but the artifact was integral to both containing and activating it. Meaning those four keys could either contain or activate this black cube—unleashing a force they cannot master."

Hana glanced up from her screen, her expression

tight. "Then we need to stop them before they figure that out the hard way."

Hana's fingers flew across her keyboard as she sifted through encrypted files and digitized Templar manuscripts. Marcus and Michael worked in parallel, combing through physical texts, their pages yellowed with age. The room buzzed with focused energy, each of them driven by a sense of urgency.

"I've got something," Hana said suddenly. She turned the laptop toward Michael and Marcus, pointing to a section of text in a digitized Templar codex. "This is from a council document written just after the creation of the seals. It mentions something called the *Ordo Clavis*. The Order of the Key."

"I've seen that term before," Michael noted. "It refers to a subgroup of Templars tasked with ensuring the seals remained separate. They were the precursors to *Custodes Umbrae*."

"Right," Hana said, scrolling further. "But here's the critical part: the document says the seals weren't just scattered to hide them—they were scattered to hide a final piece. Something called *Umbra Ordinis*—the Shadow Core."

Marcus leaned forward, his pulse quickening. "The Shadow Core? The texts that accompanied that thumb drive referred to the Covenant's core as an 'engine of corruption.' Is this the same thing?"

Hana shrugged. "The text doesn't say much, but it refers to the Shadow Core as the heart. The seals are tied to it, and it can't function without them."

Michael's expression clouded over. "If the splinter

group has the other two keys, they might already know this. They could be searching for the Shadow Core, which is the core of the Covenant."

Hana scrolled further, her eyes narrowing. "Here's the other piece of the puzzle. The Shadow Core isn't hidden at any of the sites we've identified. It's... here."

"Here?" Marcus repeated, his voice incredulous. "You mean in the Vatican?"

Hana nodded grimly. "According to this, the Shadow Core was smuggled into Vatican custody centuries ago, placed in a secure vault. The Templars believed it was the only place safe enough to keep it hidden. This gives the actual location in the Secret Archives."

Michael's voice was tight. "That means we've been sitting on the answer to everything this entire time!"

MINUTES LATER, the team stood before another heavily reinforced vault deep within the archives, its oak door adorned with intricate carvings and Latin inscriptions. Michael's hands trembled slightly as he entered the electronic access code given to him by Father Cordi, his mind a flood of ideas given the implications of what they were about to uncover.

With a deep groan, the door swung open, revealing a small, dark chamber. At its center stood a stone pedestal, and atop it rested a cube-like object, its surface black and reflective, pulsing faintly with an almost imperceptible rhythm. The Shadow Core.

Marcus stepped forward, his breath catching. "That's it," he murmured.

Michael's voice was hushed, reverent. "The Templars hid this for centuries. They believed its power was too great to be trusted to any one group."

Hana approached cautiously, her eyes fixed on the artifact. "It looks... alive," she said quietly. "Like it's waiting for something."

Michael nodded. "It is. The seals. Reuniting the keys activates the Shadow Core."

Marcus turned to Michael, his voice tight with insistence. "Then we can't let the splinter group get anywhere near this. We need to move it, hide it somewhere they'll never find it."

Michael hesitated, his gaze locked on the Shadow Core. "Moving it could be dangerous. The Templars believed even proximity to it could corrupt. Even without the four seals near it, if we mishandle it—"

A sudden sound interrupted him—the faint creak of footsteps echoing through the corridor outside. Hana spun around, her voice intense. "Someone's coming."

Michael quickly stepped toward the door, locking it from the inside. The Shadow Core cast an eerie glow over the chamber as the three of them exchanged tense glances.

"Whoever it is," Michael said, his voice steady, "they've found us."

The tension in the room thickened as the footsteps drew closer, stopping just outside the vault door. A low voice called through the heavy oak.

"You can't keep it from us forever," the voice said,

calm and commanding. "The seals are already in motion. The Shadow Core will fulfill its purpose, whether you are part of it or not."

Hana glanced at Michael and Marcus, her hand hovering over her bag where she kept her taser. "What do we do?"

Michael exhaled slowly, his expression hardening. "We hold our ground. Whatever happens, the Shadow Core cannot leave this room."

Marcus nodded, his resolve firm. "Let them come. We're not giving this up."

Outside, the voice grew louder, more insistent. "This is bigger than you. Bigger than all of us. Open the door, and we can finish what the Templars started."

Michael glanced at Marcus and Hana, his voice low and steady. "No one opens that door. No matter what."

The footsteps outside stopped. Silence fell, thick and oppressive. Then, without warning, a loud boom echoed through the chamber as something heavy slammed into the vault door.

"They're trying to break in," Hana said, her voice edged with panic. "What now?"

Michael stepped back toward the Shadow Core, his expression implacable. "We protect it. No matter the cost."

THIRTY-TWO

The chamber trembled as the Shadow Core pulsed with chaotic energy, its black surface glowing brighter with each passing moment. The splinter group's leader stood near the shattered vault door, his face a mixture of triumph and desperation as his followers gathered behind him.

"You don't understand what you've found," he hissed, his eyes darting toward the chalice and blade still resting on the altar. "The keys aren't just artifacts. They're the only way to harness its power."

Michael stepped forward, placing himself between the leader and the artifacts. "Harness it? Or use it? The Templars designed these to prevent anyone from touching it, not to wield it."

The leader's lip curled into a sneer. "That's what they wanted you to believe. But the truth is far more complicated. This isn't just a danger—it's an opportunity. One that can reshape the world."

Marcus picked up the blade, holding it protectively. "You mean an opportunity for corruption, chaos, and destruction. We've seen what happens when people try to control things they don't understand."

"Which is why you're unworthy," the leader snapped. "The seals were never meant for you. They were meant for those strong enough to master what lies beyond them. Which is why the New Order contacted us. They've supplied us with what we need, knowing we can unlock the seals when they can't. Only they don't realize we will never hand it over to them."

Hana, her taser still in hand, stepped closer to the Shadow Core, her gaze flickering between the leader and Michael. "So that's your plan? Master it? You don't even understand what it is. You're playing with something the Templars themselves feared, let alone the Nazis."

The leader's voice softened, almost reverent. "The Templars feared their own failure. But the world has changed. We've learned. We know what must be done."

Michael's tone sharpened. "And you think unleashing this will save the world?"

"Not save it. Recreate it."

The Shadow Core pulsed again, sending a wave of energy through the room. The robed figures staggered but quickly recovered, their determination unshaken. The leader stepped forward, his voice low and commanding.

"Surrender the seals. This is your last chance."

Michael raised a hand, gesturing for Marcus and Hana to hold their positions. His gaze locked onto the leader's, unflinching. "If you want them, you'll have to take them."

At the signal, the leader's followers surged forward. Marcus swung the blade in a wide arc, forcing one attacker back. Hana jabbed her taser into another, sending him collapsing to the ground with a grunt. Michael intercepted a third, his movements quick and deliberate as he wrestled the man to the ground.

The Shadow Core pulsed brighter, its energy growing more erratic. Michael glanced toward it, his voice urgent. "It's reacting to the conflict. The two seals are keeping it stable, but if this keeps up—"

"It'll overload!" Marcus finished, using the blade to block another swing from a baton-like weapon. He shoved his attacker backward, his heart pounding.

The leader lunged for the altar, his eyes fixed on the chalice, but Hana intercepted him, blocking his path. "Not happening," she said, snatching the chalice and raising her taser.

The leader hesitated, his gaze flicking toward the vibrating Shadow Core.

The energy radiating from the Shadow Core began to distort the air around it, rippling like heat waves. The glow intensified, illuminating the entire chamber with an unnatural light. Everyone stopped moving, as if the air itself pulsed like a fist around them, holding them in place.

Michael turned to Marcus and Hana, his voice calm but firm. "The core is sensing the conflict and the absence of the balance of virtues. If all four of the keys are absent, the core is dormant, as it has been for centuries now. If all four are present, it would be in balance, contained."

The shimmering air now hummed with a mind-numbing vibration.

"And with only two of the keys here?" Hana asked.

The priest stepped over to Hana, holding her close, the chalice still clutched in her hand between them. "We hold tight to our faith, Hana. Hold tight."

The hum crescendoed, the entire room morphing as the air pressed in on them all in tumultuous waves. Marcus stumbled back but cradled the blade to his chest.

Through the deafening hum, the unmistakable screams of the splinter group leader and his men brought a sickening realization to Marcus, Michael, and Hana.

The video they had witnessed was being repeated.

Horrific seconds turned to agonizing minutes, and suddenly, all sound ceased. The tremors in the chamber slowed, the air becoming less oppressive.

"Michael?" Hana said, her voice filled with cautious hope, her head still tucked into his chest, her eyes closed against the horrors she had heard.

Michael tentatively responded, "It's over."

The threesome looked at each other, Marcus with the blade and Michael still holding Hana with the chalice. They nodded to each other. Then their eyes witnessed the bodies of their assailants. Stiff limbs stuck out at odd angles, as if flash-frozen in anguish, their mouths held open, their eyes wide. Marcus cautiously approached the leader and knelt to feel the man's neck.

He turned to the others. "Alive, but"—he looked again at the bodies—"not living." He stood. "We need to leave. Now."

Michael nodded and quickly gave the sign of the cross with his right hand as his left arm held Hana close to his side. They backed toward the door. "What about them?" he asked, gesturing toward the splinter group.

"We'll send someone," Marcus said, his tone somber.

As they emerged into the night air, the silence of the Vatican grounds felt almost deafening.

THE THREE STOOD in the moonlight, their breaths visible in the cool night air. Hana finally broke the silence. "What happened? Why weren't we..." She couldn't finish.

Marcus looked to Michael, who answered her. "My guess is that the blade saved Marcus. The blade of justice represents both the dangers and decisiveness necessary to 'act righteously,' as stated in that text you found, Hana. I know of no one stronger in his sense of justice than Marcus. Somehow, even without the stability of all four keys, Marcus was immune to the danger of that artifact by embodying that virtue."

Marcus looked at Hana. "And you had the chalice. The virtue of faith."

"But"—she shook her head—"I'm not that religious..." She looked at Michael. "It should have been Michael saved, not me."

Marcus shrugged, looking out over the cobblestoned street before them. "The text called it 'faith to endure the trial.' You held the chalice, the symbol containing faith, as Michael held you in his love. The two of you have endured the trials of life's personal journey, just as you've endured the trials of this mission." He sighed. "And... regardless of our understanding of it, we are safe."

The three stood silent for some time, thinking of the last few hours, few days, of how much they had learned. And of how little they still knew.

CHAPTER

THIRTY-THREE

The Gold Train lay silent, its cavernous hold illuminated by floodlights as Vatican officials, historians, and a handful of trusted experts combed through its contents. Rows of gold bars stacked like bricks of lost history gleamed in the harsh light. Artifacts, crates of stolen art, and boxes sealed for decades lined the train's corridors. It was the end of one mystery—and the beginning of another.

Marcus stood near the last railcar, his gloved hands carefully holding the Templar codex they had surreptitiously recovered before any Vatican officials saw it. Its weathered leather cover bore the unmistakable insignia of the Knights Templar, the same symbol they had seen etched into *Eisenkreuz* and scattered across the artifacts retrieved from the Shadow Core's chamber. The book was heavy in his grip—both physically and metaphorically—as though the centuries of secrets inside it were pressing down on him.

Marcus lifted it reverently. "This isn't just treasure," he whispered. "This is history."

At the far end of the cavern, near the entrance to the tunnel, Hana snapped a photo of a team lifting a crate bearing the image of the Nazi Imperial Eagle. She lowered her camera and turned back to Marcus and Michael, her expression somber.

"You know this isn't over, right?" she said. "The New Order isn't going to let us walk away with this win. If they've been hunting these relics and blueprints, this loss won't stop them."

Michael folded his arms, his gaze sweeping the gold-strewn train. "They've been playing a long game—longer than any of us realized. *Operation Eisenkreuz*, the containment unit, the Gold Train... It's all connected. They were planning something, and we've only seen the surface."

Marcus looked down at the codex in his hands. "And the Templars had something to do with it. They left warnings behind. The seals, the Shadows' Keepers, and now this book..." He trailed off, his brow furrowed. "This codex might be the key to understanding the New Order's next move."

As the last of the crates were removed from the train, Vatican officials gathered near the entrance to the tunnel. The air was cool and heavy with the scent of earth, but there was an undercurrent of tension, like the calm before a storm. Cardinal Severino had arrived to oversee the final transfer of artifacts.

"Father Dominic," Severino called as he approached, his voice perfectly measured. He glanced at the codex in

Marcus's hands before fixing his gaze on Michael. "You've done an admirable job ensuring the safe retrieval of these treasures. The Church will ensure they are protected, as is our duty."

Michael's expression didn't waver, though Marcus could feel his tension. "And the gold?" he asked, his tone careful. "What of the families it was taken from?"

Severino's eyes flickered, betraying the faintest hint of annoyance. "Rest assured, a process will be established for restitution—discreetly, of course. These matters are delicate."

Hana, standing slightly behind Michael, smiled. "I'll be keeping an eye on your progress on that. It will be of the utmost interest to the public, and I appreciate the understanding that I'll have an exclusive on the results."

Severino's gaze slid toward her but returned quickly to Michael. "It would be unwise for this discovery to become public knowledge at present. You understand the chaos it could cause."

Hana stepped forward. "I will be sensitive to that, of course, as I report each effort on your part to bring proper restitution to completion."

Michael, to his credit, held firm as well. "Truth isn't something we get to hide. Not forever. People deserve answers—just as much as they deserve justice."

Severino's lips curved into something that resembled a smile but held no warmth. "In time, Father. All in God's time." Then the cardinal cocked his head and turned to Marcus. "Speaking of time, Marcus, it took a bit of time before you revealed this location. Time enough to..." He left off the sentence, his eyes scanning the cavern as if looking for something missing.

Marcus gazed about as well, as if puzzled. "Is there something missing, Cardinal?"

Severino stiffened. "Not that I know of."

"Then I guess nothing is amiss, right?"

Severino glared at the archeologist, then walked away.

Marcus smirked. "He can't accuse me of moving the unit without admitting he knew about it all along."

One of the Vatican officials approached Michael, his expression tense. He handed the priest a small, yellowed document pulled from a crate they had just opened. "This was found among the blueprints, Father. I thought you'd want to see it."

Michael unfolded the brittle paper carefully, and the team leaned in.

It was a Nazi schematic, detailing what appeared to be an underground facility—not in Poland, but farther west, in the Bavarian Alps. At the bottom, scrawled in German, were the words:

"Phase Zwei begins here."

Marcus's pulse quickened. *"Phase Zwei...* Phase Two?"

Michael nodded, his face pale. "The Nazis' next move. This was bigger than gold or even *Operation Eisenkreuz.* They were planning something else."

Hana glanced between them. "And if the New Order still has pieces of those blueprints..."

"They'll be looking for whatever this other place contains," Marcus finished.

The realization hung in the air, dark and oppressive. The New Order had lost the Gold Train, but this schematic was proof that their plans were far from finished.

Marcus tucked the Templar codex carefully into his satchel, his thoughts spinning. "We stopped them here, but this isn't over."

Michael nodded grimly. "No. The New Order will regroup. They're too entrenched, too organized to let this one public discovery stop them. If this map is right, they're already moving on Phase Two."

Hana stepped back, taking a long look at the now empty train. "So we won today. But the war?" She exhaled. "We're just getting started, aren't we?"

Marcus turned toward the tunnel's mouth, where the first slivers of dawn crept through the mist. "Yeah," he said quietly. "And next time, they'll be ready for us."

Michael clapped a hand on his shoulder, his tone determined. "So will we."

As the three of them walked out of the cavern, leaving the Vatican officials to their work, the weight of what they had uncovered—and what lay ahead—followed them.

The New Order was still out there, its plans unfolding like a shadow over the world. The Gold Train was secured, but its secrets had revealed far more than anyone had bargained for.

The fight wasn't over. Not yet.

. . .

HOURS LATER, deep within a hidden bunker miles from the Owl Mountains, Klaus Jäger poured himself a glass of dark whiskey, savoring the way it burned his throat. Across the table sat Cardinal Severino, his hands clasped tightly, betraying his nerves.

"It's done," Jäger said, his voice smooth. "The Vatican dogs have their prize, but they'll never know what's missing."

He gestured to a crate that had been airlifted under the cover of the chaos. Inside lay stacks of brittle Nazi documents—scientific blueprints, notes on *Operation Eisenkreuz*, and coded instructions for other hidden caches.

Jäger handed Severino an envelope sealed with wax bearing the Covenant's insignia: a dark, stylized Iron Cross. Severino hesitated for only a moment before taking it.

"And Russo?" Severino asked, his voice measured.

"He knows too much already. And the containment unit is missing."

Jäger smirked. "Let him believe he's won. He'll dig deeper. They always do. But the New Order doesn't lose. We simply... wait. When the time is right, we'll return to what's ours."

Severino's expression betrayed nothing, though his voice dropped to a warning murmur. "If Marcus Russo uncovers the others—"

"We'll deal with him." Jäger's tone left no room for argument. He raised his glass. "To the future."

"To the New Order," Severino replied.

· · ·

MICHAEL SAT beside the hospital bed, his hands clasped in a final prayer for the old priest lying before him after administering last rites. He had taken Father Bernard Corvi straight to the Vatican infirmary after their encounter with the Shadows' Keepers in the archives. Only later did Michael learn that the old man's breathing and pale face were the least of his health issues. Or learn of his spiritual issues as well, detailed in the final confession he had given Michael a day later.

It seemed the priest had suffered the guilt of knowing about the relic and its dangers as well as the internal strife within the Shadows' Keepers ranks. He had kept secret his ongoing struggle with cancer, fearing what would happen to the relic in his care if he were to be replaced, potentially by another sympathizing with the splinter group that would loosen this danger on the world. So, when Michael approached him to visit that section, he felt it was an answer to his prayers. But the encounter that day only served to frighten the old man.

In confession, Michael had attempted to alleviate the priest's final fears, but the priest insisted only one penance would suffice. Michael was reluctant until the priest explained what he wanted.

Now Michael stood, making the sign of the cross over the old priest's body for a final time. He walked away, knowing that Father Corvi had served God's purpose. And knowing that the containment unit now moved from the Owl Mountains to yet another undocumented room, one that had been known only to Father Corvi himself, would be safe in the vastness of the Vatican Secret Archives.

EPILOGUE

The late afternoon sunlight poured through the tall, arched windows of Marcus Russo's study, bathing the room in a soft golden glow. Outside, Rome murmured with life—the hum of scooters, the occasional church bell, and the chatter of tourists blending into a familiar symphony. But here, within the quiet refuge of his book-lined walls, the weight of recent events lingered like a shadow.

Marcus sat at his desk, the Templar codex open before him, its pages carefully weighted with smooth stones. The fragile script, written by hands long dead, spoke of mysteries and secrets that had cost lives— secrets that still held power to shape the future. His hands rested on the edges of the pages, unmoving. He wasn't reading. Not yet. Instead, he stared out the window, his mind replaying the events of the past weeks.

The Gold Train. The firefight. Klaus Jäger's escape. And the silent, knowing look from Cardinal Severino.

Hana Sinclair entered the room quietly, carrying two steaming cups of coffee. She placed one in front of him and took a seat on the worn leather chair across from his desk. Her smile was faint, but it carried warmth.

"You're still brooding," she said lightly, though her voice betrayed her own exhaustion.

Marcus exhaled, his lips tugging into a weary smile. "I'm thinking."

"Thinking," she repeated with a tilt of her head. "About Jäger? Or Severino?"

"Both," he admitted. He picked up the coffee and took a sip, the heat grounding him. "Jäger's still out there. Severino's probably part of it—though proving that is another matter entirely. And this codex..." He gestured to the book, his voice trailing off.

Hana leaned forward, resting her elbows on her knees. "The codex is important, Marcus. We know that. But so are you. You found the train. You stopped them from taking everything. By making it known openly, even if within only the Vatican and select experts for now, the New Order can't just run off with any of it. There will be records of it now and inventories others know about. I'll keep tabs on the man, be sure the truth comes out, even if slowly. That's no small feat.

"And we know the dangers of that black core, that 'engine of corruption,' will be well protected by the Shadows' Keepers again."

Marcus knew that to be true. When he called on

them to collect the bodies of their dissidents, the response had been immediate and chilling. They would mercifully care for the living husks that remained of their once comrades. It would serve to reinforce their vows to safeguard that core, no matter the cost. Yet still…

"It doesn't feel like enough," he said after a moment. "Not when they're still out there, planning their next move."

Hana's gaze softened. "It's never enough, is it? The work. The fight. We uncover one layer, and there's always another underneath. But you've done something remarkable. You've given us a chance to understand them—and to stop them."

Her words hung in the air, and for the first time, Marcus allowed himself to believe them. He nodded slowly, a flicker of resolve lighting his expression.

IN ANOTHER PART of the Vatican, Father Michael Dominic knelt in prayer inside the Chapel of the Holy Cross. The room was dimly lit, the faint scent of incense lingering in the air. Before him stood the reliquary containing fragments of the True Cross—a reminder of faith, sacrifice, and perseverance—transferred from the Gold Train to its rightful place in the Vatican.

He folded his hands tightly, his fingers brushing against the cool beads of his rosary. His prayers were silent, his thoughts loud.

The Covenant of the Iron Cross still existed, the

Templars' remaining Shadows' *Keepers possessing renewed vigilance in their vows. Also remnants of the reign of Nazis still existed in the New Order with their web of power stretching further than he had imagined. And Cardinal Severino—his one-time mentor, his superior—had betrayed everything the Church stood for.

Yet even here, in the midst of doubt, Michael found solace. He recalled Marcus's determination, Hana's courage, and the quiet strength of those who had fought to preserve the truth. Evil would persist, but so would those who opposed it.

Rising slowly, Michael gazed at the reliquary one last time. "You won't win," he murmured, his voice steady, his faith unshaken. "Not while we still stand."

LATER THAT EVENING, the three of them gathered on Marcus's balcony overlooking Piazza Navona. A light breeze carried the scent of freshly baked bread and the laughter of diners below. The day had faded into twilight, the sky a watercolor blend of gold, pink, and indigo.

Hana leaned against the railing, holding a glass of wine. "Do you think they'll come after us?" she asked, breaking the silence.

Marcus sipped his drink, his eyes scanning the square below. "Probably," he said matter-of-factly. "But we'll be ready."

"That's a very Marcus answer."

Michael, seated on a nearby chair with a glass of water, smiled faintly. "He's right. They'll come. But every step they take to find us exposes them a little more. Their power is rooted in secrecy. Bring them into the light, and they'll lose."

Marcus looked at Michael, his respect for the priest deepening. "You think that's enough? Truth and light?"

Michael met his gaze steadily. "It's always enough. It may take time, it may come at a cost—but yes, it's enough."

For a moment, they let the quiet settle around them, the sounds of the city filling the space.

Hana turned to Marcus, her voice gentler now. "And what about you? What happens next?"

Marcus considered the question, his mind turning over the possibilities. "We keep going," he said finally. "We study the codex, figure out what it can tell us. And we keep digging—into Jäger, into Severino, into all of it. We don't stop until we've uncovered the whole truth."

"And if we don't?" Hana asked, her tone cautious.

"We will," he said simply, his voice calm but firm. "The New Order wants us to believe they're untouchable. That they're everywhere, but they're wrong. They can be beaten."

Hana raised her glass. "To fortitude, then."

Michael lifted his own glass in response, his smile genuine. "To faith."

Marcus clinked his glass against theirs, a faint but determined smile crossing his lips. "To justice and the wisdom to bring it about."

As the stars emerged one by one in the night sky

above Rome, the three of them sat together, knowing the road ahead would be long and uncertain. But they also knew this: no matter how deeply evil rooted itself, there would always be those willing to fight against it.

And sometimes, that was enough.

FICTION, FACT, OR FUSION

Many readers have asked me to distinguish fact from fiction in my books. Generally, I like to take factual events and historical figures and build on them in creative ways—but much of what I do write is historically accurate. In this book, I'll review some of the chapters where questions may arise, with hopes it may help those wondering where reality meets creative writing.

PROLOGUE:

The **Nazi Gold Train** is one of the most enduring legends of World War II, a tale of a train laden with gold, priceless artworks, and other treasures looted by the Nazis as they retreated in the war's final days. Allegedly hidden in a secret tunnel system in the Owl Mountains of Poland, the train has never been conclusively found, despite numerous expeditions and ground-penetrating radar surveys in recent years. The story gained renewed attention in 2015 when treasure hunters claimed to have located a train near Wałbrzych, though no evidence was ultimately recovered. While skeptics argue that the train is a myth, created from wartime chaos and post-war folklore, believers contend that its disappearance was part of the Nazis' deliberate efforts to hide their plunder for a potential resurgence. The train's existence remains unproven, but its legend persists, captivating archaeologists, treasure hunters, and historians alike as a tantalizing mystery waiting to be solved.

The Nazis, particularly under Heinrich Himmler and the SS, displayed an avid interest in the **Knights Templar**, though this interest was part of a broader fascination with medieval and mystical orders. Their focus on the Templars was intertwined with their ideology, myth-making, and quest for legitimizing their vision of Aryan supremacy and a new Germanic empire.

CHAPTER 5 AND ELSEWHERE:

The Nazis, particularly through Heinrich Himmler and the SS, had a keen interest in **Norse runes and the supernatural** as part of their effort to construct an ideological foundation rooted in Aryan mysticism and Germanic pagan traditions. They appropriated ancient symbols like the runic alphabet, especially the Sieg (victory) rune, used in the SS logo, to evoke a connection to an idealized, warrior-centric past. This fascination extended to occult practices, esoteric rituals, and pseudo-scientific theories, often blending mythology with fabricated history to support their racial ideology and reinforce the mystique of the Third Reich as a modern reincarnation of ancient Germanic greatness.

CHAPTER 18:

Though the technology did not exist during the time of the Nazis, volcanic thermal energy is now used to generate electricity, but it is more commonly referred to as **geothermal energy** when harnessed for human use. Geothermal energy relies on heat from the Earth's interior, which can be especially accessible near volcanic regions. And, in fact, Iceland is a global leader in geothermal energy, deriving about 25% of its electricity from geothermal power. Its location on the Mid-Atlantic Ridge, with high volcanic activity, makes it ideal for this purpose.

Projekt Riese ("Giant") was a massive and secretive Nazi construction project during World War II in the Owl Mountains of modern-day Poland. Initiated in 1943, the project involved building an extensive underground complex of tunnels, bunkers, and chambers, potentially intended as a bomb-proof military headquarters for Hitler, advanced weapons research facilities, or storage for looted treasures. Constructed by the Organisation Todt using forced labor, including concentration camp prisoners, the project caused significant loss of life due to brutal working conditions. Although several sites, such as Osówka and Włodarz, were partially completed, the project was abandoned as the war ended in 1945. Today, these tunnels remain subjects of speculation and intrigue, particularly regarding their purpose and rumors of hidden Nazi treasures.

Keeping in mind that the legendary **Gold Train** has yet to be discovered, the contents described in the cars are obviously fictive, as is the Nazis' assumed use of volcanic thermal energy to power the mountain systems. But I had to keep the lights on somehow, didn't I?

As I mentioned earlier, *"Projekt Vulkan"*—the use of geothermal energy during the 1940s—was purely fictional.

AUTHOR'S NOTE

Dealing with issues of theology, religious beliefs, and the fictional treatment of historical biblical events can be a daunting affair.

I would ask all readers to view this story for what it is—a work of pure fiction, adapted from the seeds of many oral traditions and the historical record, at least as we know it today.

Apart from telling an engaging story, I have no agenda here, and respect those of all beliefs, from Agnosticism to Zoroastrianism and everything in between.

Thank you for reading *Covenant of the Iron Cross*. I hope you enjoyed it and, if you haven't already, suggest you pick up the story beginning with the earlier books—*The Magdalene Deception, The Magdalene Reliquary,* and *The*

Magdalene Veil—and look forward to forthcoming books featuring the same characters and a few new ones in the continuing *Vatican Secret Archive Thriller* series, and the new *Vatican Archaeology* series.

When you have a moment, **may I ask that you leave a review on Amazon**, Goodreads, Facebook and perhaps elsewhere you find convenient? Reviews are crucial to a book's success, and I hope for all my books to have long and entertaining lives.

You can easily leave your review by going to my Amazon book page; just search for *Covenant of the Iron Cross*. And thank you!

If you would like to reach out for any reason, you can email me at gary@garymcavoy.com. If you'd like to learn more about me and my other books, visit my website at www.garymcavoy.com, where you can also sign up for my private mailing list.

With very best regards,

Gary McAvoy

Made in United States
Troutdale, OR
03/04/2025